THE MAGICAN PROTOCOL

HARMONICS
BOOK 1

COLLIN EARL

CHRIS SNELGROVE

SILVERSTONE BOOKS

The Magican Protocol

Harmonics: Book One

By Collin Earl & Chris Snelgrove

ISBN-13: 978-1-967473 15-1

CONTENTS

PROLOGUE

They built what could not be constructed: a weapon light-years ahead of its time. A weapon so superior it defied the known laws of physics. Seven years ago, they were on the verge of unleashing its power. Then... they lost it. Now, they are on a desperate hunt to reclaim what they stole. Following the trail of unexplainable deaths, they frantically search for what may become their ultimate demise. But what if the project doesn't want to be reclaimed? Join their hunt, wading through political power plays, corporate corruption, domestic terrorism, and the greatest enigma of their time—the infamous assassin known only as The Magician.

CHAPTER 1

DESERT WARFARE

Time: Five years ago
Scene: Unmarked Desert Base

"'Gone'? What do you mean 'gone'?"

Two nondescript Lab Coats stood in front of a Suit wearing expensive black glasses. This Suit was the sort of man who answered to no one about nothing. He looked very angry.

"Just what I said. Both projects are gone. It's as if neither ever existed," the Lab Coat's voice lamented. "So many years of research. And just after we get the Alpha 1 prototype up and running and Beta 1 finally showed signs of the phenomena, this happens. Up in smoke. Both projects gone, just like that."

"Control yourself, Doctor. I'm not interested in your

emotional turmoil. What I'm not understanding is, how does a multi-part research project worth billions just disappear from one of the most secure facilities in the world?"

"We're not really sure. I checked the weapon last—"

The Suit stepped forward and struck the Lab Coat in the jaw, sending him sprawling to the floor.

"We don't use that word around here, Doctor. This isn't that sort of facility. I assumed you were aware of that."

The doctor spat blood as tears ran down his face. "I apologize, sir. What I meant was that I checked the data feed from the project just last night, and everything seemed to be in order."

The Suit sneered. "This is getting us nowhere. Get me security; let's see what they have to say about all of this."

"Security is dead, sir." The doctor fidgeted, still on the floor. "That's why we called you. Everyone else is dead."

The Suit flinched. "They're dead? All of them? I hand-picked those men myself from the United Delta Force. There is no way that all of them are dead. Not unless they were up against a small army."

The second doctor reached into his pocket and held a shaking hand out to the Suit. "No army, sir. We didn't even hear anything. I think you need to see this."

The Suit removed his sunglasses and took a small security drive from the doctor's hand. He gave the Lab Coat a withering look, then walked over to a large display screen, touched a number of on-screen commands, and the system began interfacing with the drive. A security reel started to show a slideshow that none of them would soon forget.

The Suit's eyes widened. "Oh my—"

Death scenes, one after another, flipped across the screen as if the display were nothing more than a family picture album. The Suit examined the time stamp of each still image. The images were taken less than an hour ago. "This... this is impossible."

The scenes depicted stalagmite-like protrusions jutting from random places in the room, most running cleanly through bloody, fatigue-wearing men. The next slide loaded. More images of what the Suit could only assume were the security force, completely wasted. Several lightweight Series 7 Vector machine guns were strewn across the floor in each image, but the guns were the only things easily distinguishable; the rest was a charred, smoking mess. The scene flipped again. Yet more destruction: doors torn off hinges, terminals and other equipment destroyed, and many more dead in gruesome and deliberate ways.

The Suit spoke, his voice very quiet. "You're telling me that the entire research facility's security force is dead and no one saw anything? What about the rest of the staff? The scientists in charge of the project? Are they dead as well?"

The Lab Coat shook his head. "I have no idea, and I don't intend to find out. We are leaving right now—"

"Who gave you permission to leave? We still have work to do, Doctor, like figuring out what happened to the projects. Luckily, all the research should be backed up to the remote data drives. So really, we just need to contain this incident."

"Sir," the second Lab Coat interrupted, "I don't think you get it. There is no containing this incident."

The Lab Coat pointed as the last of the reel loaded. The three men stared up at the screen. The Lab Coat's face beaded up with sweat, fear shining through as the Suit's face darkened.

The screen depicted a cave-like room. Large servers, huge fans, and suspended steel-framed walkways connected a variety of different exits and stairways sprouting off in all directions. Easily recognizable, this room was situated deep underground. It was the brain of the entire desert facility. The room was designed to withstand anything a military could throw at it, from bunker-buster bombs to nuclear warheads. It was ironic, really. The company had designed this place to be impenetrable from the outside, but no one could anticipate every threat.

"What the hell...?" The Suit's words faded away. He barely comprehended what he saw. In the middle of the picture, resting directly between two of the largest cloud frames, sat a huge multi-layered crate. Affixed to the crate was a banner with two words on it.

"Good-Bye?" The first Lab Coat's eyes squinted at the chicken scratch painted in huge red letters.

The Suit started swearing. He turned and opened a comm channel. "MESA One, this is Outpost Whiskey. We have a security breach. The Farm is compromised. We need full tactical support. Send in Containment and S&D teams, priority one!"

The Lab Coats stumbled over their words. "Sir, do you really think both Containment and S&D are needed? The threat seems to be gone; all the departments are sealed."

"Fools," said the Suit, walking over to a weapons cache, unlocking it, and pulling out a Tiger 35 Assault Rifle. The Suit loaded a clip and slid the action back. "Look at the bottom of the picture. Do you know what that crate is?"

The Lab Coats looked again at the final picture of the morbid slideshow. The crate was mostly covered by the banner, but there at the bottom, two more letters could be made out. Two more characters that read clearly,

"X9," mouthed one of the Lab Coats. "That crate is a palette of thermobaric explosives? Oh Lord. How could they have—no, this isn't happening!"

"That isn't the half of it," whispered the other Lab Coat, still staring at the image. "Is that a clock?"

All three of the men stepped closer to the massive screen. The Suit touched the screen, zooming in on the corner of the image. The second Lab Coat was correct. There was a small clock, and its numbers were moving.

The three men stared, reaching out as if to touch the

clock through the screen. They watched the numbers count down. 10, 9, 8, 7...

"Isn't this a compilation of security feed stills?" questioned the Suit. "How—how are the numbers moving?"

The question went unanswered as the countdown hit zero.

CHAPTER 2
THE GOOD DOCTOR

Time: Late at night, five years later
Scene: Private Apartments of the UON

Hans Bloomquist took his job very seriously. Years of military training and special ops had honed him into the disciplined soldier he was today. Throughout the years, he had guarded military attachés, council members, heads of corporations, and had even been on the chancellor's detail once. He had been assigned to the UON for almost a year now. Despite the lack of prestige, Hans treated each assignment as if it were his only assignment, and guarding Dr. Shu was no different.

Sure, the little scientist had his faults. Hans was loyal to the Collective, and the fact that Dr. Shu had defected from the Jade Empire didn't sit right with him, a Northern-born man. But he had always put his personal feelings and politics aside when on duty. Even Dr. Shu's constant nagging and whining about being protected had not shifted Hans's focus. There were times, when Hans was off duty, of course, that he would have liked to wring the little man's neck, but those thoughts were always kept outside of the job.

It wasn't like Hans didn't have skeletons in his closet as well. Mostly just one big ugly skeleton stuffed into a very small closet. It was this skeleton that had almost seen him court-martialed and subsequently forced him into the private sector. He just needed a few more years of babysitting UON officials to pay off his debt. He wasn't sure what he would do after his coerced tour of duty was up, but he'd think of something.

Hans felt for his sidearm through his jacket, a habit he had established early on in his career. Next, he checked his timepiece, smiled inwardly at his stunningly accurate sense of time, and radioed in to the main guard post. A series of beeps and tones relayed down to the post, and a shorter sequence replied moments later.

Hans settled back into his mental patrol of the empty hallway. He recalled the briefing on Dr. Shu earlier that week. The man was not necessarily a high-profile target, but chatter on the nets had indicated an increase in threats against him. Mostly it was from naturalist groups, and of those, only a handful had ever been linked to violence, but you never could tell with those wack-a-doos. Hans never understood people's aversion to using computer/human interfaces to improve the standard of living. CHIs, as they were called, had greatly helped many of his former comrades in arms who had lost limbs during various conflicts. He had never thought of it before, but Dr. Shu probably had a hand in helping his buddies get those interfaces. Maybe the little man wasn't so annoying after all.

Hans's feet started to tingle a bit, a sure sign that he had been standing in the same position too long. Unfortunately, per his duty instructions, he could not leave the inside of the doorframe. He flexed and relaxed his leg muscles and shifted his weight more evenly on his feet before settling back into the silent sentinel routine. A few minutes later, his feet were still tingling. He stood on one foot, shook the other, and then switched. Even more tingling. He must not have realized how asleep his feet had become. He could feel the pins attacking the sole of his foot as it tried to regain its normal blood flow.

He picked up his foot again and heard a faint creaking noise. Reflexively, his hand found the grip of his sidearm. He really hoped no one could see him leaning to one side, one foot off the ground with his other hand gripped to his sidearm; he imagined it looked comical. But he stayed stock still, listening for the sound again. After a few moments, he set his foot back down softly and slowly. His other foot felt like it was on fire, like a thousand tiny needles were flowing across it. He lifted his foot one more time and gave it a good shake and heard the noise again. This time the gun came out of its holster as Hans replanted his foot squarely back on the floor.

The noise had echoed from a distance. Hans could not quite get a bead on where it was coming from. His training kicked in, and he slowly swept his weapon from side to side. Nothing. Hans reluctantly stepped out from the doorway and stood still. He listened for the slightest of sounds, ticking off the seconds in his mind. One second turned to ten, then twenty. One minute. Two minutes. Three minutes. Nothing. Hans counted off another thirty seconds before returning to the doorframe and holstering his sidearm. The two or three-step reprieve from his statuesque pose, however, did not seem to do anything for his tingling feet.

Just as he resumed his visual patrol, the floor suddenly jerked upwards, catching the sentinel off guard and driving his head into the top of the doorframe, crushing his skull and snapping his neck. Hans toppled forward, unresponsive arms unable to break his fall. His mind screamed to grab the sidearm even as blackness overtook him.

"Yes, that's right, Reed. From the dossiers, he is the one who is most vulnerable. Of all the potential candidates, we can leverage his circumstances most effectively."

Dr. Shu sipped his jasmine-infused sake as he spoke with the small image of his contact emitting from the projector.

"I will relay your choice back to the committee," the image replied. "How is your imposed incarceration going?"

Dr. Shu harrumphed. "Damned naturalists. It's not like they actually pose a significant threat. If it hadn't been for those last few anonymous communications that were intercepted, I wouldn't be here. They just popped up last minute, right when things looked like they were going to settle down. Now I have some Northern Territory bear guarding me."

The contact laughed.

"No, seriously, this guy could pass as a Ganga for sure." Shu could feel the sake burn as he tipped back his third cup. "Well, that's it for me. Anything else you need?"

"No, we are good here. I will arrange the meeting with the Vice-Chairman later tonight. Yuon? Yuon, what's the matter?"

Dr. Shu had turned to listen to something he thought he had heard. When he didn't hear it again, he turned back to his contact. "Oh, nothing. Just thought my incompetent guard was saying something. Anyway, let me know how the meeting goes. I think the Emperor will be very pleased with the information that Reed is willing to share. For the right price, of course."

The contact chuckled a knowing laugh. "Well, Yuon, get some sleep. You look tired. After I arrange the meeting, I'm stopping off in the Burning Plains to facilitate an acquisition. I'll be leaving tonight and may not have comm coverage down there, so just leave a secure message with your update if you can't reach me."

Dr. Shu didn't quite hear this last comment. His attention

had again turned back to the noise at the front of his apartment. "Huh? Oh, fine. I will be in touch."

Dr. Shu severed the comm uplink and turned to leave the room. As he stood, he swayed a little. Perhaps that third cup had been a bit too much. He unlocked the door and ventured out to find out what that grizzly bear of a guard was doing that had made such a ruckus.

His apartment was dark, and in his altered state of mind, Dr. Shu could not for the life of him remember disabling the light dimmers. However, there had been many a time when the automatic lights waking him had done nothing to help his sake-induced hangover, so the fact that he had disabled them made sense, in a turned-around sort of way.

"Hank? Hank!?" Wait, that wasn't the man's name. What was it again? Harry? Horse? Ham? Yes, that was it, Ham. "Ham! What's going on?" Dr. Shu continued through the sitting room towards the front of the apartment. "Ham! Answer me! What was that noise? You in heat or something? You find a nice girl bear to mate with?" Girl bear. That was funny. Yep, third one was definitely one too many. "Ham! Ha—"

Dr. Shu stopped mid-yell as his slowed brain pieced together what his eyes saw at the front door. The door was open, and it looked like it no longer fit into the doorframe. The bottom part of the floor jutted up in a weird fashion and bowed the rest of the frame outwards. Ham was on the floor. What was Ham doing on the floor?

Dr. Shu slowly took in the scene and then noticed that Ham's neck was cocked at a very unnatural angle. Sluggishly, the adrenaline started to kick in. It flowed freely, trying to overcome the effects of the sake. Dr. Shu started to breathe very rapidly as his brain told him to find the panic alarm. He spun around and groped the wall. His hands were shaking now. Where was it? Stupid dimmers! Why had he disabled them? He threw his hands all along the wall, desperately feeling for the plastic box. At the end of the wall, his fingers brushed it. There it was! He fumbled to get the safety shield open. The adrenaline coursing through his veins combined with his impaired fine-motor function made his fingers shudder and shiver. Just as the shield slid upwards and his hand was about to come down on the button, a vice-like grip clamped down around his arm and spun him into the wall, his back smacking against it. All of his breath escaped as the force of the impact propelled the air out of his lungs. Even if Shu's alcohol-addled brain would have thought to scream at the black apparition that now stood in front of him, there was no air left inside of him to make a single sound.

———

Scott had the best gig of any of his buddies. Ever since the situation in the Burning Plains, Scott had figured he would spend the rest of his life hauling refuse or chaperoning some rich dude's kid at the brat's weekend parties. He wasn't sure which career would have been worse. And then, his lucky break; a way out of his mess with only a few years' payment to make. And to make things even easier, he basically just sat around and watched vid feeds, radioed posts, and kept the visitors log up to date. Talk about cushy.

It would have been heaven if that stupid scientist had not been sequestered in the apartments at the last minute. Total buzz kill. To make matters worse, the doc's assigned guard gave Scott the most ridiculously complex check-in schedule. None of this on-the-hour, every-hour stuff. First check-in was followed by a second 17 minutes later. Then 38 minutes, then 12, then 2, then 27, and so on. The latest of these absolutely excessive check-ins was about ten minutes ago. Scott looked at the schedule, which he had hidden from the beefy man because he certainly was not going to memorize it as instructed. The next check-in would be in one minute.

Scott had learned the hard way after his first botched check-in that he had exactly 5 seconds to reply to the guard's radio before he comm'd down to the main post. Scott was late only that one time. No way this d-bag was going to get Scott reassigned away from his cushy job.

Three, two, one and...nothing. Scott looked at the desk clock. Then he checked the crumpled-up piece of paper, fearing he had missed something.

Nope. There it was, 7 minutes from the last one. Scott waited a few more seconds. Weird...that guy was never late.

Scott pulled up the hallway feed to Dr. Shu's floor. There was the burly man guarding the empty hallway. Everything seemed fine. Scott reached for the comm but then hesitated. Should he really do that? If he pointed out that this guy had missed a check-in, could that bear of a man somehow twist it so it looked bad for Scott? He checked the time on the sheet and the clock again. No way! He was totally on point. The big dude had messed up, and this was Scott's opportunity to let him know it.

He linked the comm open. "Hey, Hans. You, uh, miss something?" Scott muted the mic and snickered. This was totally brickin'. The big man in the vid didn't budge. Oh, tough guy, thought Scott. "Hey, Hans. You're two minutes late. You're slipping, man." Again, no movement from the guard. Scott checked the comm settings and then tried the secondary channel. "Uh, Hans...Hans? You there, man?" Nada.

This guy was starting to piss him off. First, he gives him this ridiculous schedule, and then when Scott calls him on missing a check-in, he pretends he can't hear him. Scott linked Dr. Shu's room. He'd just let the doctor know that his bodyguard wasn't responding. That would get the guy in trouble for sure. "Dr. Shu? Sorry to disturb you, but I just wanted to see if you were all right."

Oh, this was gonna be fan-frickin-tastic. Scott could tell that the Dr. guy didn't like Hans in the least; this would seri-ously set him off. "Dr. Shu? I really hate to call like this...I just need to check in with you." Nothing again. Maybe the comm system was acting up.

Scott called up the vid feed from the doctor's apartment. All dark. He checked the room sensors. All green. This was getting really weird. There was no way the stupid guard got Dr. Shu to go along with his ignoring game. Scott pulled up the biosensors. Two heartbeats. Well, at least the old guy wasn't—

The two signals dropped out. Scott stared at the monitor, now fully convinced that the system was broken. Oh crap! That meant that the burly guard could have been trying to radio the main post and he'd missed it. He started to pull up the hallway feed again. He would try to get the guy on the emergency link.

Except the vid feed that came up was entirely different than the one that Scott had just seen. Hans was no longer standing in the doorway. In fact, all Scott could see of him was the man's leg halfway out the door. He cycled to the feed inside of the apartment. Still dark. He logged in and tried to manually raise the lights. Nothing. Scott looked at the biosensor again. What if the system wasn't failing? What if—

Scott was in full panic now. He reached for the master alarm and then stopped. A memory came from the back of his mind and stopped all thoughts of hitting that alarm. Scott remembered the details of his "deal." He sat back, reached for his personal comm, and linked into the untraceable number he had been given when he was assigned to the main desk.

What was he going to say? He had never even dreamed of having to use the number. The comm line opened.

"Yes."

"Uh, yeah. This is—"

"We know who this is. Do you have anything to report?"

"Uh, right. Of course you do. Um, yeah. I think something is going down here. That doctor guy isn't responding, and I think his bodyguard is...well, dead."

Scott listened as the silence on the other end grew.

"Hold."

Scott sat at the desk looking around nervously. The seconds seemed to crawl by. How long had it been now? The voice returned to the comm suddenly. Scott sat up and listened to the instructions he was given. He made one or two confirming noises as the instructions rattled off in his ear. Then the line went dead.

Scott logged in to the system with the credentials the voice had given him and suspended the vid feed recording the secured floor. Then he sat back in his chair. He had no idea what was going on now. He looked at the clock and waited. Two minutes. Five minutes. Nine minutes. Twelve minutes. At seventeen minutes, Scott reached over and hit the master alarm.

———

Jorge listened carefully as the voice issued instructions. He had heard the voice only one other time in his life, and that was when he had found himself in quite the pickle. He had listened to the voice that time too and had been very thankful ever since. The voice spoke rapidly through the comm. Jorge listened intently, making mental notes about his assignment. The voice finished, and the comm went dead. Sixteen minutes. Jorge checked his timepiece and started for the elevator.

After pulling on gloves, he pulled out the security card that an anonymous man had slipped into his pocket the first day on the job and directed the elevator to the secured floor. Upon exiting, Jorge turned up the hallway.

Fifteen minutes.

The dead guard was lying just inside the door. Jorge had expected as much. The doorway itself was scrunched upwards from the floor, and the sides bowed outward, giving it a funhouse look. Jorge drew his sidearm, stepped over the guard, careful not to touch the body or anything around it, and entered the apartment. The light filtering in from the hallway was the only thing illuminating the room. The seconds ticked by.

Fourteen minutes.

Jorge sparked his torch and drew it alongside his gun. He swept the room and then proceeded to the kitchen, bathroom, bedroom, and finally the study. He paused to steady his breathing.

Eleven minutes.

Jorge found Dr. Shu in his study. Blood covered most of the wall. Jorge checked the floor. There was no way around treading on the blood-soaked carpet. He quickly holstered his sidearm and stepped into the room. He put two fingers on Dr. Shu's neck, confirming what he already knew. Jorge took out a small vid feeder and logged in to the encrypted server with the credentials the voice had given him.

Nine minutes.

Jorge started to stream vids of the room, close-ups of Dr. Shu and the blood-spattered walls. He walked backward out of the room and got shots of the remainder of the apartment and finished with the doorway and the dead guard.

Five minutes.

Jorge stowed the vid feeder and pulled out another small device and waited for it to boot up.

Four minutes.

He flipped it open and then ran it above the guard, the floor of the doorway, the doorframe, and just outside of the apartment.

Three minutes.

He checked the readings, and like the vid feeder, stowed the device. Jorge moved down the hallway and hit the stairwell. He flew down the stairs and exited one floor beneath the secured floor. He raced down the hallway as he pulled the small device out once again.

One minute.

Looking up at the ceiling and the end of the hallway, Jorge found the spot right below Dr. Shu's apartment. Again he reached up and passed the device below the ceiling and around the area. He checked the readings and sent the log to the same encrypted server as the vids. The master alarm sounded.

Jorge started back towards the stairs just as someone came around the corner at the end of the hallway. Jorge reached for his sidearm, but then stopped as the man approaching him held out his ID badge. The tactical gear, assault helmet, and Tiger 35 rifle also made Jorge think twice about pulling his weapon.

"That hallway clear?" called out Jorge to the man. The visor of the helmet nodded up and down. "Good, I'll check the floor above."

Jorge quickly moved past the man before he had to answer any questions about his assigned floor duty. Once in the stairwell, Jorge checked that the file had uploaded successfully and then ran upstairs as if for the first time.

———

Canderous entered the main lobby, flanked by the elite members of his Containment squad. The men spread out across the lobby, taking up positions by the elevator and stairwell. Canderous walked calmly to the scrawny-looking man at the main desk.

"You call in the incident?" barked Canderous.

"Uh, yeah, I did. And I followed all my instructions. Master alarm was tripped eight minutes ago."

Canderous nodded and then told his comm officer to check to see if the files had been received. The man logged into MESA's secure server, spot-checked the vids and logs, and confirmed their receipt to Canderous.

"Good." Canderous linked to his team. "Now, the master alarm will have locked down the building. Since we are the first ones on scene, we have a small window of opportunity to recover the package. S&D will be on-scene in 10. I want—"

"Uh, sir?" Scott cleared his throat. "Sorry I didn't catch your name. But, uh...about being first on scene." Canderous slowly turned to glare at the man. Scott continued. "I gave an update to the prelim scout you sent. He should be back any minute now."

"Son, I don't have time for your babbling. I got a situation to contain here," Canderous responded impatiently.

"Ok, right. No problem. Like I said, he should be back any minute now."

Canderous turned back to his team and started to finish his orders, but then stopped. He turned back to the stringy man. "Who's gonna be back any minute?"

Scott gulped. "Uh, that guy you sent ahead of your team. He said you would be here in a few minutes and then said he needed to start securing the perimeter, so I unlocked the side entrance and let him out."

Canderous grabbed the man by his uniform and pulled him closer. "And why on god's green earth would you let anyone out of this building when your instructions specifically said not to!?"

"He was your advanced team!" Scott stammered. "He was tact'd out just like you—gear, helmet, assault rifle. He said you sent him ahead and that you would be coming in just a few minutes! I swear!"

Canderous barked for a man to clear the side entrance. Moments later, the man came back holding a tactical gear belt, assault helmet, and a Tiger 35 AR—all exact matches to the gear that the Containment team sported.

Canderous's eyes went wide with rage.

———

Somewhere in the gathering crowd of onlookers, a nameless man removed his tactical gloves and dropped them to the ground unnoticed as he gawked with the multitude at the congregating influx of emergency, security, and medical personnel.

CHAPTER 3
TREASURE TIME

Time: Late afternoon, five years and two days after the desert facility was destroyed
Scene: Sacred Temple deep in the Burning Plains

Using the old map he had borrowed from an older native, Dirk wound through the sparse underbrush of the plains. In this broken and godforsaken land, his lips were parched, his face was sweaty, and the sun bore down on him like a 16th-century taskmaster. He was almost out of water, too. If he didn't find something soon... But the map, his little savior, showed he was getting close. If he could pull this off, it would be one of his biggest finds. Dirk could taste the credits now.

Dirk could have kissed the old, wrinkled parchment. The old man's map was a boon from the gods and would save Dirk some serious time and effort. Combined with all the other information he had gathered about the relic, it was almost too easy. And that's what worried him.

Dirk had long ago accepted that he and fate were not on speaking terms. He had often wondered what personal vendetta fate was pursuing against him and realized early on in his career as a relic hunter that he would have to work for everything he got. So when the old man had mentioned the map, the one thing that Dirk had not counted on having, he almost—almost—let it go. The map could be a dead end, or a curse, or a portal to another dimension. Not that Dirk believed in any of that mumbo jumbo—gods, demons, aliens, and curses, nonsense every bit of it. But then again, he did believe in fate.

Ultimately, Dirk took the map; he couldn't help himself. His mother had always said, between sips of cheap vodka, that you should never punch a gimme bear in the face and never kick a gift donkey in the stones. He wasn't sure what that meant, but then again, his mother was drunk. A lot. Dirk just hoped the old-timer wouldn't start missing the map until he was far away from the plains.

He rounded the last outcropping on the map and saw the canyon that lay before him. He spun the map around in his hands, lining it up with the ledge of rock that he now stood upon. He studied the markings on the map and periodically looked at the rock formations in front of him. Then his skin tingled. Dirk looked at the map and then at a spot one hundred meters across the canyon. He broke out his nocs and focused the lenses. A small opening in a cliff came into view. Dirk smiled. It was treasure time.

Two days. Only two stinking days, and he had already had enough. Roman Kowalski would be thrilled if he never again set foot anywhere near the Burning Plains. In fact, if it weren't for his orders coming directly from the top, he might have told them he could not locate his target and called it a day. His inclination was to do just that, but without realizing it, Roman found himself heading to yet another nameless village in this desert hellhole.

He could not remember if this was the fourth or fifth village he had visited trying to track down his target. This man, this relic hunter, seemed to snake through these backwater areas like a thief in the night. But the man was indeed a thief, and from what the intel had shown, the time of day did not seem to matter, night or otherwise. At least his target was consistent.

The rickety old transport slowed, and Roman stood to exit. Once off the moving death trap, he asked around to locate the local enforcement station. He had found in the first two villages that this was the easiest way to confirm if his target had been in the area.

Roman found a shopkeeper who pointed him toward the center of the village, and after a good walk, he found the ramshackle office that represented the government in the area. "Government" was such a misnomer here. A loose association of corrupt warlords was a better description, but Roman hadn't found a word that fit that definition yet.

He gathered his motivation and pushed through the doors. It was bad enough dealing with law enforcement when you were a local. Add the fact that Roman was a foreigner, and it just complicated everything he was trying to accomplish. His resolve slackened as he saw the line of locals snaking out the door. This was going to take forever. Roman's motivation slipped another notch.

———

After unpacking his rigging, Dirk secured his line above the opening in the cliff. Slowly and methodically, he lowered himself down to the ledge at the mouth of the cave. Once he had good footing, he slackened his line, took a few steps into the cave, and started to unhook himself.

Now unhindered by his gear, he cautiously moved deeper into the space. His helmet lit up as the ambient light around him waned. He checked the section of the map that detailed the cavern. He knew there would be ancient catacombs that he would need to explore, but with the map, Dirk was saved a heap of guesswork. He chose the entrance to a smaller tunnel leading off to the south and started to creep down the moist rock.

Using the forward-looking beam and cascading side and rear floodlights of his helmet to light the way, he wound down the dank path. Each time he passed an offshoot in the tunnel, he checked the map to ensure he was on the right course. Normally he would never have put so much faith in a map, but his tingling skin told him that he was close. And Dirk's skin never lied.

A number of slips, near tumbles, and a few falls later, he noticed the walls of the tunnel widening. He pressed forward, seeing the light of his helmet dim as the surrounding light grew. He walked upright into a large room with walls reaching ten meters into the air. Far above his head, cracks between rock formations allowed beams of daylight to illuminate random spots on the ground. He scanned the room, marveling at its construction, searching for the treasure that had brought him here. He passed over the smaller relics that lined the floor as he swept the room.

He smiled as he saw it. On the far side of the cavern, resting on a large outcropping of stone, Dirk saw what he had come for. Restraining the excitement that his electrified skin was igniting in his body, he moved across the room toward the relic. As he approached, he saw just how magnificent it was.

The gold of its hilt gleamed in the sunlight shining down from the ceiling. The jewel-encrusted guard was dusty but nevertheless shimmered each time his helmet light hit it. But what was beyond description was the blade of the large scimitar. He eyed it, studying the gloss of the metal. Steel? Dirk moved in closer. No, it was platinum! The blade was made of pure platinum! Dirk's skin did yet another little dance.

———

Roman shuffled forward in the never-ending line of locals as they each in turn relayed their grievances to the enforcement officer at the desk. Story after story of robbery, property destruction, illegal gambling, and the like assaulted Roman's patience as he eavesdropped on the conversations.

It wasn't until an old man started telling the haggard officer of the theft of a family heirloom that Roman's ears perked up. From what he could gather from the man's adamant explanation, he had been swindled out of a family document that was very old and very precious. The officer asked the same set of questions that Roman had been hearing for the last two hours, but it wasn't until the old man started to describe the culprit that Roman realized that his luck was about to change. As he continued to listen to the story, Roman became convinced that the old man was talking about his target.

Once the office took the man's report and gave the customary "don't call us, we'll call you" speech, Roman gave up his position in line and followed the old man out of the decrepit office. A short distance later, he checked to be sure there were no enforcement officers in the area and then carefully approached the old man.

"Excuse me, sir," said Roman in the man's language as the old man continued to shuffle away from him. He turned and looked at Roman, instantly apprehensive. Roman played the authoritative foreign diplomat card. "My name is Roman, and I am a foreign diplomat visiting here under a security assignment." Roman took out his holo-ID and showed the man his credentials. "And you are?"

The old man's apprehension seemed to ratchet up a bit at the sight of the official-looking badge. His eyes flicked from the badge to Roman, then back again. It didn't seem to Roman that the badge was having the desired effect. He needed the old man to talk, not cower. "Pardon my intrusion, but I overheard you speaking with the enforcement officers about a document that a man stole from you. I think we can help each other with our mutual problem."

The man's eyes narrowed. He obviously did not like someone eavesdropping on him. "I assure you," Roman continued, "that I am only here to help. You see, I believe the man that stole your document is the same man I am looking for. I would love to get some details from you to see if I could be of any assistance in retrieving your stolen property."

The man continued to stare at Roman, still not making any indication that any of this was working. Roman tried a more direct approach. He started to reach behind him, and the old man's face dropped in fear. Roman slowed his movements as he spoke. "Perhaps we can find a more comfortable, private place to discuss the matter?" Methodically, Roman pulled out a stash of BP credits from his back pocket. The old man's apprehension instantly evaporated at the sight of the money. He surreptitiously looked around, then nodded for Roman to follow him. Roman fell into step right behind the old man as they set off for a darkened alley away from the bustling street.

———

Dirk carefully lifted the blade from the mounts. It was heavier and longer than he had anticipated, but he wrapped protective cloth around it as best he could. Now that he had acquired his prize, he took in the whole of the place. Almost instantly, strange hieroglyphics caught his eye. Dirk had seen these before in various other places he had borrowed items from. He had absolutely no idea what they were, but they always seemed to accompany the best of his finds. He looked around at all the other treasures in the stone room. It wouldn't hurt if he just perused the merchandise a bit. He set about examining the various holy relics strewn about the area.

———

Roman had him. He was sure the person the old man had described was the target. He could finally get out of this wretched place. He was now making his way back to the enforcement office to grease the wheels, so to speak. Roman had a large amount of grease, and all he needed to do was find the right man in charge.

Once there, Roman scanned the layout of the enforcement office. He saw the haggard intake officer. He wouldn't do at all. A few file clerks. Nope, too far down the totem pole. Then he saw the office at the back with the unmistakable markings of seniority. That was the man Roman had to talk to. Walking past the long line of plaintiffs, Roman flagged down the intake officer. Ignoring the complaints of the small old woman at the front of the line, he flashed his credentials at the officer. Immediately the man's bored demeanor changed. Roman spoke in the local dialect and told the man that he needed to see the Major, and that anyone who helped in his assignment would be greatly rewarded. Roman had accidentally on purpose let his wad of credits slide out from behind his credentials, which had the desired effect.

Moments later, Roman was in the Major's office, explaining the lucrative venture that the Major could be a part of. The man sitting behind the desk was listening with rapt attention.

Twenty minutes later, Roman, the Major, and two squads of officers headed out with the old native in tow.

———

After procuring some additional assets, Dirk secured his cargo and started to make his way back through the maze of tunnels. He had stayed way longer than his original plan had called for, but sometimes you just had to stop and smell the gold.

Using his mental map of the route, Dirk continued back through the various parts of the network of tunnels. An hour or so later, he found the entrance and started to hook up to his line. He checked his stash to make sure it was secure, engaged the climbing motor to eat up the slack, and steadied himself for the ascent.

A few meters up the line, Dirk's skin felt uneasy. Immediately he stopped. He had learned the hard way never to ignore his skin. He reached back and checked his find. Secure. He looked at the line. It looked just fine. He checked the climbing equipment. Nothing seemed out of place. He was just about to continue up when a few small rocks fell past him to the valley below. The hair on Dirk's skin stood on end. He looked up to find a rather large group of enforcement officers at the top of the ledge. This was bad.

———

Roman could taste it. While he recognized that it had only been a few days, he was elated that his efforts looking for this infuriating target had finally come to a close. After the old man recounted the circumstances of having the document stolen, Roman had probed further, inquiring what the document was exactly. Upon the old man explaining that his native ancestors had buried a sacred sword deep within a nearby cliff and that his family were descendants of those charged with keeping the sword, Roman's target had apparently posed as an archaeology professor from a visiting university to gain the man's trust. With the confirmation that the document was stolen and that it led to a priceless relic, Roman was now sure the thief was the same man he had been tracking.

Roman had paid the old native for both drawing a replica of the map from memory and to come along with the enforcement officers to apprehend the thief. Using the old man and his replicated map as a guide, the group had easily found the spot of interest, and upon discovering the rappelling equipment, Roman could not have been more pleased.

All they had to do now was wait. If he wasn't dead, the target would come up eventually. One of the squads moved in close to the ledge. This was it. Roman had him.

———

This was not happening. Not again. Dirk seriously considered finding a new profession. Maybe a teacher or a writer. Something that did not involve angry enforcement officials. Dirk quickly thought through his options and realized he only had two: go up and be caught, or go down and hopefully not be caught. Well, that was an easy one. Dirk readied himself. He took one last look down to make sure his path was clear and then hit the release on the brake. Gravity took over, and Dirk heard the line spin through the motor's grips with an ever-increasing whine. He was falling rapidly towards the valley floor. He had to time this just right.

Dirk kept looking down at the fast-approaching ground. Just a few more seconds. Dirk hit the brake, engaging the clamps. The line smoked and moaned at the intense friction. He closed his eyes, hoping that he had timed it right. If not, two broken legs would definitely not help in his escape attempt.

———

Roman heard the descending whine, and his heart sank. He scrambled to the edge of the rock face on his hands and knees, looking for its source. All he saw was a blurry image of a man falling towards the bottom of the cliff. Roman called to the Major to secure the line and start pulling the man up. The pit in Roman's stomach grew a little larger.

———

Dirk felt a sharp tug on the line and was momentarily lifted a half meter off the ground. He needed to get out of this rig, and fast. Removing a knife strapped to his boot, Dirk quickly sliced through the line. He landed deftly on his feet and used the knife to swiftly extricate himself from his gear. Once free,

Dirk looked at the top of the ledge, checking to see how far he had fallen. There was no way those goons could get a clean shot off at him from that height. He breathed a small sigh of relief. He wasn't out yet, but not having to worry about gunfire was a definite bonus. He quickly scanned his surroundings, taking in the valley floor. There was no time to see if the map had any pointers for escaping, so he relied solely on what he thought the floor would look like compared to the details of the rock face surrounding it.

He chose to go back the way he came, hoping there was a slope or ridge that he could climb to make it back to the outskirts of the village. From there he could arrange transport out, and everything would be fine. But as soon as he started off, his skin had other ideas. Dirk stopped dead in his tracks. Well, if he couldn't go that way, then he'd have to take his chances around the rock face in the other direction.

Dirk set out, weaving his way through the brush, not noticing what his skin was really trying to tell him.

———

Roman watched as the seven or eight men pulling on the line staggered back and fell to the ground as the weight at the end of the line suddenly disappeared.

"He must have cut the line!" yelled Roman to the Major. "Where is your second squad?" Roman knew he wasn't in charge, knew that he had absolutely no authority in this situation, but he desperately wanted to get out of this place. He wanted to get his target and go back to the motherland. Thus, Roman took a few liberties in sidestepping the official chain of command.

Remembering the reward Roman had promised him, the Major barked out orders to an officer, who radioed down to the second squad. Roman heard their reply, and his anxiety lifted slightly as they confirmed they had seen the target and were moving in to apprehend him. Oh, he was close, so close.

———

Dirk's skin was on the fritz. It was jumping at every tree and bush he encountered. He must be more shaken up than he initially realized. The vegetation was growing thicker, and he wasn't exactly sure where he was going. Then he saw movement just beyond a tree in front of him. Dirk skidded to a halt, rustling the dried leaves and dirt beneath him. He stood still as his skin warned of some apocalyptic doom about to befall him. Except Dirk had no idea what that doom was. He cautiously looked around him, his knife at the ready.

Then they emerged from the trees and bushes. Dirk could not believe it. He had been staring right at a spot where there had been nothing but trees one second, and the next there were scary-looking natives all with weapons pointed at him. One of them started yelling to the others. Dirk swung his head to the side to see what the yelling was about. It was then that he noticed the glint of gold reflecting back onto his face. He craned his neck farther to see the hilt of the scimitar fully exposed.

Dirk looked back at the native. She was pointing directly at him and screaming to the others. Now this was very bad. Dirk spun around and bolted back the way he came. He got past the edge of the forest and was just starting back towards the rock face when he ran smack into a squad of enforcement officers. This just was not his day.

————

It took quite a long time to backtrack around the rock face and meet up with the second squad, but Roman had been spurred by the radio chatter he overheard indicating that they had the target in custody. It was over. He had won and would now claim his prize. They had been after this particular acquisition for years, and only recently had there been enough intel to mobilize.

Roman rounded the last bit of rock with the first squad in tow. He could see the second squad with the target in restraints, but he did not expect to see the addition of a number of natives. Roman saw the animated, angry faces before he heard the harsh yelling directed at the squad and the target. The elation that Roman had experienced mere moments ago started to drain away.

As he approached, the Major shoved past him to speak

with the squad leader. After a bit of explanation, the Major started to converse with the natives. While Roman was fluent in the local dialect, this conversation was absolutely foreign to him. The Major's face continued to darken the more he conversed with who Roman assumed was the leader of the natives.

Things were going downhill fast. Roman had to do something. He stepped up to the Major and asked what was going on.

"It seems that this man has stolen a very holy artifact from a sacred temple," the Major replied to Roman.

"Well, that shouldn't be a problem. Just give them the artifact back, and I'll take my man and be on our way," stated Roman.

"It is not that simple. You don't understand the local politics in play here. Their tribe is part of a larger population ruled by one of the local warlords. If I do not turn this man over for trial, there will be serious repercussions from their lord." The Major's face looked torn, obviously remembering his payment being contingent on Roman taking custody of the man.

"Isn't there anything I can do? Perhaps give the tribe credits?"

"They are not interested in credits. Perhaps their ruling lord is, but I have no way of making the introduction, and if you walk into their lands, I'm afraid you will not come out."

"There must be something that can be done," pleaded Roman.

"Believe me, I am just as upset as you are," said the Major curtly. "Since I can't turn him over to you, I am out the credits you were to pay me, and I have this native dispute to deal with."

Roman looked at the man. He was stuck. He had no authority here, and there was no way he could strong-arm the Major. Not with all the officers around. "So what do you suggest, Major?"

The Major rubbed his chin, his scheming mind working through the problem. "Maybe all is not lost. I must take this man into custody. The local native liaison council will determine his fate. Maybe I can make some introductions there, and you could persuade the council members to release him into your custody."

"Of course. If you can arrange that, I think we can come to an amended sum for your efforts." Perhaps this wasn't a complete failure.

————

Roman sat at the dingy bar, looking at the drink that sat before him and thinking about yesterday's ordeal. He had located his target and had executed a foolproof plan to take him into custody, but now the thief was sitting in a jail cell waiting for his fate to be decided by the local council members. Despite the Major promising to introduce Roman to some of the more prominent council members, he had also explained that it would not be a quick process.

In a matter of minutes, Roman's hopes of leaving the Burning Plains were dashed into very small pieces. There was no way he could leave now that the target had been positively located. Roman had spent the last few hours gathering up the courage to report the series of events that had led him to this predicament.

He decided to check his secure messages before placing the dreaded call. Nothing. Roman tried to log in to the comm server. No luck. The coverage down here was spotty at best, and he hadn't been able to log in for a few days now. Maybe he could postpone the dreaded call after all. He thought back to his conversation with his contact a few days ago and then to the fact that the lucky stiff was not in this grimy bar.

Roman set down the interface and picked up his drink, a feeling of delayed doom replacing the impending one. He knocked back the spirits and started to get up from the bar when the news vid caught his eye. It wasn't the reporter or the station that he recognized. Rather, it was the building in the image that the anchor was talking about. Roman knew it from somewhere.

He studied it for a moment, his mental processes trying to pull out the reference. Then it hit him as the scene changed to a previously recorded clip. It was the UON apartment building that Shu was in. Roman barked at the barman to turn up the feed. He watched as the news report relayed that there still were no leads after the horrific scene at the apartments three nights ago.

Roman's feeling of delayed doom gave way to full-blown panic. If Shu was dead, that meant... Cho.

Roman snatched his interface. Still no coverage. He had to warn Cho. Roman just hoped he wasn't too late.

CHAPTER 4

COLD AS ICE

Time: Five years, three days after the desert facility was destroyed

Scene: Remote island estate, nighttime

The German shepherd sniffs the fence as his handler leads him along the perimeter of the estate. Other dogs trot along the opposite side of the property, each with a gun-toting handler. While none of them wear an official uniform, their fatigues all match in color. Dogless guards patrol the inner property line closest to the house. Invisible to the untrained observer, FLIR cameras dot the property and swing in a steady rhythmic motion from one side to the other.

A short way off from the fence, near the top of a tall pine, a man lies prone on one of the outermost branches of the massive tree. Wrapped head to toe in a black synthetic material, the man looks through his night vision lens at the sentries below. Through the blue-lit haze of his display, he watches as the sweeping beams of infrared track along the ground around the estate.

He is almost ready for his insertion.

Slowly, methodically, he pulls out a grappling gun and levels it along the branch of the pine. Using the gun's sight, he adjusts the minuscule laser dot shimmering off the side of the estate. Silently locking the gun's mounts into place, the man reaches down and wraps his arm and hand around the thick branch that is supporting him.

He closes his eyes and remains still for many moments. Slowly, he raises his foot off the branch at the trunk of the tree and swiftly brings it back down. Gripping the tree branch tightly with his wrapped arm, he squeezes his eyes closed. Moments later, he hears the barking begin, shortly followed by a low crash. Opening his eyes, he watches as handlers attempt to restrain dogs that are now pulling them to the opposite side of the estate. The FLIR cameras all sweep to one side to scan the far side of the house. Calmly, the man squeezes the trigger of the grappling gun. With a quiet compressed-air pop, the hook launches across the lawn and embeds itself squarely in the house. Quickly, the man connects his harness to the outstretched line and slides silently across the span in a matter of seconds.

Once at the side of the house, he effortlessly flattens himself against the brick, blending in with the shadows created by the overhanging roof. The man quietly slaps his thigh with his free hand and then reaches out to touch the brick of the house. Astonishingly, he hangs from the brick. Unhooking himself from the line, he stretches out his other hand, repeats the same process, and begins to shimmy across the face of the wall.

Down below, a guard and his dog come around the corner of the house, running toward the group of others gathered at the far end of the estate. The man flattens himself tighter against the brick, motionless as the guard passes him without notice. Tapping his hand against the brick, the man continues to ascend the wall. Finding himself at the topmost floor, he moves laterally across the wall toward a darkened window. He stops and rests the side of his head against the brick, just out of reach of the faint light emitting from the window. Closing his eyes, he remains there, intently focused on something that only he can hear. A wide grin slowly creeps across his face.

———

Vice-Chairman Reed sat across the mahogany table from the small Jadian man. Reed hated the little gooks, as his great-grandfather called them. Years of fighting them didn't soften easily, despite the requirement of political cordiality. But if there was one thing that Reed could do well, it was put on a show. Whether it was stumping on the campaign trail making empty promises to moms and veterans or sitting across tables from small, slant-eyed weasels who were trying to advance their pathetic empire, his ability to change the color of his true emotions was second only to a chameleon.

Finely aged scotch with ice in a crystal tumbler swirled in a mesmerizing motion. Vice Chairman Reed inhaled deeply; at least they had really good booze here. "I'm not sure how they do things in your part of the world, Mr. Cho, but the less I know about you and your organization, the better I'm going to sleep tonight."

Mr. Cho listened as his translator relayed the comment. The Jadian man nodded and spoke rapidly to his lovely intermediary.

"Mr. Cho understands your apprehension, Chairman Reed. He asks you to please understand that his efforts to evolve our empire's science programs are strictly peaceful, and that our scientists are only looking to protect our sovereign nation from rogue organizations outside the UWC that would seek to take away our people's freedom."

Reed could barely contain the sarcastic guffaw that welled up inside him. Perhaps he had imbibed enough scotch for the night. No use letting the juice compromise his ability to maintain his composure. People's freedom, he thought. The only thing free about their people was the amount of free income that they forked over to their oppressive leaders.

Reed eyed the small man across the table. His eyes roamed to the soft skin of the attractive woman sitting next to the man. Reed's mind started to wander as his eyes did the same. What I wouldn't give, thought the Chairman. His mind snapped back to reality. Had he any control over his wandering libido, he wouldn't be sitting here trying to deal with the devil to save his own skin. Reed did the math again in his head. If he could squeeze this little man out of at least seven and a half, he might just be able to avoid the repercussions of his indiscretions.

"You see, it's not that I don't trust you, but... Well, how do I put this delicately? The fact of the matter is, I'm up for reappointment in a year, and none of our 'business' here tonight can ever get out," said Reed.

Another stream of translation and instruction came. "Mr. Cho could not agree with you more, Chairman. There are many organizations in and out of the UWC that our empire is under scrutiny from. This... business, as you call it, will be kept under the tightest of security."

Reed nodded. Maybe he could get eight. Yeah, eight sounded like a good number. "Well, let's get down to that business." Reed set down the tumbler. "Now, I can't get you all of the specs at once. That would cause too much heat. But what I can get is the initial blueprints and research notes, followed by each subsequent release of the schematics."

More translation. "Mr. Cho is quite earnest in his desire for all the program files. While he can consent to a piecemeal transaction, he wonders what timeline you are suggesting."

Earnest, thought Reed. More like desperate. He picked up the scotch again. The timeline was going to be a problem.

Too stretched and his eight turned into five. Too quick, and even eight wouldn't matter as a resident in a three-by-two cell. He swirled the scotch around and around as he thought. "Timeline's tricky. The last thing you and I can afford is to have people sticking their noses where they don't belong."

The translator started speaking and then looked like she was thinking through this last statement. Finally, she spit out a last little bit very rapidly. Mr. Cho looked at Reed and nodded.

"What do you say about a twelve-month schedule?" asked Reed. "You'll get the first part in a month, then the remaining three iterations once a quarter over the next nine months." Mr. Cho listened to his translator and then sat contemplating. He motioned for a younger-looking Asian man to come over and then whispered something in the young man's ear. The young man bowed deeply and then replied in an equally hushed voice. Reed didn't pay much attention to any of this. He was too busy noticing the skirt length of the translator, or rather the lack of length. Mr. Cho cleared his throat, which brought Reed back to the conversation. He spoke to his translator, who then looked at Reed.

"Mr. Cho is agreeable to that timeline. In an effort to secure the transaction amicably, he is willing to offer five point seven."

Reed the chameleon did not let his emotions out of their cage. Despite his mind racing to redo the math, his face was calm and collected. Five point seven, he thought. That would leave him at least two and change short. Reed cleared his throat. "Well, that is a mighty fine offer, Mr. Cho. A fine offer indeed. I was, however, thinking more in the neighborhood of eight and a half."

Mr. Cho looked passively at the Chairman. As he relayed his lengthy response to the translator, she spoke to Reed. "Mr. Cho understands the risk that is involved with this particular transaction and is also well aware of the Chairman's fine tastes. He is willing to pay seven in addition to..." The translator quickly looked at Mr. Cho. She bowed her head and asked him a question. He repeated his response to her. She looked dumbfounded. She started to ask something else and was quickly cut off by a rapid flow of guttural sounds. She bowed her head even lower and returned her gaze cautiously to Reed. "Seven in addition to my personal services to you."

Reed's eyebrow shot upwards. "Not to be ungrateful for your generous offer, but what personal services could I possibly want from Mr. Cho?"

The translator hesitated at this statement. As she started to speak, she was interrupted. "Mr. Reed, I was not offering my personal services, but rather the personal services of my lovely translator. I understand you will be here for a few more days. Let her show you the sights and scenes of this great area."

Sneaky greedy... now I remember why I hate these little... Reed did not let his expression change. Inside, he could barely restrain the flow of adrenaline that was coursing through his body. He looked at the translator, who was staring at the floor. He knew he wasn't going to get a better offer. "Well, I suppose we have a deal th—" Just then, a loud crack sounded. The young man grabbed his radio and spoke rapidly into it. Mr. Cho barked orders to the man, who swept out of the room quite suddenly. Then he turned to Reed.

"This estate is surrounded by a very old forest. Branches fall all the time. There is nothing to worry about."

"Branches, you say? Just how secure is this place?"

"The highest level of security and detail was put into your visit tonight. Rest assured you are well protected."

For the first time in as long as he could remember, Reed's stoic face sagged just slightly. He had known this was a bad idea. "Well, Mr. Cho, let's get our business concluded and then I will be on my way." Reed glanced at the translator. "Or I guess, we'll be on my way."

Mr. Cho opened his mouth to reply when he noticed the air in the room dropping in temperature. His breath fogged as he started to speak. He looked around. Everything seemed to be normal. Then his eyes stopped at the far end of the room. Something on the wall looked out of place. The paint seemed to be changing color along a vertical line that started just above the floor and ran up the wall and then continued along the ceiling. The odd line seemed to stop right at the fire sprinkler. Mr. Cho gazed at the line, wondering if he was seeing things. He called to another man in the room and pointed toward the wall. Just as the man started to walk across the room, the clattering began. Pipes jangled and clanked in the walls. Reed had followed Cho's gaze and was now watching the far wall as well. He dropped his scotch.

———

The night had gone exactly as Cho had anticipated. Despite having to reveal that he did not need his translator, Reed's weakness had shone through just as Cho had planned. Bringing the lovely woman along to the meeting had been sheer genius on his part.

If it wasn't for that disturbance outside, he would have considered the whole thing a complete success.

Cho saw the Chairman's face dip slightly. "Well, Mr. Cho, let's get our business concluded and then I will be on my way." There it was; like clockwork, the man's lust took control. "Or I guess, we'll be on my way."

Cho was just about to reply when he saw his breath cloud from his mouth. What was going on? He looked around the room. Nothing seemed out of place. But then why was it so cold all of a sudden? Something across the room caught his eye. Something about the far wall seemed... off. Cho saw a vertical shimmer start from just above the floor and continue up past the darkened window to the ceiling. He watched as the odd discoloration continued across the ceiling and terminated at the fire sprinkler. He called to one of the remaining guards and told him to check out the wall.

Suddenly, there was a loud metal clanging. Cho looked around the room, trying to figure out what was happening. He caught sight of the Chairman, the panic painted on his face, and the now empty tumbler on the floor. The banging grew louder and louder. Cho whipped his attention back to the far wall. The paint and plaster were starting to crack and crumble to the floor. He stood up and started to back away from the wall. Just as he saw Reed start to stand, a copper pipe burst through the ceiling. Reed screamed and covered his face with his arms, but nothing happened. No water, no mist, no nothing. The clanging had stopped.

Cho watched as Reed peeked out from behind his arms. The Vice-Chairman stared at the frosty pipe hanging rigidly from the ceiling. Reed slowly turned to Cho with a questioning expression on his face. Cho started to speak, but just then a hollow pop sounded. Cho watched in slow motion as a column of ice rocketed out of the hanging pipe and skewered Vice-Chairman Reed through the chest.

———

Somewhere far beyond the reach of the FLIR cameras and German shepherds, a man dressed all in black runs through the forest at breakneck speed.

CHAPTER 5
THE PROJECT

Time: Five years, 14 days after the desert facility was destroyed

Scene: Boardroom of MESA Labs

"In our top story tonight, a ranking member of the UON Science and Technology Advancement Committee was brutally murdered at his secure apartment home. While authorities are being tight-lipped about the murder, anonymous inside sources spoke with us about the event. Mark Brown has more."

"A gruesome scene unfolded last night in the apartment home of Dr. Yuon Shu, a member of the United Organization of Nations Science and Technology Advancement Committee. Dr. Shu was best known as a leader in cutting-edge research on computer-human interfaces over the last ten years. At his new post in the UON, he was in charge of approving funding for various companies around the Collective that sought to improve the standard of living by introducing much-needed advancements in healthcare, agriculture, and education. All that work ended here in a bloodbath late last night. Sources inside the UON investigation confirmed that Dr. Shu was at his apartment under guard due to recent death threats made against him. Before we were escorted off the premises, we were able to obtain this still of Dr. Shu's apartment."

The image moved alongside the reporter as other footage of the scene played in the corner.

"As you can see, the doorframe was split in two by what looks like an earthquake of some sort. But my source tells me investigators found no evidence of any other part of the building being affected, nor were there any geological events last night. Further, rumors indicate that Dr. Shu's personal guard was found just inside the door.

"Initial reports show that the guard appeared to be killed as a result of head trauma caused by the shifting floor. Any additional details about Dr. Shu's death are sketchy at best. It seems there are a number of unanswered questions, the most pressing being how an assassin gained entry into this high-security residence, took out a personal guard, and accessed the secured apartment without the use of explosives, rigging, or heavy equipment."

The videos of the scene minimized off-screen as the vid of the reporter filled the space.

"Now, my source tells me that investigators have not ruled out some sort of portable mechanical device to jack the underlying floor, but upon inspection of the floor below, no evidence has been found. The UON is holding a press conference later today, and we will bring you any further details."

"Thanks, Mark. With so many unknown questions surrounding this high-profile death, do the authorities have any leads on the assailant?"

"Tina, from what I can gather, investigators are searching for details that will help them find the person or persons responsible. But I will say that as we have been reporting from this location, we have heard a number of whispered conversations among investigators and other news feeders about another possible strike by the famed Magician. However, we have not heard anything official confirming that."

"Well, thanks again, Mark. Keep it tuned to this feed. We will bring you updates as this story progresses. Now, a look at the markets. In heavy trading this morning..."

"Turn it off. I think we have heard enough," said the old man at the head of the dark cherrywood boardroom table. The holographic image of the newsfeed faded out, leaving a company logo spinning slowly above the projector. Men in dark suits lined one side of the table and sat opposite a line of lab techs, all in white coats. Monitors with floating heads hung just behind the seated men, and more came online as others joined the meeting from remote locations.

"This recording of the incident two weeks ago marks the latest use of the lost project," the old man said in a low voice. "The media can speculate all they want. Our plants inside the UON have confirmed the modification of the floor of the apartment. No explosives, no mechanical devices. Preliminary vids taken right after the incident show that the floor was simply mod'd to jut up three feet in that isolated location. Warrick, load the feed."

A younger man tapped some commands on an interface, and the spinning logo faded to a display of charts and graphs. Warrick cleared his throat.

"As you can see, the spectral analysis of the floor shows a slight increase in residual energy. I believe that—"

"Slight is the key word here," interrupted a white coat at the other end of the table. "Your residual energy blip is less than the fluctuation in the calibration sequence. Before you go sending us on another covert op to chase down yet another dead end, don't you think we should have some more proof that this is a result of the missing project?"

Warrick looked unfazed. "Doctor, I appreciate your healthy skepticism regarding the retrieval of an asset your department lost. I'm sure we all understand how your past attempts to recover the long-lost project have jaded you and perhaps dampened your hopes in recovering it. But please, and I mean this in the kindest of ways, shut up."

"I will not shut up, you sniveling little punk. I was splitting atoms when you were still setting fire to your hair with your home chemistry set. As I have voiced many times before, I know my project. I know what it was capable of. I have the test results just prior to... well, the most recent data we have. There is just no way it is capable of this type of complex modification."

"Doctor, your test results are five years old. As we have discussed previously, we are in the dark as to what its capabilities would be if left unmonitored or, worse, found and further developed." Warrick enlarged the graph to show the small blip in the otherwise flat line. "This spectral evidence confirms that molecular modification has occurred."

"Do you even understand what you are talking about?" the doctor blurted out. "Who would even have the resources to further develop the project? In the past, we have seen copious amounts of residual energy being left at the scenes of these so-called assassinations. First responders have even filed reports of the trees and earth around the modifications being warm when the ambient temperature is quite cool. What you are inferring, Warrick, is that whoever is using the prototype has somehow learned from our attempts to track its use and has started to police its brass, so to speak, by cleverly dissipating the residual energy that ensues after structure modification. Do you have any idea how asinine a theory that is? We are talking about a technology that, when we last saw it used, was barely able to bend a toothpick.

And that feat was accomplished after months of intense work!"

"And yet its use has graduated from bending toothpicks to high-tech assassinations. Oh, and let us not forget these images from the night when you lost the project." The charts faded into holographic images of skewered guards and charred hallways of what looked like a research facility. This seemed to put a damper on the doctor's protest. Warrick continued.

"Besides, our recovery team was first on scene and confirmed the use of the prototype. Our local agents have made the needed arrangements with the UON investigation and with the local LEOs. Standing gag orders have also been issued to those who have advanced knowledge of this situation."

The old man stood from his chair and walked to the full-length tinted window of the conference room. He stood staring out for a few minutes before he spoke. "Gentlemen, while we will pursue this new development in recovering our property, we must press forward with our efforts. Kingston has a report on the good professor that I believe all of you should hear."

Warrick passed the tablet to a man in an expensive-looking black suit. He tapped out a few commands, and the face of a middle-aged man began to rotate at the center of the table.

"As most of you know, Dr. Eli Thurman has been a part

THE MAGICAN PROTOCOL 61

of our efforts here for quite some time now, although the good doctor doesn't really know that. It was Thurman's early work into M-theory and resonant frequencies that led us to borrow his research, which eventually led to the interface lab. We have been keeping tabs on Thurman and his work for a number of years, but the rebuilt interface lab has recently indicated that it may be time to acquire Thurman as an official asset to MESA. Developments in user acceptance testing have suggested that success may be just around the corner."

Kingston changed the holographic image to a vid of Dr. Thurman in a lecture hall.

"Currently, Thurman heads a university research lab that has limited resources. We at the company have obviously progressed far beyond their work; however, the interface lab has yet to produce a working model as advanced as the project is. Seeing the rising cost associated with the increased quantity of coding needed, it has been suggested that we start our efforts to bring the doctor on board."

"I understand that most of you share my concern about the doctor finding out how we used his research for the advancement of our goals," said the old man, still staring out the window. "Kingston and the head of the interface lab have begun to develop a plan that will give us access to Thurman and keep him at a safe distance from the more sensitive efforts that are currently being undertaken."

"Yes," confirmed Kingston. "The head of the interface lab has been working on this acquisition for a number of years now. It is his opinion that when Thurman comes on board, we could be looking at building another prototype on par with the perceived current specs of the lost project," Kingston glanced at the white coat at the end of the table, "in a minimum of 12 months."

"And what developments has the lab made, and why do we even need Thurman if we've progressed so far beyond his current research?" asked a nameless man in the middle of the line of suits.

"Well, short of giving you the entire briefing," replied Kingston with a smirk, "the head of the interface lab has reported that they have run into a challenge with current prototypes accepting the coding. However, this latest iteration has shown slightly less adverse declines in performance after the coding trials but is still hampered by its side effects. While the lab has mitigated these with the advanced U/I that they have developed, this is only a temporary solution. The head of the lab believes that Thurman will be able to fill in the gaps to make the interface seamless."

"Do you really think Thurman has the ability to advance us further than what we've been able to accomplish?" asked the nameless man.

The old man turned from the window. "Eli Thurman is the reason this company has been so successful in our interface pursuits. Eli Thurman combined the needed theories to produce the science that allowed us to build the prototype. Eli Thurman is unmatched in his understanding of quantum dynamics and Tesla's works. Aside from his moral objections to some of the things we do around here, Eli Thurman could advance this company into the next century with the knowledge he possesses." The old man walked over and sat in his chair. "With the combined talents of the head of the interface lab and Thurman on board, we would finally be able to change the recovery of the project into the termination of the project and eliminate those who perpetrated its theft. We would be able to produce what we have been trying to craft for almost the last decade. So in answer to your question, yes, we believe that Thurman has that ability. Gentlemen, I believe that will be all for today. Please file your reports with your respective division heads."

The floating heads faded into spinning logos as the men around the table stood and started to exit the room. Kingston docked the tablet, listened as the old man whispered something to him, and left the room as well. A trip down the elevator, four biometrically sealed doors, and three guard posts later, Kingston stepped into the office of the head of the interface lab.

"The old man wants to come down and see the new prototype," said Kingston softly.

The man behind the desk raised his head slowly to look at Kingston.

"Is it... online?" asked Kingston.

Without replying, the man stood from his desk, walked past Kingston, and continued down a separate hallway. The two walked in silence as they passed entry after entry. At the end of the hall, they came to another biometrically sealed door. The man stooped to scan his eye and then waved his hand across the screen. A moment later, the viewing port slid to one side. The man indicated for Kingston to look for himself. Kingston stepped up to the small window and peered into an almost pitch-black room. As his eyes strained to see the contents of the room, a dark outline anchored to a table slowly came into focus.

CHAPTER 6
LADY IN THE LAKE

Time: Seven years after the desert facility was destroyed, early morning

Scene: Academy City 676

Ok, ok...you need to focus. I know you don't want to, but you just need to do it if you want to pass.

Sam took a breath and started to read, but almost tripped as she did. She hated walking to school. It wasn't that she didn't like school; school was just fine. It wasn't that she disliked walking either. In fact, she rather enjoyed walking. What she didn't like was walking to school while attempting to finish an essay for her stupid critical writing class. That was really annoying. And of course, the dumb essay was due on the very day she was going to meet Richard to—

Focus, Samantha!!

Sam refocused, her attention locking onto the holographic

screen projection a half-meter in front of her, trying to find the place where she had left off.

Decades after the recession of the early 21st century, the difference between the exceedingly poor and ridiculously rich was so great that the world entered a Post-Industrialization Feudal Age. Now the rich are disgustingly rich, and the poor have become the exclusive and sole responsibility of the government.

Sam stopped, making a mental note. She needed less personality in the essay, less of the incendiary adjectives. She could almost smell the attitude. Sam continued to read.

The transformation of the world economy occurred after World War III broke out. The war started when extremists in the Central Eastern countries, or modern-day New Nicrawmini, attacked their longtime Zionist rivals, or modern-day Esai. The war lasted ten years, eventually engulfing all the major world players, and exacted a cost of over three billion lives and forty percent of the livable land in the world.

The end of the war brought the rise of two new super-powers: the United Western Collective, or the super-government made up of the old United States of America, Canada, Mexico, and South and Central America, and the Jade Empire, made up of the old European Union states and many Asian countries. The next fifty years produced a cold war like the people of Earth had never seen, creating a landscape where the rich got richer and the poor were taken care of by the newly established conglomerate governments. Now there are very few in-betweeners, or people of the middle class. Not to say they are totally gone; the rich would never let that happen, as there has to be someone that buffers the poor from the rich in the world. In my town, that is where Partial Palace comes in. Partial Palace is where I live, and I believe it should be dismantled as a matter of public policy.

Sam shook her head; she had slipped into the first person again. She hated when she did that.

Thousands of other communities like Partial Palace can be found in every town in the United Western Collective. My community is located in the middle of T. Tracks in Academy City 676, in the State of Bush.

Sam stared at the passage. There was more to this place, a more expressive description, a deeper and livelier introduction, but really it was more or less the same as most other UWC towns. Further description probably wasn't needed; it would just create unnecessary clutter.

Sam took her finger and, with a few quick strikes, erased the last sentence. Ms. Diablo wasn't going to like that description; it was just too boring. Sam would have to change that later.

The T. Tracks aren't really tracks, as their name suggests. There might have been real tracks on this particular stretch of land at some point, but ever since the advent of cellular bio-fuel and cold-fusion transport, the bullet trains of the 22nd century were bound to fail. Now, where 150 years ago a train might have once traveled, there is a park that would embarrass the old United States National Park, Yellowstone. The park is complete with a lake as deep and blue as a ship-sinking glacier and hybrid trees tens of years old that shadow the vast expanse of lush grass, flowers, and other vegetation.

Beauty came at a price, however. In truth, this park that the townsfolk call T. Tracks has a single purpose: it divides the high part of town from the low part, High Tracks and Low Tracks, or the really rich and the quite poor. In all actuality, T. Tracks acts like a barrier to any who might venture out of their station. The park thus becomes a scene of serenity but also a symbol of division.

Sam highlighted this sentence. She liked that one; it had some great imagery.

The T. Tracks and other landmarks like it are not out of the ordinary in government cities like this one. In fact, it is not that much different from every other Academy City in the Collective. This similarity comes from their purpose of policing mandatory education from six to eighteen years of age throughout the Western Collective.

Sam made another note; she needed to add "United" before "Western Collective."

This Academy city, which like most Academy cities is about 85% students, holds one major difference. The preconceived roles of the rich class and the poor class are less embraced among the student body. In sharp contrast, other Academy Cities across the Great Collective have socioeconomic strife, or fighting within their student population. But here in Academy City 676, it isn't all that bad being poor. The government pays for just about everything from healthcare, school, food, and housing to entertainment. Practically name it, and the government takes care of it. While everything isn't roses and butterflies, for the most part, the residents of Academy City 676 have their needs met. This, in my opinion, is probably the reason that people here are a bit more accepting of the Post-War Feudal System. The aftermath of the war created needs, not wants. People needed for so long they forgot how to want. Now that it's been years since the end of the war, the residents of the world, excluding a select few, still haven't remembered how to want, and in my opinion, that is where the problem is found.

In Academy City 676, a person's social position or socioeconomic status, whether you are from High Tracks or Low Tracks, determines everything about them: what classes they take, who they sit with at the lunch table, the people they talk to—everything. It is for this reason that living in Partial Palace leaves uncertainty where conformity should have resided. And as anyone from Partial knows all too well, there are few things worse than uncertainty. Being from Partial makes me very uncertain, as I have no real place where I belong. I'm not accepted by either the High or Low Tracks crowds. There is just me.

Sam reread the paper, fixing the punctuation as she did.

She would probably have to change that last portion. It sounded sort of whiny.

She took a deep cleansing breath as she walked artfully through rays of early morning light. Sam could already see the revisions she would make later. She was never very good at these writing assignments. That was why she had to—

Her concentration broke as a buzzing scream rent the peace of the morning, splintering the calm in a stab of noise. The abrupt change stopped Sam dead in her tracks, her adrenaline heightening her senses. She spun around, searching for the source of the noise, the scream fading in and out, going quiet and loud, quiet and loud, over and over again until any semblance of rational thought felt like a distant memory. The sound burned with fire, skimming the surface of her brain and scorching her calm. Sam tuned into the burn as words, some jumbled and confused, others twisting in somewhat coherent patterns, jumped to the forefront of her thoughts while strange companion emotions pushed at her own emotional core. Sam's eyes went blurry as a tingling sensation took over. Her vision grew dark.

Then blackness closed in...closed in until...until...the nip of the breeze startled her. Her eyelids fluttered, and she scanned her surroundings, taking in the light of the yawning sun and the shadows of the springtime trees. Nothing seemed out of place, not a single indication of what had just happened or why.

Sam paused in her contemplation and whispered to

herself just to make sure she wasn't dreaming. "What on earth was that? What just happened?"

Sam tried to collect her thoughts, but the questions kept running laps around the track of her mind. It was all so fuzzy. She grasped at a thing, something. She wasn't even sure what it was. For some odd reason, she couldn't seem to remember.

"HEY SAM, SNAP OUT OF IT!"

Sam whipped around, going for the gas-blaster in her bag.

"Whoa!" said a cute Latina girl with crunchy brown hair. "I am so going to sue you if you gas-blast me."

Sam's finger relaxed off the button as she slackened her grip. "Oh Cammie, it's only you." She gave Cammie a small shove. "Why were you yelling like that? You scared the church out of me."

"'The church out of you?'" Cammie grinned thoughtfully. "Maybe I should scare you more often. I could use more church in my life."

"You mean more morality."

Cammie shrugged. "Don't get so, like, wrapped up in the details, Sam. Besides, you are in no place to talk about morals. Hello! You totally almost gas-blasted me. Me! Your best friend! Do you have any idea how bad that stuff is for your skin?"

Sam put her fingers to the bridge of her nose, squeezing the pressure point there. "So let me get this straight. I almost gas-blast you, and you're worried about whether it negatively affects your skin?"

Cammie nodded vigorously. "Love is a battlefield, Sam. Don't ever forget it."

Sam paused. "Uh...what are you talking about? Wait—never mind. I don't really want to know. Back to the gas blast—how would you know what it's like to be gas-blasted? This doesn't have something to do with your restraining order, does it?"

Cammie scowled. "You set one tree on fire because a boy breaks up with you, and you're branded for life."

Sam laughed. "You're lucky all your dad was able to pull some strings and get you probation."

Cammie sighed dramatically. "Ahh, no one understands me."

Sam placed her hand on Cammie's shoulder. "It's rough being you, isn't it?"

"Of course, being a diva is tough stuff. Ok, sidebar conversation."

Sam rolled her eyes. She hated it when Cammie called a sidebar conversation; it usually meant that she was about to go off.

"Samantha OMGWB, what are you wearing? I thought we talked about this. No more frumpy jeans and formless shirts. What happened to the Liquid Light sundress I gave you?"

At this, Cammie rolled the hem of her own strategically placed skirt. Cammie wasn't the cutest girl on the planet, but she made up for it with sense and style. She could dress for her body type like no other person Sam knew.

"Cammie, I've explained this ten times to you already. Samantha," Sam pointed at herself, "isn't like that. Those sorts of threads don't look good on me. They—they just aren't me."

"Um, the two boys staring at you with 'stalker eyes' on Friday seemed to indicate otherwise. Besides, that red high-cut Jadian quju was a hot little number. Even the store manager was gawking, and I'm pretty sure he's gay!"

Sam rolled her eyes. "He's not gay, Cammie, just really happy."

"Uh, I wasn't aware there was a difference." Cammie dipped her head, leveling her gaze at Sam's chest. "Sam, you're trying to be more feminine, remember? Well, at least you're wearing a bra today."

Cammie reached out and gave Sam a squeeze before she could react. Sam squealed in surprise, slapping Cammie's hand as her face blushed scarlet. She glared with her arms crossed over her chest. "Pervert."

Cammie grinned. "Well, if the shoe fits—"

"Then buy the whole store."

"You sure are pissy today. Is it that time of the month?"

"Yes, the time of the month when I need a new best girlfriend."

Cammie looked at her, scandalized. "I thought I was your best friend. Oh, don't tell me that Dick beat me out."

"Don't call him Dick, and yes, he did beat you out because he doesn't fashion grope me on a regular basis."

Cammie's expression soured. "Only because he doesn't have the guts to."

"Cammie, you're impossible."

A squelching noise, like the sound a cat might make if it was drowning, reoriented Sam's thoughts. That weird noise that had assaulted her... She had been trying to figure out where it had come from.

She leveled her gaze at Cammie, who was busy entering her Vii Space page. Sam spoke quickly, knowing that the social site would completely destroy any chance she might have to talk to her friend. Well, face-to-face at least.

"Moving on from Richard, why haven't you said anything about that screeching noise a few minutes ago? It's not like you to just ignore an unexplained phenomenon. It might have been aliens, you know."

"Ha-ha-ha, Sam, everyone knows that aliens only attack at night and they don't scream. Nice try. If you are going to make fun of me, at least make it a bit more—Ashley, OMGWB I can't be-li-eve he asked you..."

Sam stopped listening. Cammie was in Vii Space now; she was gone for the time being, causing their walk to come to a dead stop.

Stupid social cloud. What a waste of time, thought Sam as she looked out over the water, watching the waves ripple.

She sighed heavily. "Richard, where are you when I need you?"

A glare from the water caught her attention. An unnatural shine seemed to move with her. The light, which was of a curiously soft nature, deteriorated immediately, leaving only a glowing trail. Sam stepped away from Cammie, venturing towards the edge of the lake. A few feet from the bank, settled low in the clear water, sat a shimmering metal box. Sam studied the box from the shore.

"Now what on earth are you?" she said, squinting in an attempt to make out the box. A few minutes passed in idle contemplation until Sam made a decision.

"All righty then," she said, speaking aloud. "Into the water we go."

Sam removed her shoes and socks, pulled her pant cuffs up as high as they would bunch, then moved cautiously into the water. She neared her target, the water coming up much higher than she had originally anticipated. The box was right in front of her, but she didn't know if she wanted to spend the rest of the day drenched. A brief spell of calm water momentarily gave Sam an unimpeded view of the box. She again considered her options.

You're already here, she thought. Might as well...

Sam leaned over into the water and barely made contact when—"Sam! What on earth are you doing?"

The call startled her, and without further preamble, Sam slipped and—splash!

Sam, now completely wet, came up out of the water holding the box in her hand.

"Sam, are you ok?" Cammie came rushing to her side, barely able to control her laughter as Sam stomped onto the marshy grass. "Why on earth did you go in the lake?"

Sam shook her mane of matted hair and held up the box. "Wanted to see what this was."

Cammie laughed again. "Nice, Sam, a tin box. How dumb can you be?"

"Thanks a lot, Cammie, that was really sweet."

Cammie's eyes went wide and innocent. "Uh, I'm pretty sure it's not my fault you decided to go for a mid-morning swim." Cammie looked Sam up and down, lingering on her soppy clothes and waterlogged hair. "Though I have to admit, Sammie, I think it's an improvement."

Sam scowled and pushed past Cammie, who scrambled after her.

"Hey, come on, Sam, it was just a joke," said Cammie, attempting to sound contrite. "Sorta."

Sam had already had enough of this day, and the stupid thing had barely started. Falling on her butt in the lake was a bad omen. She was going home to shower and hide under the covers. A whispered conversation directly behind her told Sam that even as Cammie was following her, she was back on Vii Space. Oh, how Sam hated that—

"Samantha!" called Cammie, sounding more than a little excited. "Weren't you supposed to meet Dick this morning?"

Sam came to an abrupt halt, cursing her luck. "Yeah, I'm supposed to be feeding the ducks with Richard. Crap! He's going to be so mad at me. I've got to get home and change."

"I don't think he's thinking about that right now, sweetie." Cammie slid her fingers across her screen. The display reacted, enlarging and reversing a vid for Sam to see.

Sam put a weary hand to her forehead. "Oh no, not again." She turned on her heel. "Come on, Cammie. We have to stop this before someone gets hurt!"

Cammie rolled her eyes. "What? Sam, do we really have to do this? Again? It's just a couple of pics and some vids, no big deal."

"If they get carried away, he could die, Cammie!" screamed Sam as she turned and started to run in her sopping clothes.

"You're overreacting as usual, Sam. He'll be just fine. He always is." Cammie walked reluctantly after her, mumbling in a low voice, "And even if he did die, at least he wouldn't make you late all the time."

"I heard that, Cammie!"

Cammie cracked a smile. "Why can you always hear me, Sam?" She shrugged to herself, hurrying to catch up to Samantha.

CHAPTER 7
THE LION AND THE LAMB

Time: Current day, early morning
Scene: T. Tracks Park

"Come on, Dick, you're going to have to do better than that if you don't want me to flatten your fat face!"

Sam could hear the taunting before she could see what was happening. She had run all the way to the T. Track's Hamster Wheel, which was really just a cute way of saying playground equipment. A huge multi-story castle of a jungle gym, which included towers, walkways, and battlements, was only one part of the Hamster Wheel's amenities. The park, affectionately called Camelot, was a place that many of the older Academy City 676 residents liked to gather in those rare moments of free time. This tendency to congregate almost guaranteed that if there was something interesting happening, they could get the deets at the base of Camelot.

This morning wasn't any different; there was already an expanding crowd of students whooping at the current proceedings. Sam and Cammie pushed their way through the crowd. Sam groaned in unison with the spectators as the people around her flinched back at the sound of a sharp smack cracking against exposed skin.

Sam took a deep breath. "Why? Why do you have to deal with this..." Her voice drifted off as the scene continued to unfold.

Two boys were circling each other. The first, a boy with tight spiral locks of hair, had his hands up, mimicking the old 20th-century boxing pros while he danced around the second. Curly-q's shirt was off, his body glistening with just the right amount of sweat to accent an almost perfect physique. The second boy, a chubby kid with massive girth, was sweating gallons as he tried to fend off Curly-q. Fatty's defense was desperate, his footwork slow, and his punches pitiful. This fight was the equivalent of an old fat lamb trying to take on a young overzealous lion while the rest of the jungle watched the disembowelment.

The crowd "ooed" and "ahhed" as Curly-q connected a punch to the side of Fatty's face. Fatty crumpled to the ground, spitting blood. Curly-q threw his hands up as the crowd cheered.

"Don't even think about it, Sam," whispered Cammie in a not-so-quiet voice. "You'll only embarrass him."

Sam turned to face Cammie. "But come on, Cammie, you saw that punch. He's really going to hurt him this time!"

"You say that every time, Sam, and it never happens. I'm starting to think this is more for show than anything else."

Just then, Curly-q landed another shot, this time to the body. Fatty went down again. A round of high fives from some of his goony friends ensued as Curly-q danced to the enthusiastic cheers of adoration from the onlookers. Fatty was spitting blood again and was nursing a fat lip. Curly-q knelt down in front of him.

"Dick, I thought you were taking a mixed martial arts class. Weren't you supposed to be getting better at this? It's getting really old just beating your blubber all the time."

"We cannot all be as physically gifted as you, Dyson. Though it does make me speculate how your performance may suffer when you have opponents that will actually fight back."

The crowd started to laugh, but it almost instantly sputtered and coughed into a hushed mumble. Dice Danni Dyson XIII was a high roller, even in the High Tracks crowd. But at just over one and a half meters tall and only 59 kilos, it was hard to be intimidated by him personally. His Ganga bodyguards, on the other hand, were rumored to be byproducts of failed attempts at crossing humans with polar bears.

The Ganga population became completely loyal to Dyson's

father after the business mogul donated crates of the legendary cleaning configurations to the fragmented government of the Burning Plains. Nestled in the heart of the unlivable lands of the South, the Burning Plains were some of the most inhospitable land on good old mother Earth, and the Ganga called it their home. Because of Dice Danni Dyson XII's act of kindness, or perhaps his ploy to cement the Ganga into forced indentured servitude, the Ganga were tied to the Dyson family and probably would be for the foreseeable future.

Then there was Sam's best friend, Richard. Sweet, good-hearted Richard, who just happened to be the smartest student to ever attend Academy City 676. This was Richard's blessing and curse. While he was one of the smartest people in all of Academy City 676, he wasn't a fighter despite his hulking 2-meter and almost 145-kilo frame. No, Richard wasn't a fighter; an eater, yes, but not a fighter.

The Ganga's threatening glares stifled the giggles that snapped and popped behind cupped mouths, but not before Dyson heard them. He gave Richard a swift kick to the gut. Richard groaned in pain.

"Stop laughing immediately!" Dyson called out to the crowd, his voice going shrill. "Or you will suffer. I will make you all suffer. I'll show you! I'll show all of you!"

Dyson snapped his fingers. The Ganga snapped to attention. "Get him up. We're done playing around."

The Ganga followed orders, grabbing hold of Richard and hoisting him up. Now on his feet, the Ganga threw

Richard against one of Camelot's support beams. The gathered crowd started to mutter amongst themselves. Richard closed his eyes as his leg started to shake violently, a habit that Sam knew all too well. Richard was scared. Dyson walked around as if he were about to start a school lecture.

Sam felt a tingle as Dyson continued to jeer at Richard. A strange sensation traveled up her spine and nuzzled into her brain. "Don't even think about it, Dyson," she blurted out.

Too late. Dyson's punch was already speeding for the center of Richard's head. Sam took three big steps, her body acting on its own, fully knowing that she wasn't going to make it in time. She could already see the bloody mouth, broken teeth, and broken nose. But would he stop there? No, he wouldn't. Dyson would feel the strength of the position and strike again and again, until... until... Involuntarily, she closed her eyes at the last second; she did not want to see it.

A thud and yelp of pain was followed by a chorus of laughter. Confused, Sam opened her eyes to see what had happened. Over the din, Sam heard Cammie shout.

"Dyson, you're such a goof. How did you miss? He was a half-meter in front of you!"

More laughter sounded, including the Ganga, though they at least attempted to hide it. Dyson was enraged. He held his hand gingerly; it looked broken. He yelled at the Ganga to get Richard, who was already scrambling and tripping over his own feet in desperate flight. Sam looked at Richard's chubby face. The idiot had his eyes closed.

"Richard, you fool, open your eyes!"

Richard's eyes popped open, his expression wild as he continued to scramble away from the Ganga. He scrambled along the border of the fence, trying to find an opening he could get through. No such luck. He turned and again ran back down the incline to Camelot's base. He hadn't run more than a few meters when—

Smack!

Richard hit something hard, something that had not been there earlier. Everyone was holding their hands to their eyes, the glare of sunlight making it difficult to see into the early morning sun. The Ganga's chase had stopped all while Dyson was whimpering and swearing, but in a subdued tone. He was even cowering a bit. What Sam could make out through the glare took her a second to understand.

"Whoa there, buddy," said a playful voice. "You'd better watch where you're going, or a face plant into a wooden beam could be in your near future."

Sam shifted her position until she could finally see a tall boy steadying Richard. With shaggy blond hair, clear blue eyes, and perfect bone structure, he stood in front of one of Camelot's structural supports and spoke to Richard in a low voice. Sam whispered his name without realizing it.

"Coda."

Cammie, on the other hand, was less than subtle. "Oh Kra-ckle! Coda made an appearance. One more and I'll win

Beautiful Boy Bingo. You hear that, Ashley? Put that in your old school bong and smoke it. Boo-ya!!"

Cammie's comment let the cork out of the rest of the spectators. They started to laugh. Coda was laughing right along with them as he walked towards the gathered crowd.

"Camille," Coda nodded towards Cammie, "you're always such a treat."

Cammie shot him a mischievous smile and mouthed, "Call me!" Coda laughed again, but Dyson wasn't going to let it go.

"This is a private matter, Coda." Apparently, Dyson had found his courage, because he was now walking slowly up to the boy. Dyson's play, however, was less than intimidating since Coda towered above him.

"If it's a private matter, Dice, I suggest you leave the Ganga out of it. I know that I haven't been here long, but I've noticed they have a funny habit of showing up in your 'private' matters. Maybe you should give them a day off and then pick a fight with Richard."

"Are you saying I can't win against Fatty?" bellowed Dyson, looking around the crowd, his face going a shade of red. "You think that Dick over there could beat me? I've trained since I was five, Coda. I'm the youngest Master in Boran history."

Coda smiled. "I think that Richard can hold his own. I don't care what sort of rank you have. I know all about you, Dyson. You've never fought anyone who could or would fight back. You have an awfully high opinion of yourself, and from what I know of Richard here, he isn't one to call you on it. But if you would like to find out, I would be happy to give you a real opponent."

What Coda said next was too low to hear, but it was short, perhaps a single word. Whatever it was, it shocked Dyson. He took a step back, watching with a calculating look. Then Dyson pulled up his interface and began tapping the screen like mad. After a few seconds, he tore his gaze away from the screen, but this time his expression was very different. His eyes went wide as if he had just witnessed something he didn't like. He seemed almost scared.

"I suggest you run along, Dyson, before something bad happens." Coda nodded towards one of the Ganga. "Besides, you wouldn't want me to bloody your nose. I know how your mother hates that."

Sam whistled and shook her head. Coda had just pushed Dyson's biggest button. Anyone that was even remotely wired in Academy City 676 knew that Dice Dyson was the world's biggest momma's boy. It was common knowledge; common knowledge that threw Dyson into a rage whenever someone mentioned it. Coda had obviously known this and was either trying to pick a fight or was dumber than a fence post.

Dyson's already red face lit up like a carnival balloon and beads of angry sweat began forming on his brow. Sam watched him until she became a bit dizzy, then realized she was holding her breath. She exhaled and turned her attention back to Richard. She found him, and as expected, he had his eyes closed. Sam looked back at Coda. He motioned towards the buzzing comm in one of the Ganga's hands.

"You'd better take that, Dyson," Coda said. "Gives you the opportunity to walk away."

Dyson hesitated a moment longer, then ripped the comm out of the Ganga's hand.

"I'll take care of you later, Coda," spat Dyson, touching the side of his ear. He started in the opposite direction. "I'll see you. Though probably sooner than you think."

Coda smiled. "I look forward to it."

Dyson retreated and the group dispersed. Sam launched forward, trying to get to Richard. By the time she pushed through, Coda was already there helping him.

"Richard!" Sam rushed to his side and hugged him.

"Samantha, delightful to see you," he said, apparently unfazed. "I am sorry that I missed our date this morning."

Cammie made a rude sound, something that was somewhere between a fart and a sarcastic laugh.

"Yes, Camille? Is there something that I can help you with?" asked Richard in a calm, inquisitive voice.

Cammie glared at him. She hated it when people called her by her real name, Coda, of course, being the exception. He could call her whatever he wanted.

"I was just taking the time to correct you, Dick. You said date. I just wanted to let you know, only people who are, like, together, go on dates."

Richard shook his head wearily. "Camille, are you really suggesting that I take vocabulary advice from someone who not only wrote the essay 'Why I Love Shopping,' but actually spelled 'shopping' incorrectly in the process?"

Laughter erupted from Sam and Coda, the latter actually holding his gut while he chuckled. Cammie glared, which was less than serious; she was trying not to break out in a smile.

Coda's guffaw subsided just enough to be understood. "Richard, I swear man, you need to become a comedian. Your dry wit is almost too much."

With giggles barely in the background, Coda, Richard, Cammie, and Sam gathered their stuff to leave. They still had a fair distance to walk and class would be starting soon. It wasn't more than a few steps before Richard's burning gaze narrowed in on Sam. A look Sam knew all too well. Richard had questions for her.

She thought through their homework from the previous night. The chem lab they were supposed to be preparing for, their physics class, and the dramatic monologue for their drama course. Sam filed through each of the subjects one after another, ready for any questions Richard could throw at her. Cammie's inquiry beat him to the punch.

"It was really lucky that you were passing by, Coda, but how did you know that Dick was in trouble? I thought you weren't connected to the Inter-cloud."

Coda gave Cammie a jovial smile. "Actually, it's funny

you ask; it's quite the story. See, I was walking to class this morning—"

"Samantha?" said Richard, asking the question as if Cammie and Coda weren't there. Sam noted a touch of concern in his voice. "This may not be any of my business, and you know better than anyone that I'm open to all types of styles, but do you really think it wise to attend a learning institution sopping wet?"

Sam's face flared red as she realized she was still soaking wet in her white shirt! She had been so worried about Richard that she had forgotten her earlier mishap. She cringed in embarrassment. Most of her section had been at that fight, and she had just been standing there letting the group see her practically in her underwear. Richard, seeing her anxiety, removed his jacket and handed it to Sam. Sam smiled warmly at Richard and put it on.

"And that's when he told me about Richard and Dyson at the base of Camelot, so I rushed over there as fast as I could," Coda finished with another suave smile. Cammie giggled, a reaction that Coda followed. Both were in their own world, oblivious to Sam's problem.

"I can't believe he actually spoke to you," fawned Cammie. "He's been here for three months and I've only heard him talk once."

Sam's ears perked up. "Are you two talking about Adam? Was he the one that told you to come and help Richard, Coda?"

Coda flashed Sam a wicked smile. "Why are you asking, Sam? You haven't been taken in by Adam too, have you? Man, I've never seen someone get so many chicks before in my life. Cammie I understand, but you? Cheating on Richard, is that what a good wife would do?"

"Ha ha ha, Coda. I was just curious."

"Sam, did you realize that you're totally wet?" Coda searched Sam up and down. "And wearing a lacy cream-colored bra that is completely visible to Richard and myself?" Coda's eyes went a little wide. "Wow, Sam, have you offered thanks to the gods recently, because they've certainly blessed you. Man, what a rack!"

Sam spun on her heel, punching Coda on the arm as she continued to walk backward. She adjusted Richard's jacket to properly cover herself. "Stop looking at my 'rack,' Coda. Listen, guys, I've got to go back home and change. I'm totally wet and—"

Sam stopped mid-sentence as she backed into something hard.

"Whoa there," came a voice that was soft and warm. "Careful now."

Sam's face lost all its color and her voice seized up. "Ah-a-a-a... hi-hi, Adam."

CHAPTER 8
HOUDINI'S FAILED ESCAPE

Time: Current Day, lunchtime

Scene: School lunchroom

"Mackie, your explanation of the attack patterns and weaponry clearly doesn't match the types of wounds inflicted or the residual chemicals and fragments found in the wounds. Not to mention the mapping of the bodies is all wrong."

What happened to this morning? thought Sam as she weaved through a group of classmates filling the tables in one of the school's many lunchrooms. Was I sleeping through my morning schedule or what?

It was just that type of morning. After the excitement of Richard's fight, she had run into Adam, made a complete fool of herself babbling like an idiot and being completely soaked, and since then had been having a hard time focusing or thinking straight. It had been like this through History,

English, Physics, and now lunch. Well, at least she was dry now.

Sam's thoughts were jumbled as she walked directly into the back of a boy's chair. He ignored her, continuing to tinker with a holographic projection that took up the length of the table.

"You have the mental capacity of a drug-addled Ganga. This is a precise and detailed execution of his attack map and his most likely weapon use. Watch again, but closer this time."

The boy tapped on the projected keyboard as the group refocused its attention on the board. The animation was the kind that graphic show directors used to model scenes for Vii-movie experiences. What seemed to be the head boy at the table spoke at length about various things, tapping different buttons on the touch board. Periodic tables, diagrams of different weapons, and long names like Aikido and ninjutsu rolodexed their way across the length of the board, ending with a smiling face on a black screen. The boy who had been tapping spoke with a conspiratorial tone as the other boys and Sam leaned in.

"It's him. Watch the reenactment; there's no one else it could be."

Sam watched, fascinated, as the lead boy tapped a large projected red button on his screen. The holo-board sprang to life as a strange, highly detailed fight sequence began to play out with five-inch holographic representations. Quite unique, the scene reminded Sam of the old classic Kung Fu movies that were filmed before the rise of the Jade Empire. Sam watched as the main combatant performed impossible acrobatics, including flips, kicks, walking on walls, and jumps of incredible height. Ordinary physics, including gravity, didn't seem to be an issue for the little avatar. But these impossible feats paled in comparison to his odd ability to seemingly pull weaponry out of nowhere. Blade weapons thrown with deadly accuracy, hand-held explosives, and strange concussive shockwaves ravaged groups of energy-blaster-wielding guards.

The man's actions made Sam's mouth go dry. She refocused, zeroing in on the depiction. He was taller than the other little holo men and appeared to be very strong, as evidenced by the way he was cutting, shooting, and burning up assailants left and right with little or no hesitation. Something about him seemed surreal, like he was a work of fiction or part of some sci-fi adventure. His single-minded action was captivating.

The man's battle culminated in a fevered chase where the hero tracked down a second holo-man. Sam struggled to make out this part of the action. The holographic scale really didn't include infrastructure, making it hard to understand the venue and environment. It didn't matter, though; the more she stared at the figures and the boys watching them, the more she could not help herself. She wanted to know what was going to happen. The culmination of the scene came abruptly with the brutal destruction of the main character's target. While this made her cringe, it made the boys at the table cheer.

Sam shook her head, partly because of the violence and partly because she couldn't shake the feeling that she knew that man. She looked back at the table as again the main character stood triumphantly in the middle of the board. Sam decided then and there that she would take the old-school 2D players any day of the week. This was too real for her.

A second clumsy bump into another chair and a sharp pain in her leg brought Sam back to reality. She hadn't even realized she had been walking. She really was a klutz.

"Sorry about that," said Sam in an embarrassed voice. "I didn't mean to, well, you know."

The boy in the chair turned to address her, both anger and milk dripping down his face. He was going to yell at her, she could tell; he was going to verbally assault her in the middle of the cafeteria. His mouth opened, and she waited for the fireworks to come, but then nothing. It didn't happen. He didn't yell at her but instead opened and shut his mouth like a mute attempting to kick the silence habit. After a bit of a struggle, he found his voice and was able to mumble, "Uh...it's okay."

He turned back to his friends, who were all staring at Sam. She scratched at her head, confused. An awkward silence followed, during which the group of boys watched her with bug-eyed disbelief, an expression that baffled Sam. With nothing else to say, she slowly turned and walked towards a far table. The boys stared on, the seconds seemingly snow-balling into minutes as Sam continued her sluggish pace. Behind her, the boys appeared to get over whatever was ailing them, and their conversation resumed.

"Charles, I'm telling you, this is the most likely hypothesis for the types of wounds inflicted, the compounds found, and the evidenced fighting style."

"Your explanation has about as much potential validity as your thesis on android women. There is absolutely no conceivable paradigm in which this representation is accurate."

The boys' conversation dwindled as she walked farther from them. Not that she really understood what they were talking about anyway. Richard would probably know. Maybe she would ask later if she remembered. The boys at the table weren't the only ones staring at her, however. Now that she thought about it, lately she seemed to be getting a lot of atten-tion wherever she went. Just like when she and Cammie had gone shopping the week before for dresses. Now that had been a trippy experience. Cammie had been right; those guys had been looking at her. The changes over the last few weeks had been subtle. She had hardly noticed, but something was different. She was different. She felt it now, standing in this lunchroom with all these people. The knowledge that some-thing was different made her feel very alone.

But it wasn't just her; others seemed to notice a change as

well. People that she had never talked to or even seen before were starting conversations with her for no apparent reason. It was totally bizarre, and not in a good way.

"Hey, Samantha."

The voice startled her, notwithstanding the incessant amount of noise in the room. Sam turned to face a burly boy with long black hair. Moses Rair stood smiling not a half-meter in front of her. She didn't know what to say. What was the most popular guy in school doing talking to her?

He spoke again, his voice deep and accented. "Samantha, how do you do?"

"Umm...hi, Moses. Umm...I...I do fine, and how do you do?"

Moses beamed. "You know my name; I'm flattered."

Sam's eyebrows compressed. 'You know my name, I'm flattered'? Sam thought. Moses Rair is saying this to me?

"Oh my yuck, Moses," came another voice from just behind him. "What are you doing talking to someone from Partial Palace?"

A girl stepped out from behind Moses and struck a pose as if she expected the lights to dim and spotlights to shine. Another person Sam knew of, but until now had not really seen in person. High Tracks debutante Sariah Grey switched between incensed anger and demure pouts as she looked back and forth between Sam and Moses. "Come on, Moses, they have the fat-free, sugar-free, taste-free chocolate pudding today. I want some."

Sariah pulled on Moses, who followed, though quite reluctantly. He watched Sam as he walked away.

The two left, leaving Sam speechless. First, the super-hot transfer student Adam talked to her, and now Moses Rair stopped her in the lunchroom. Why was this happening? A thought struck her. "The box!" she said aloud. "Could this have anything to do with that weird noise?"

That couldn't be right. She had just found that box this morning, and though it was weird, it couldn't account for the changes she felt. Still, the box pulled at her mind in a strange way, and she didn't have any idea why.

Sam shook her head. Of course, this didn't have anything to do with that silly box or that— that scary noise. Sam pushed it out of her mind.

She found Richard sitting at a table, eating an array of particularly unappealing food. A range of uncooked vegetables, artificial soy protein, and supplements went one after another into Richard's mouth. He chewed unenthusiastically as he read a book.

"Hey, Richy." Sam sat down next to Richard. "I can't believe you're still reading those things. You know you can get just about any book you want on Vii Space, right?"

Richard didn't say anything, causing Sam to sigh a little louder than was necessary.

"Still not talking to me, huh?"

Richard looked up from his book and swallowed. "Actually, I wasn't talking at all. This tendency towards silence has a proclivity of transpiring when someone, i.e., myself, has half-masticated artificially enhanced protein in their mouth. However, if you are asking whether I am willing to engage in average everyday small talk with you, the answer is still an unequivocal no."

"Come on, Richard, I don't even know what I did."

"You not knowing something is shocking, I assure you."

Sam ruffled his hair. "Don't try that crap on me, Rich; it's not going to work. Now tell me what is bothering you."

"Ignore him, Sam, he's just pissy."

Cammie and Coda, coming from different directions, plopped down next to Sam, which instantly made the situation comical as Cammie shot daggers at Richard and hearts at Coda. "Dick over here is just pissed at how you got all goofy with Adam earlier."

Cammie angled her body, giving Richard a view of her profile; the move highlighted a severely snotty look. "I thought you said that jealousy is an ill-redacted instinct, Dick."

Richard put a hand to his forehead, rubbing the length of it. "Ill-adapted, Camille. Once again, your burning intellect leaves us all in admiration. And for your information, I didn't get jealous. I do not get jealous. I was just surprised that Samantha's instinctual biological predisposition to 'hot guys' was as devolved as the rest of yours. I could scarcely conceal my absolute and utter disappointment that she was not using higher cognizant functions in developing her surreptitious romantic infatuation."

Richard paused, leaning forward so he and Cammie's faces were uncomfortably close. He studied her vacant expression. "Surreptitious means secret, Camille."

"Ahhh, I see. Continue, but hurry and get to the 'however.'"

"However," cut in Richard again, sounding annoyed, "it is neither my function nor desire to orate on the discombobulated capitulations of female/male mating instincts. Suffice it to say that while I hold certain informational privileges as Samantha's best friend—" Richard paused and then nodded towards Cammie. "Yes, Samantha told me you were demoted."

Cammie swore. "Oh my George W. Bush, Sam!! You actually told him he was the best friend?"

Richard continued his discourse, ignoring the comment. "While I have those certain informational privileges, it would be arrogant for me to comment on the adequacy or inadequacy of any particular suitor Samantha may or may not be interested in. I do not have to comprehend nor approve of her decision. I accept it regardless of whether it offends my gag reflex or not."

Sam's face blazed scarlet, a repeat of her encounter this morning. They all knew he was talking about Adam and doing it like she wasn't even there.

"You know, now that you're freely discussing this, Rich," said Coda, who was playfully poking and watching the resulting jiggle of a sizable tower of Jell-o, "what I don't understand is why you dislike Adam. On the last competence testing, he took like second in the school, right after you. He was behind you by like 10 points or something, if I remember correctly."

"14.134 points actually," snapped Richard. "And only because of the influenza virus I caught."

"Not the point, Rich!" exclaimed Coda. "What I am getting at is Adam is smart, handsome, and kind—yes kind, Rich. Bet you didn't know that he was the one that told me to save your chubby butt this morning, huh? Speaking of which, how was it that Dyson didn't knock your head off? It was like he just missed. Who seriously just misses? Anyway, to my point, which is Adam is a nice, smart guy, and Sam likes him. Why don't you like him, besides the fact that he almost beat you on a test?"

Richard pulled out his tablet. He centered it in front of him and cracked his knuckles.

"Oh no, I know that look," whispered Sam. "Remember what you promised? No hacking into government mainframes."

"That was an unfair promise. 90% of nets are government. I didn't know what I was agreeing to."

"Are you kidding me?" spouted Coda and Cammie at the same time. "Sam got a concession from the mighty genius?"

Richard sneered. "She made a 1950s Chicago-style deep-

dish pizza and then made me promise not to hack any government systems before she would serve me any. Thick crust,
real mozzarella cheese, fresh tomato sauce just tantalizing me.
I would have agreed to Lamarckian evolution as a viable
scientific theory at that point. But we digress in the conversation, which lacks relevance to the actual topic at hand. What
I was preparing to do, Samantha, was show you something on
the school's network."

After a few lazy taps on his interface, Richard brought up
the school's vid-net. Various live feeds displayed in neat little
boxes stacked across the screen. The others moved in around
Richard, once again amazed at his resourcefulness. Richard
was talented, and they all had grown accustomed to his
unique brand of ingenuity, but even with this conditioned
behavior, they could not help once in a while feeling astonishment at Richard's innate ability to pretty much do whatever
he wanted when it came to technology.

"Rich," asked Coda, sounding awestruck but eager, "is
there any way that you can set me up one of these feeds?"

Cammie scratched at her head. "Why would you want
one of these feeds, Coda?"

"I would have thought the answer to that question would
have been exceedingly obvious." Richard tapped on one of
the windows marked Changing Room.

The image blew up, and a feed loaded the live image of a
girl about to change into a school-issued swimsuit.

Cammie gave Coda an extremely dirty look.

"What?" he said innocently. "It's for research, for a book I'm writing."

"What's the title?" asked Sam with a slight giggle. "Pervert 101: How to Get Caught in Voyeurism?"

Richard tapped the tablet again, and the feed diminished and darkened.

"Richard," said Sam sternly. "I don't want to think that you are spying on girls while they're changing."

"Come on, Sam, we've already had this conversation!" cut in Cammie. "Richard doesn't li—"

"I'm going to cut you off right there, Camille," interrupted Richard, talking over her. "I appreciate your feeble attempts at humor as much as the next imbecile, and I understand you have the attention span of a precocious two-year-old, but let's return to the task at hand."

They all closed in around the screen.

A second feed blew up to show the very lunchroom in which they were sitting. The view of the camera was scanning the many doors that led into and out of the lunchroom, panning on a prescheduled routine. Richard tapped out a few more commands, and the camera stopped on a single person.

Sam spoke with more than a bit of breathiness. "Richard, I know that you are trying to show us why you dislike Adam, but wouldn't it be easier to just tell us? Do you really need to hijack the vid and watch him?"

"Hush, Samantha," replied Richard. "Hush and watch."

Adam Smith's presence was captivating. Strikingly handsome, his sandy-colored hair and fiery eyes gave off a feeling of warmth that was almost feminine. Not that Adam was feminine by any stretch of the imagination. He was actually quite athletic and excelled in all the physical education classes and defense training. His stoic attitude, refined beauty, and quiet nature were almost magical and made him extremely popular with all the girls. He was, in fact, so popular that a few of the younger girls had started an Adam Fan Club.

Surprisingly enough, at this particular moment, his massive group of followers had yet to notice his presence. He stood just inside the door, looking slowly from his left to his right and back again. His normally casual attitude seemed absent as he surveyed the room with what felt like practiced motions. He did this twice more before he walked fully into the room and was instantly mobbed. Richard then closed the feed, looking satisfied.

"There," he said smugly. "Now you know why I cannot trust him."

"You can't trust him because he's more popular than you?" asked Cammie. "If that's the case, all I can say is well, duh."

"Cammie, if only abortion hadn't been outlawed decades ago. Your parents would have greatly benefited from the institution."

He looked to Coda and Sam. "Did you catch it?"

Coda answered thoughtfully. "That he's popular? Yeah,

totally, but we already knew that. Well, I didn't know he was that popular. Umm...you don't think he's more popular than me, do you?" Coda leaned back slightly, interlocking his fingers behind his head. "If so, I can see why you don't trust him, Richard. Anybody who's more popular than me can't be trustworthy. I mean, who transfers schools in their last year of generals? Really, who does that, and how could they not be suspicious?"

Sam rolled her eyes. "Coda, didn't you transfer schools in your last year of generals?"

"Technicalities, my dear."

A ringing sound silenced any further conversation, and a loud voice echoed around the lunchroom. "All students please report to your pod. This is a code three. Please report to your pod."

The atmosphere instantly changed. Men wearing dark uniforms walked in and started to escort the students to reinforced lockable classrooms that were more akin to bomb shelters than places of learning. The conversation about Adam was instantly forgotten.

"Rich, what's going on?" asked Sam as they were pushed with the flow of students. "Why are we going to the pods, and what's a code three?"

"A code three means that there is some kind of danger that could be threatening the school. Security is to heighten their alert level, though even this seems excessive."

Sam wasn't given the opportunity to ask more questions

as suddenly she and Richard were surrounded by the very group of boys that had been watching the holo-board earlier. "Richard! Sir, Richard please. We need you. Will you help us? It's about him, we need him, we need you, we—need it—answers—"

"Mackie, handle yourself more appropriately. What is it? You are rambling incoherently."

"We need you to hack the school's cloud-net. It might be the only way for us to find out. It's probably misinformation again, but we have to know."

"What is it that you are attempting to ascertain that would require me to commit such a blatant violation of Academy Code SP-171?"

Another much younger boy, probably only a fourth year, pushed his tablet up towards Richard's face.

"Um... this is why, Mr. Richard, sir."

The headline on the tablet read, "BREAKING NEWS: Headline – 16 dead, 57 injured, top secret military technology missing. Police have a man in custody they believe to be the legendary assassin known only as the Magician. Again, the Magician has been apprehended."

CHAPTER 9
EVERYONE IN THE POOL

Time: Current Day, late afternoon
Scene: School Pool

Sam and Richard were sitting on the benches at the school pool. The lockdown had lasted less than half an hour. During the short-lived event, they had watched armed guards run up and down the hallway, shouting incoherently and generally causing chaos. Now they were already back to their regularly scheduled programming. At the moment, they sat huddled together, watching the Western Media breaking news report.

"The scene was horrendous here at the Obama Center for Hope Ever After when assailants from the terrorist organization, The Republicans, assaulted the research facility. From what witnesses can tell us, the battle lasted well over two hours. The total death count is into the twenties, with another fifty or sixty wounded. General Sheen had this to say."

The screen flipped to an aged gentleman wearing a red military uniform.

"Being a medical research facility, it is unclear what these terrorists were after or how they were able to procure such advanced weaponry. Fortunately, the facility's security forces were able to repel the invaders before they could obtain their objective, whatever that might have been."

The reporter's voice came from off-screen. "General, is there any truth to the reports that this attack was carried out by a single assailant?"

The General answered, his voice becoming irritated. "No, absolutely not. This facility has some of the most advanced security in the Clinton Providence. It is ridiculous to think that a single individual could attack and live to tell about it."

"So the rumors that the Magician assaulted the facility are false?"

"Of course they are. A single individual attacking an advanced medical facility without the aid of intelligence or even modern weapons, relying on some obscure magic tricks and martial arts? Preposterous! This was a team of highly trained individuals who probably had weeks of recon and cold runs. This so-called 'Magician' is no more real than Santa Claus."

"So it wasn't a false alarm?" asked Sam, sounding scared. "Should we really be out of the lockdown rooms?"

"Let your mind be at peace, Samantha. A threat to the school is essentially a threat to the entire city. The Republicans are an anti-government force; they aren't going to attack an Academy City. The lockdown is just operating procedure from the Great War."

"I don't know, Richard," said Sam, a little unsure of herself. "I think that General guy is lying. They aren't telling us the whole story."

Richard gazed at her, a little surprised. It was an unflattering expression for Richard, perhaps because she wasn't used to it. "What makes you think he was lying, Samantha?"

Sam shook her head. "I don't know; just a feeling, I guess. I can't really explain why."

"You're just being paranoid, Samantha. It's just like that time you made me watch all those classic horror movies with you. Your imagination is running away with you."

Sam shook her head a second time. "No, really, Richard. I'm serious. There is something about this whole thing that stinks..." Sam's voice trailed off. "Wait a second, wait just one bricking second." Sam put out her hand, requesting the tablet. "May I?"

Richard handed it over. She had a hard time with the upgraded interface. She was never very good with technology. After a bit of a struggle, she started to replay the video that she and Richard had just finished.

She smiled triumphantly as the recording finished up. "I knew something weird was going on."

Richard sighed deeply. "You mind sharing your findings with those of us who are less savvy with conspiracy theory as an emotional paradigm?"

Sam ignored Richard's sarcasm and launched right into her explanation. "He said that the Obama Center for Hope Ever After was just a medical research facility. But if it's just a medical facility, why would they have such tight security?"

Sam smiled smugly. Richard didn't say anything but continued to stare at her.

"He's totally hiding something, Rich, can't you see that? Why would an anti-government organization attack some medical center?"

Richard was unconvinced. "Samantha, it's a government facility. Of course, it has high security. Chancellor Himms is one of the most paranoid people on the planet. There is a reason that the Continental Security Force has the biggest budget of all the agencies."

"But Rich, come on, you can see it on his fat little face. He's totally lying."

"You can believe whatever you want, Samantha, but don't be disappointed if the official report undermines your theory."

Distraction came as more students, boys and girls, exited their respective dressing rooms, all wearing the required school bathing suit. Over the din of nervous laughter, Sam could clearly hear Cammie complaining.

"Who picked these crappy new suits? OMGWB, they

are, like, totally formless. I can't even show off my cleavage! I should write the city council. This is ridiculous!"

Richard turned to Sam. "The fact that she hasn't been cited for some form of sexual harassment remains a mathematical quandary to me. Probability alone says she should have been incarcerated by now."

"That's Cammie for you." Sam zeroed in on Richard's face. "Rich, can I ask you another question?"

"It's not about your ridiculous conspiracy theory, is it?"

"No..."

"Then feel free."

"Who exactly is the Magician?"

Richard laughed, something else that was a little out of the ordinary for him. Laughing was probably an overstatement; he gave an ironic sort of chuckle and then took back his tablet just as he was about to answer.

"'Who exactly is the Magician?' You're joking, right? Please tell me you're joking."

At that moment, the group of boys from the lunch table with the holopad, the same group who had petitioned Richard to hack the school server, trotted right up to Sam and Richard, forming a half-circle.

"Easy, Mackie," Richard said calmly to their leader. "I realize that you have been eavesdropping on Samantha, but alas, she remains a youth in the proverbial world of the nets and doesn't have time to stalk fictional characters like your comrades and yourself."

Sam started to ask what Richard was talking about, the words right at the tip of her tongue when she paused, swearing she had heard wrong. Did Richard just say that they stalked a fictional character?

Mackie ignored Richard's slight and addressed Sam directly. "And here I thought everyone knew of him. You have been ill-educated, my lady. Allow me to school you in the ways of the Magician."

Mackie posed dramatically, apparently looking for some sort of encouragement. When nothing came, he continued in a slightly put-out but informational voice, very reminiscent of the anchor from the news report. Mackie pointed at Richard's tablet.

"First, I must address the propaganda you've been forced to endure. I can see that you've been watching Western Media. You do realize that Western Media has strong ties to the State, right? I mean, the sell-out journalists bring up the Magician just so the State rep can deny his existence and then pontificate about how absurd the whole thing is. And let me guess, their version of the story said that the deaths at the Obama Center for Hope Ever After were related to terrorist violence. They probably claimed that a radical group, nick-named the Republicans, attacked a government research facility about 35 kilometers north of Academy City 676, taking many lives and injuring many others in their assault.

"No doubt they assert that it was unclear as to what the Republicans were after, but their weaponry was highly advanced and their attack was greatly organized, and that while it is still unknown what their goal is, the invaders were beaten off before they could obtain any significant foothold on the grounds of the facility. Subsequent official reports by the Continental Security Agency will obviously verify this 'official' description, and then everyone will move on with their lives, not the least bit concerned about the happenings at the Obama Center for Hope Ever After, not knowing that the real story, the truth, starts more than a week ago."

Sam cut in. "I'm sorry. Mackie, was it? What are you talking about, 'a week ago'? The assault on the center was a few hours ago. You know, when they supposedly caught the Magician and reported the 'breaking story.' Though apparently, they really didn't catch him; it was just Vii Space's misinformation as usual."

Mackie laughed, then looked to the other boys as if to invite them to join in on the joke. "Of course they did, sweetheart." He picked up his monologue again. "Now, as you so kindly pointed out, Samantha, Vii Space is way ahead of the government in matters of information collection and distribution, which brings me to this."

Mackie pulled out a tablet, tapped the screen, and loaded an encrypted file. He spoke as the file loaded. "This is the 'medical facility' mentioned in the report. These pictures are from a hacker code-named John Adams. Notice, if you will, the heavily armed guards, the Extra Sensory perimeter fence, and mounted plasma sentry guns. Do you all see how nice and pretty that base looks?"

They all nodded, including Sam.

"So, now that you've seen it in its wonderful glory," Mackie tapped the tablet again, "you'll be pleased to see it after the so-called foiled attack, which actually happened one week ago. And I think you all need a copy of this to really get a feel for it." Mackie gave his buddies a wink. "I've been saving this for just such a moment."

Mackie recommenced his vigorous tapping, finishing with a flourish. The other boys who had tablets with them, including Richard, pulled the picture up as they received it. Their expressions instantly turned to awe.

Chaotic destruction was the only description for the scene captured on the still frame of Richard's JX23 Interface screen. Bodies were butchered and strewn across charred grass, the fence had been ripped clean in two, and the mounted sentry turrets appeared to spark in complete disrepair. Buildings were in ruins, vehicles were burning, and massive craters punctured the ground randomly across the landscape. So widespread was the devastation that the pictured venue was hardly recognizable. Sam's eyes rose slowly from the illustrated pandemonium.

"You know," she said in a whisper, "the government's story is sounding more and more plausible."

"The small army story?" Mackie sneered disdainfully. "Ugh, they seriously need to come up with a new headline."

He pulled up another encrypted photo and sent it on to the others. "The Republicans attacking that facility is bull honky cloned donkey. This is who attacked the facility."

The picture loaded onto Richard's tablet but seemed to take a lot longer than it should. Sam held her breath with anxiety. She exhaled abruptly, the air making her lips flap. "Mackie, you've got to be kidding me."

The picture showed the gate of the base from a higher angle, but still low enough to get the breaking light of the setting sun in the picture. A single unarmed individual stood silhouetted against the glare. No details could be made out, but whoever this was seemed just average: average height, average build, just plain average. Or maybe it was just the angle; Sam wasn't sure. Regardless, the scene seemed fairly unremarkable, but then something about it made her pause ever so briefly. Again it was that feeling in the pit of her stomach. She put her hand on Richard's shoulder and leaned in.

"What's wrong, Samantha?"

Sam shook her head. "I don't know. I feel like... I feel strange. Like something about this scene feels familiar."

Mackie started up again. This time his voice was low. "This picture confirms his existence; it's one of my greatest treasures."

"Ok class, we will be starting warm-ups in 10 minutes, so disrobe and start your stretching!"

Mackie looked slightly irritated at being cut off, but his eyes brightened at once when Ms. Swan said the word "disrobe." All the boys, excluding Richard, stared at Sam in slobbering anticipation. It wasn't hard to guess what they were waiting for.

Sam's face turned an extreme shade of red, despite feeling rather flattered at their interest. Still, she didn't dare remove the robe she was wearing.

"Ok, you animals," said Cammie, moving in right behind Sam and the group of mega-nerds. "Don't devour our dear Samantha quite yet. Give the girl some time to adjust to this newfound position of power."

The boys turned to look at Cammie but didn't move otherwise. Cammie rolled her eyes. "Get a move on, you miscreants!"

Cammie gave Mackie and a few others a good kick to the rear, which finally stirred them from their stupor. They slowly stood to leave. Once she was sure they were gone, or at least a good distance away, Cammie turned back and inspected Richard and Sam.

"So we know that you totally pass, Sam. Your body is slammin'."

"Thanks," said Sam, again embarrassed. "I think."

"As for you, Dick, you really should go on a diet. No one is going to want to get with those jelly rolls. You know that there are supplements for unwanted fat, right? And they only cause mild amounts of erectile dysfunction. Not that you'll ever need little Richard anyway."

"You know, Camille," replied Richard, completely

unshaken, "if you're having a hard time understanding why the men in your life suddenly disappear, I could formulate a couple of highly probable theories for you, most of which have to do with the phenomena of you irritating them until they develop suicidal tendencies. I would venture to say that you have a zero percent probability of even finding a male that could possibly withstand your annoying nature, let alone actually snagging him as a potential mate. I would say you should explore the option of some sort of same-sex relationship, but in all actuality, you'd probably just irritate any female partner to death as well. That being said, I will now offer you several moments of uninterrupted silence while you attempt to work out what I just said."

"Yeah, yeah, Dick. I know I'm dumb and you're super smart. At least I'm not going to die of a heart attack. Why aren't you in your swim trunks?"

Richard lifted up his tablet. "I have a note. Can't swim. Asthma."

Cammie let out a little puff of air, a gesture that always accompanied her annoyance at any given situation. "You do know, Dick, they cured asthma like a billion years ago, right? Pssh, whatever. If you want to get fatter and never find a woman, that's fine by me."

For once, Richard kept his mouth shut.

Cammie turned her attention to Sam. "And you! You're almost as bad as Dick over here. What in the name of Michael Jackson the Third are you still doing in your robe?"

Sam scowled. "Don't judge me, Cammie. Not all of us are as bold as you."

"Samantha, you get your cute butt out of that robe right this instant," stomped Cammie with an air of authority. "I heard that Moses talked to you during lunch. How could you ignore such a development? You need to strike while the iron is hot!" Cammie ran to Sam's side and started tugging on her robe. Sam gripped it like it was a life preserver.

"'Strike while the iron is hot'? I don't even know what that means."

"Samantha, look who's watching you right this very second!" Cammie attempted, unsuccessfully, to point inconspicuously.

Sam's curiosity was piqued. She struggled to look without appearing too obvious. Contact came in the form of two pairs of eyes. One was searching while the other was waiting to be found. What Sam found made her heart skip a beat.

Adam...

Deep blue eyes, like the sky after a rainy day, were fixed directly and unmistakably upon her. He was looking at her and doing so with a strange amount of warmth. Her blood was rushing, her face was going red. She could feel the pounding of her own heart as it tapped rapidly upon her eardrums. Twice. Twice in one day. TWICE in ONE day! He had taken notice of her. Today was the best day ever.

Embarrassment and fear caused her to break the contact,

and it was then she noticed. Adam wasn't the only one looking.

Every boy in the 5th slot physical education class had their eyes locked directly on her. Oh, the feeling. The feeling of having hundreds of eyes glued to your form. It was a feeling of power mixed with overwhelming vulnerability.

A cold chill surged up Sam's back, followed by unreal clarity.

No. It wasn't her vulnerability she was feeling. She did not feel vulnerable. She felt... she felt... protected, powerful. Such a unique and exquisite feeling; one that made her realize, made her understand. She wasn't afraid because the eyes weren't staring at her in judgment, but rather in anticipation.

Sam, without realizing it, let her robe drop to the floor, and with it, the anticipation turned into satisfaction.

CHAPTER 10
BOOM GOES THE METHANOL

Time: Current day, early afternoon
Scene: Chemistry class

"Richard, I told you it's not my fault. It was the biggest suit they had, and I haven't been able to get a new one."

Sam removed her school interface from its protective case and placed it in front of her, taking a long moment to pair her touchscreen with the project holoboard in front of their desk. Richard turned from Sam and gazed soberly out the window.

Sam sighed. "I don't know why you are so mad; the suit wasn't that revealing. I was mostly covered up."

Richard's eyebrows scrunched, a clear sign that he was annoyed. "Samantha, if your swimming attire can double as floss, it's too revealing."

The comment would have been funny in any other circumstance. She thought back to the week before.

"You have the chance of a lifetime, Sam," Cammie had said, eyes glowing with anticipation mixed with jealousy. "You've got the goods, and now you can show them off; all the other girls have to wear the new models. You're the only one that gets to wear a cute suit. You're a swan in a lake full of cows."

Sam remembered shaking her head. "First of all, lake full of cows? That doesn't make any sense. Second, no way, Cammie. I wear something like that, and it's bordering on public indecency. I will just have to skip that—"

"Sam! You don't have time to be shy. You've got to be bold. Adam is going to be there. He won't be able to resist you. Show a little skin and gain a lot of ground. That's what my mom always used to say."

Sam's eyebrows creased. "I have a hard time believing your mother used to say that."

Despite her argument with Cammie, Sam took the swimsuit and afterwards didn't look for another. Two days before her "unveiling," she had tried on the swimsuit and looked at her figure in the full-length mirror. If she was being truthful, she felt embarrassed; incredibly embarrassed. But aside from that, she liked it—she liked what she saw in the mirror.

Later that night, embarrassment beat out her potential ego boost. She sat in bed telling herself it was just a school swimsuit. Not that big a deal. It wasn't that revealing. Her head knew better, of course. She had been trying to convince herself otherwise ever since, but now, thinking of Richard's remark (who didn't pull any punches when it came to the truth), she had always known.

She really wasn't sure her actually wearing the suit was the problem for Richard. The suit just represented something deeper, like his inability to articulate what was really bothering him. She protected her own by falling back onto her excuse. Adam was there, and she didn't get many chances to impress him. Plus, she reasoned, it wasn't really her fault that the school suits were on backorder! What else could she have done?

Sam sighed. She could have done any number of things, really—she knew it. Richard knew it. Ultimately, she didn't know why she chose to wear it. Sam figured it had something to do with her trying to change her own perception of herself as much as it was trying to get the guy of her dreams to notice her.

Still, she couldn't place her finger on the source of her recent behavior. She simply did not know.

Nevertheless, there was no way that she was going to let Richard know that. She would never hear the end of it.

Sam tried to keep her face from lighting up and glared at Richard. "This makes no sense. You've never commented on what I wear before, good or bad, sexy or unisex. I wasn't even aware that you actually saw me as a girl."

"If you want to objectify yourself as some sort of item rather than a person in an attempt to invoke coitus or a coitus-bearing relationship, then it's none of my business, but,"

Richard turned and steadied his gaze on her, "I am well aware of your feminine charm, Samantha. Trust me, I'm well aware."

An awkward silence passed in which Richard tapped half-heartedly upon his screen, deep in thought. Sam was at a loss for words.

He's aware of my feminine charm? she thought. *What in the name of the Old Catholic Church did that mean? Did that mean he saw her as a girl? Like someone to, like, like? And why was he saying this now? He never talked like this.* She didn't know what to do and definitely was not sure how to react to this new Richard. He rarely showed this much of himself, even to her. As a matter of fact, he only became this open when—

Then Sam understood. She understood why he was acting so funny.

"You're going into the health center again, aren't you?"

Richard glanced at her, obviously taken aback. "N-no. No, of course not. I would have told you if—"

"You're lying, Richard. I can always tell when you're lying."

"Samantha, don't be silly. Of course I'm not going into—"

"Stop lying, Richard!" Sam's voice carried, causing the other students to look her way. She fumed, breathing heavily. "What is it this time?" she said more quietly.

Richard studied her briefly. She could tell he was debating whether to tell her or not. "My heart."

"Again?"

"Yeah, it seems my body might be rejecting the modified one."

Sam slumped down in her chair. Unbidden thoughts traveled back to the previous year. Richard had been in the hospital for his heart then as well. And now he was going to relive it. He was going to do it again; she knew it. There was a problem. There had to be. Richard had played it off the first time around too. A tune-up, he had called it. Nothing serious. The really stupid thing was she had believed him.

The first time around, she had to pry the whole heart condition/medical leave thing out of him. That's when he told her that when he was a child, he had received a genetically modified heart...and that his body was rejecting it. The defect was rare due to modern technology, but not unheard of, and one that Richard's siblings had fought and lost. Richard didn't talk about it much.

The battle between Richard's heart and body raged on and was the source of his continued weight gain despite his ridiculously healthy habits. One never would have guessed how klutzy Richard the super genius was.

This wasn't all, though; Richard had strange pains if he sat too long, couldn't breathe most of the time without wheezing, and probably the weirdest of all, his skin was always cold; always. It could be 37 degrees outside, and Richard's skin was cool. It was eerie. The few times that Sam recalled brushing up against it really drove it home. Richard was really, really sick.

The hardest part of the whole circumstance was Sam couldn't tell anyone. Richard valued his privacy. No one else knew about his condition except maybe the school admins, and they didn't ask a lot of questions for fear that Richard would transfer. Richard was the type of student that could put Academy City 676 on the academic map, and they didn't want to jeopardize that. As far as she knew, Richard had ever only allowed one visitor to see him in the hospital. It was an experience she would remember for the rest of her life.

Witnessing Richard strapped to state-of-the-art monitors, punctured and tubed like a long-forgotten science experiment, was another image that had hit home. She didn't know why, but it scared her more than she would have ever admitted to anyone, including Richard. She thought he might know, though. The one time she came to see him, she had left the building crying, sobbing uncontrollably. And to this day, Richard had never mentioned her visit.

"When do you go?" Sam asked in a quiet but toneless voice.

Richard spied their surroundings, attempting to find eavesdroppers. "I'm going to be gone the whole break; maybe longer if something happens."

Richard averted his eyes.

Sam slouched in her chair. Her little triumphs, those little moments she had gained that day, felt so unimportant now.

Richard was going back into the hospital for yet another surgery. Last time...last time he had almost died. Ugh...today really sucked.

Her head reeled as she attempted to find something, anything else they could talk about. She needed to show him she wasn't worried about it, that she knew he was going to be okay. The silver box nestled at the bottom of her bag popped into her mind. She mentally examined it briefly. That strange little box sat strangely present, ever nagging in the back of her head as if she was magnetically drawn to it. But then again, something else pushed upon her consciousness, telling her that it wasn't the time for that. Richard needed something else, something more.

She touched her screen, pulling up her cloud Spyder. She typed "OGCOLE," and the engine loaded. Next, she typed "the magician" into the search bar and started the engine.

The page loaded with 256,834,576,212 hits!

"Whoa," said Sam as she adjusted her holoscreen to increase the size of her viewing partition. She picked the first link in the line of results and watched the cloud load. A VIIS fan page exploded onto the screen, starting with a graphic movie that showed a rather cheesy depiction of a single individual posed in a variety of positions.

He was visible from his neck down to his waist and wearing a tuxedo of the finest quality. The head and face remained partially hidden under a corny black top hat that only revealed a nose and mouth. A smirk of a smile suggested an ironic knowledge which the rest of the world was not privileged enough to possess. The smile intrigued Sam, but not as much as what objects framed the face. The man with the knowing smile and black hat had crossed his arms atop his chest, each holding a handgun; big ones, the kind of guns that used the old metal projectiles for ammunition. The picture came as a surprise, and Sam wasn't sure how to react.

Richard glanced at the screen, sighing heavily. "You've done it now, Samantha." Chat bubbles started popping out over the projected screen.

"Hi."

"How are you?"

"A/S/L Please?"

"Are you a girl????"

Richard reached over and quickly killed the link. "The fanboys tend to come out in droves when they think a female is a fan of the Magician. Especially one they haven't pounced on yet. It's better for you to not visit that page. If they get their hooks in you, they'll never leave you alone."

"All that just because I visited a fan page on VIIS?"

"Oh, that was nothing. Like I said, you need to stay away from that page. Those guys are disturbed even by 'disturbed' standards."

"Well then, are you going to—"

"He's an urban legend, Samantha. Well, I suppose 'he' could really be a 'she,' but leaving the formalities of politically correct verbiage aside, he is someone that doesn't exist."

Richard shifted his body, clearly indicating his intention to end the conversation. Sam diverted before Richard could fall back into study mode.

"When did you become such a sucky teacher? I don't understand at all, Super Genius Richard, but if you find it difficult to tutor me, then I would be happy to find someone who can."

Richard glared at her. "The Magician, Samantha, depending on who you are, is either the world's greatest freedom fighter or the most notorious assassin in the last 300 years."

Sam paused, waiting for the punchline, the next step, but Richard offered nothing, much to her disappointment.

"So he's an assassin?"

"Or freedom fighter, yes."

"Okay...so then why do they call him the Magician?"

Richard shrugged. "Because teenagers have too much time on their hands, for one. The other reason, while not as obvious as the first, is far more obnoxious. The Magician supposedly only kills using magic."

Sam burst into laughter. He had sounded so serious she couldn't help it. Richard didn't join in; rather, he looked at her impassively. Sam's chuckles died out, and she realized—

"Oh my George W. Bush, you're serious?"

Richard shrugged again. "Is it that hard to believe? He is called the Magician, after all. Irrelevant, however, as he's completely fictional."

"So if he's fictional, why does he have such a huge following?"

Richard gave her one of his rare smiles. "Because the youth of this generation, like every generation preceding it, want something bigger than themselves to believe in. Times are dreary nowadays. A cold war already in its 50th year; nuclear and nutronic fallout resulting in many of the lands on the earth becoming unlivable except for the most formidable of persons; a line of demarcation separates the Collective and the Jade Empire, making air travel close to impossible; and of course, let's not forget the economic state of the world markets. Now, consider for a moment that a single man or woman could change that with a thought. That one person had the supernatural ability to fix it. It'd be better, right?"

Sam thought about it. "Yeah, I think it would."

"And so you finally know the legend that is the Magician. Now do me a favor."

"What's that, Ritchey?"

"Please stop talking about it."

"Okay, okay, settle down," Mr. Thomas told the class as he walked into the room holding his satchel. "Mr. Jackson and Mr. Phillips, I hope you are not online playing what I think you are playing on those school interfaces."

The two boys sheepishly tapped on their screens and set them down on the desk. "All right, class, we are continuing our exploration of combustible gases and liquids that we started earlier in our fossil fuels section. We have covered ethanol and propane; today we will be discussing methanol. Please continue to take notes as this will be covered on the exam, and I don't want to hear anything about studying outdated fuels. It's in the curriculum, so you'll be tested on it."

Students began to shuffle things around, pulling out tablets to begin taking notes. It appeared that some were resuming previously banned activities, as evidenced by their constant furtive looks to see if they had been discovered.

"Now, methanol has a composition similar to methane except that a hydrogen atom has been replaced with a hydroxide. So while methane is CH_4, methanol is CH_3OH."

Students continued their note-taking, or for some of them, lack thereof.

"Now we also know that through combustion, the methanol will react with the oxygen naturally occurring in the air. This reaction will produce carbon dioxide and water. Today we will be doing some small practical examples of this reaction."

A small snickering caught Mr. Thomas' attention, but when he turned from the holoboard, everyone seemed to be paying attention or recording their notes. He turned back to the board.

"Each set of partners will need a 100cc beaker of methanol, a plastic jug and cap, and a long match. Of course, safety equipment including goggles, fire shields, etc. is also required. Any questions? And Richard—"

Richard, who had been staring out the window deep in thought, faced Mr. Thomas. "Yes, sir?"

"I know that you've probably already finished the equation, but at least pretend to pay attention, okay?"

Richard returned to staring out the window without answering. Mr. Thomas scanned the rest of the students and caught a glimpse of a smirk from Jackson and Phillips in the back. Sam could tell that he had had it with those two.

"And since Mr. Jackson and Mr. Phillips have been such exemplary students recently, why don't you two come up and begin your experiment so the whole class can learn from you?"

Jackson and Phillips begrudgingly started towards the front of the class.

"Uh, gentlemen, you'll need to gather your supplies from the equipment closet before proceeding. Safety gear too, if you don't mind."

The two turned and headed for the closet to retrieve the list of items. As they were collecting them, a plump old woman entered the room. "Mr. Thomas, Dean Sanchez sent me to ask you something. Do you have a moment?"

"Yes, of course. Jackson and Phillips, don't do anything until I get back." Mr. Thomas followed the woman out of the classroom and closed the door behind him.

Jackson and Phillips finished gathering their items and started setting them up at the front of the classroom.

"Stupid Thomas. Why do we have to do this?" asked Jackson.

Sam spoke up. "Maybe it's because you're both cretins. Or maybe because he knows what you two do all period long in his class."

Phillips sneered at the remark. "Not like anyone could get a passing grade in this class without copying all their home-work from a science geek like fatty over there. We all know that's the only reason a hot little piece like you sits with him." Jackson pulled the large glass jug towards him and grabbed the methanol bottle.

"What are you doing, idiots?" Sam said, obviously angry. "Mr. Thomas said to wait."

"Oh, shut your trap. This isn't astrophysics." Jackson started to carefully pour the contents of the methanol bottle into the glass jug.

Sam was on her feet now, which caught Richard's atten-tion. "Morons, you're only supposed to use a quarter of that."

"Shut up, Palace. We're just going to make it a little more interesting." Phillips grabbed the bottle and emptied the contents into the glass jug, sloshing the liquid inside as he did so. He took up the jug and shook it, acting like a bartender blending a martini, all to laughs from some of the class. He motioned for Jackson to grab the long match.

"You're gonna blow us all up!" yelled Sam.

"I told you to shut up. Just watch, this will be cool."

Jackson lit the match then hesitated. He took a few steps back and then threw it towards the jug.

Sam could see it happening, but she was too slow; too slow to do anything about it. The match sailed slowly across the mouth of the jug.

Boom!

A shockwave rippled through the room, sending debris and destruction with it. The buzz of a fire alarm blared in the background as smoke filled the air. Sam felt her body pinned to the floor, different types of pain shooting up and down her frame. Images of contusions and burns danced in her mind as the various points of pain registered. The heaviest pain of all was the unidentified weight on her chest and lower body. She couldn't see because she couldn't seem to get her eyes open. She tried to move but couldn't feel her legs. Fear started to overwhelm her. How hurt was she? And if she was hurt this badly, then how badly was Richard hurt?

Fear forced Sam's eyes to pop open. What she saw made her even more confused.

"Richard, get off me."

The class was in total disarray. The teacher's desk, main holoprojection board, and terminal crackled with sparking wires. The rest of the room looked like it had been through a riot, with chunks of equipment, glass, and desks scattered about. Sam felt her face going red for about the twentieth time that day. She was really glad that no one could see her right now.

Richard held her wrapped in a fat-insulated bear hug. His face was screwed up in fear, his eyes and mouth squeezed shut. He was breathing heavily.

"You idiot," she whispered. "What are you doing jumping in front of me like that?"

Richard didn't answer. People were at their side lifting Richard up, and Richard was pushing them away. Some of her classmates pulled her to her feet and caught her as her knees went weak. She must have hit her head harder than she thought.

Teachers, security, and the medical staff showed up next. Most of them rushed to Richard first. After enduring a few moments of mothering, he started yelling, "I'm completely fine. Check Samantha, you idiots. Make sure Samantha is all right."

Jackson and Phillips were beside themselves. Jackson's face was totally pale, and Phillips had several large cuts.

"Sam, we are so sorry. Are you okay? You're not hurt, are you?"

The ringing in Sam's ears actually did hurt a lot.

"I'm fine," lied Sam. "You two are both fools. You could have gotten us killed."

Jackson and Phillips laughed uneasily. Jackson made a little cough as Phillips commented:

"Yeah, you got lucky. Dick's fat blocked the blast. We're really sorry about that."

Sam closed her eyes, trying to shake the ringing in her head. "What do you mean, Richard's fat blocked the blast?"

The two morons, trying to distance themselves from their stupid act, started to laugh again. "Come on, Sam, it's just a joke. We didn't mean anything..."

Sam stopped listening and instead glanced back to where she and Richard had been sitting. The space looked different. Something about it was...off.

Then Sam realized.

Their desk, no, not just the desk but a space about two meters wide, was almost completely free of debris of any sort. No glass. No chunks of metal or pieces of equipment. Sam continued to look around.

"No way," she said aloud. There weren't any scorch marks. How was that possible?

A familiar light glared in her eyes, increasing her headache tenfold. She moved her head and refocused. Sitting directly under her seat, faintly glowing with eerie light, sat her school bag partially open. In it, Sam could see the silver box she had found in the lake. The light from the box died out as darkness overwhelmed her, and she hit the floor for the second time.

The last thing she heard was a frantic cry of an unfamiliar voice.

CHAPTER 11

POMP AND CIRCUMSTANCE

Time: Start of the new semester

Scene: Lecture hall at an old university

"Now, we see that despite the mental instability stigmas attached to Nikola Tesla in his later years, he was the inventor of a great many things that are the precursors of the creature comforts we depend on today, mainly anything that uses electricity. Without his development of the induction motor using alternating current, cities would have been confined to a very small space. But you are not in this class to study history; rather, science.

"Tesla was an ingenious inventor. Many of his inventions were way beyond his time and still today are only represented by his theories. We will be discussing one of those theories that he put to some practical tests but never had the ability to take to larger applications. We will look at how the engineering genius of Tesla combined with recent achievements in quantum dynamics have created the world's greatest advancement of the human race."

The lecture hall was filled to the brim with preppy-looking students of all races. While each of them typed away on their various screens and holo-boards, others sat as their recording apps converted the professor's remarks into notes as he spoke. Only two of the attendees in the room seemed not to belong at the university.

"First, we'll start with mechanical resonance. Mechanical resonance is the tendency of a mechanical system to absorb more energy when the frequency of its oscillations matches the system's natural frequency of vibration, what we call its resonant frequency, than it does at other frequencies. In other words, everything that is around us has the ability to move when subjected to waves. Even the Earth itself has a resonant frequency. Most of the time, these waves do not match the resonant frequency of the matter in question, and thus the vibrations are imperceptible to the human eye. Yet once in a great while, we observe in nature when that special sweet spot is hit with just the right wave; it's almost magic. A common example of this phenomenon is pushing a child higher and higher on a swing or, better yet, watching the plump opera star sing at a crystal glass. As soon as the frequency of her voice matches the resonant frequency of the crystal, it begins to vibrate. Amplify the wave oscillations enough and..."

"The glass shatters," interjected a cute student sitting in the second row.

"Precisely," replied the professor. "The waves seem to crash into the crystal at just the right speed to amplify the vibration each time it rebounds. This is mechanical resonance. We have known about this for centuries now. Engineers use the mathematics of mechanical resonance to design buildings that sway and bridges that move, but not to the extent of our poor shattered crystal. They employ the use of dampeners to prevent resonance disasters. But alas, this is not Engineering 101, and Professor Talmut wouldn't like me very much should I choose to teach his material in my class." The students all gave a courteous chuckle.

"So, keeping this concept of mechanical resonance in mind, we look to some more modern work. Late in the 21st century, M-Theory was an attempt to describe the theory of everything. Almost two centuries earlier, Einstein, after his breakthroughs in relativity and light, had focused what some call wasted efforts on a theory of everything. He believed that everything should be able to be explained, measured, and observed. Heisenberg showed that we could either know where a particle is or how fast it is moving, but not both at the same time. Einstein just could not accept this and worked on a counter-theory until the day he died.

"Today, we have never been closer to completing the theory of everything. But more importantly, it has led us to the concept of the string. The basis of this theory is that everything is made up of smaller and smaller things. Grains of sand become molecules, which become atoms, which become protons, neutrons, and electrons, which in turn become quarks, leptons, and so forth, which eventually become strings. Now, strings are thought to only exist in one dimension, meaning they have length but not height nor width. In my own theorizing, I proposed that they have no fourth dimension, or spacetime, as well, because strings make up spacetime itself. My theory of everything is just that: a theory of every single thing in our universe—empty space, dark matter, antimatter, electricity, the entire electromagnetic spectrum—all matter and energy is made of the same thing. I also believe that this principle applies at both the macro and micro levels of matter and energy. Further, it is how these strings vibrate that determines what it is that it is."

Confused looks crossed everyone's face, except for the two men sitting quietly at the back. "Sorry, professor, what was that again?" asked a student off to the side.

"The vibration of these strings determines what it is that it is. Meaning, if it vibrates a certain way, then it is dark matter. At another frequency of oscillation, it is sodium. Yet another, it is UV radiation. If the oscillations of these strings were to change, so does what it is...uh, change."

"What was it that led you to develop your theory in that direction, professor?" asked another student.

"What a beautiful segue into what we will be studying this semester. My theory developed through my work with the metal known as harmonicum. Now, if there are any budding astrophysicists in the room, they could tell you that harmonicum is a rare element thought to be transplanted here on Earth from comets and asteroids long ago. The total quantity of the element is extremely small, and we have yet to synthetically produce it in a lab."

The students in the room looked on with interest. One raised his hand. "So what work could you have done with an element that is so rare? I mean, how do you even find the stuff?"

"Most excellent question. In fact, most harmonicum comes from a single source. It is found in a crater recently discovered in the Northwestern wilderness in the middle of the province of Palin. This particular crater is millions of years old and was so overgrown with trees and vegetation that it blended in with every hill and valley surrounding it, until recently. It was in this crater that harmonicum was discovered." The professor paused for effect.

"Now you may ask yourself, what does this rare metal do that justifies it being the focus of a theoretical physics course? Oh, my young eager minds, I answer that harmonicum does everything. As its naming convention suggests, harmonicum has a peculiar tendency to harmonize with other elements that are in proximity to it. We first thought that this metal merely had radioactive properties similar to uranium or plutonium. As a result of its radioactivity, we saw how it would break down nearby elements and change their molecular makeup in the process. It wasn't until we looked closer at this process that we saw something extraordinary."

The professor clicked a few buttons on his remote, and the lights dimmed. A projector created a central video image above him.

"As you can see, we conducted experiments with harmonicum by placing different elements in close proximity to it. In incredibly short amounts of time, the new element would begin to change. We were dealing with very minute sample sizes, so the changes were subtle but noticeable. It wasn't until we were able to use more advanced measuring equipment that we found our theory of harmonicum's behavior to be completely wrong. We discovered that, in fact, the harmonicum was assimilating the elemental properties of the nearby element. It seemed to be a mimic, taking on the structural and physical qualities of what was around it."

"You mean the metal changed to whatever it was placed next to?" asked a woman at the back.

"That would be a simple way to state it, but more accurately, the metal seemed to be able to synchronize itself with the properties of the other element. It was still harmonicum, but with a shade of the other element as well. Later we realized that this happened only when energy was introduced. The lights and electricity of the measuring equipment increased this behavior. So we tried to see what else we could do by introducing stronger fields."

"So what, you shocked the metal with jumper cables or

something?" interrupted a young man from the side. The students laughed at his question.

"Not quite that raw, but you're on the right track. Here, let me show you." The professor tapped the remote again, and the vid changed. A large clear container filled with water sat atop a small metallic disc. Wires ran all over the remainder of the screen.

"This is an early experiment with harmonicum. We attempted transversing states of matter to have the metal assimilate a gas, specifically hydrogen. We altered the frequency of electromagnetic energy fed to the disc to see if that would change anything. As a result, we stumbled upon something extraordinary."

The students looked on as the clear container sat on the screen, not doing much. Then the water line clearly started to fall. The water was disappearing somewhere.

"Professor, I don't underst—" started a student.

"Just watch; it will be over shortly."

The students continued to watch the screen as the water line faded to the bottom of the container. As soon as the water was gone, a probe with what looked like a spark plug at the end entered the container near the top. The spark flashed, and a millisecond later, a fireball erupted out of the container. The collective gasp from the students was followed by comments of excitement and surprise.

"Professor, what happened?" she asked.

"The harmonicum was able to separate hydrogen from

oxygen and convert water into two gases, as evidenced by the explosion. This was just a demonstration we produced for the media, since just watching sensor readouts doesn't produce the same 'oomph.' We conducted many experiments with the harmonicum, each showing the same result. Harmonicum can adhere to the resonant frequency of every element we have tested it with. In other words, harmonicum is the physical incarnation of the theory of everything. These early experiments were crude in their design as we had yet to apply what we knew from the principles of string theory and from Tesla. In later experiments, we were able to map two or three more elements and their harmonic frequency."

"Harmonic frequency? What's that?" asked a student.

"Oh, that's just something we coined in the lab. It combines the idea of Tesla's mechanical resonance with the theory that everything is vibrating at a different frequency."

"So harmonicum affects the other elements on an atomic level," replied the same student.

"No, the atomic level is too macro. My theory states that harmonicum taps into the ultra-quantum level—the vibrating strings themselves."

"But there is no way to prove that, right, professor?" he inquired.

"Some may think that applying normal everyday physics to quantum mechanics is a little insane, but as Tesla himself said, 'The scientists of today think deeply instead of clearly.

One must be sane to think clearly, but one can think deeply and be quite insane.'"

The student shifted uncomfortably in his seat, obviously not sure how to respond to this last statement.

"You see, there is no other element in the known universe like harmonicum," the professor continued. "Its atomic structure is like nothing we have ever seen. Thus our knowledge of how the element works is limited by our understanding. It's thought that it can be molded and shaped, but even at high levels of radiation and energy exposure, the atomic structure seems to remain intact. No other element possesses that conservation ability."

The two suits in the back of the hall seemed to perk up at this reply.

"So how did you learn to control the frequencies?" came the question from the other side of the hall. "I mean, was it all just guesswork?"

"At first, yes, it was. But I believe as we continue to document our findings, we will be able to map the frequencies of the universe. Think of it as universal DNA coding. To know what everything is made of is to know how to make anything. In the far distant future, I can see the use of an interface that would be able to use a harmonicum synthetic to give people back their sight, their hearing, bring motion back to the paralyzed. Forget all the problems and setbacks of stem cell research. Or we could use it to change harmful elements such as radioactive waste into more productive things. We could live the dream of the alchemists of old and change one thing into another. Think of it. What if we could change sand into wheat to feed the hungry, dirt into clean water for the thirsty? The possibilities would be endless."

"But these are decades away, right?" asked another student.

"Oh no, not decades. Centuries. Anything approaching a simple practical use, even on an extremely simplistic scale, would be at least sixty or seventy years out. We would need to come a long way after that before we could tackle these global issues. For now, we'll build the foundation of the future one experiment at a time. Plus, who knows what our space program in the future will yield? Perhaps Mercury is riddled with harmonicum from its many impact craters. Only time will tell."

Unnoticed by the students or the professor, the suits looked at each other and nodded something in agreement.

"So what is our semester going to look like, professor? I mean, I thought this was a theoretical physics class."

"Yes, but what is a theory that can't be proven? We will delve deep into the possibilities of harmonic frequencies this semester. This class is theoretical in basis, but you will also be required to log lab time to earn a full grade. After all, what would a university be without the ability to harvest so much free labor? We wouldn't want your thousands of credits going to waste, would we?"

This last statement was met with mixed emotions from

the students. The bell rang, and the students started to log off the classroom net. The professor killed the vid as the lights came back on in the lecture hall. Students chatted with each other as they collected their things. They all seemed to completely ignore the two people in the back row who had not moved during the entire presentation. As the students filed out of the room, these two stone-like men sat, apparently waiting for something. As the last student left the room, the two stood and strode down the steps towards the professor. The professor seemed oblivious to them as he collected his papers and remote, putting them into his faded leather bag. As the last paper was shoved in, he looked up, grabbed his chest, and stepped back.

"Sorry, professor. Didn't mean to sneak up on you like that," the first man lied.

"Oh, goodness. Well, you did give me a scare, that's for sure."

"My name is Kingston, and this is my associate, Mr. Creed." The man motioned to the taller man standing next to him.

"Well, Mr. Kingston, Mr. Creed, it's nice to meet you. What can I do for you?"

"We enjoyed your lecture very much, Professor. You seem to have some bright students this year," remarked Kingston.

"Yes, well, the semester is still young, and usually the increase in the frequency of party attendance has a negative correlation to one's achievements in my classes, so we'll see how they shake out. Are you two fellow physicists? I think I recognize you from somewhere."

"No. I could barely understand what you reviewed here today, professor," said Kingston. "My colleague Mr. Creed, however, is a whole lot smarter than me, and he thoroughly enjoyed himself." Creed smiled and nodded at the professor.

"Yes...well, I am glad. Now if you'll excuse me, I have office hours." The professor made his way between the men and started to walk up the stairs.

"My friend had one question about your lecture, professor," said Kingston offhandedly. "That last part about the timeline. You really believe that it will take centuries to be able to use harmonicum practically?"

The professor continued walking as he replied over his shoulder, "Yes, I do. Hopefully, we can trim a few decades off with the work I am doing now, but I feel it is an accurate estimate."

"Huh, well then I guess I lost my bet," replied Kingston.

The professor stopped at the top of the stairs. "And what bet would that be, Mr. Kingston?"

"Oh, it's just Kingston, and Mr. Creed and I bet that we were within a year or two of using harmonicum in practical applications. He said that without you, it'd be at least five or six decades out. There goes my hundred credits."

"Please forgive me for my confusion, Mr. Creed, but what do you mean 'without me'?"

Creed spoke up. "Oh, simply that without your contribution to our research, we would be hard-pressed to finish our practical application trials."

The professor stared at them, confused. "Practical application trials? What trials? What research are you referring to? I don't mean to boast, but I am considered the world's authority on harmonicum, and practical application trials are a pipe dream."

"We know you are the expert, professor," replied Creed, "but academia has its limitations. Namely resources, and more specifically, credits. How would you like to advance your research at a greater pace?"

"You must be joking," laughed the professor. "Where are you two from? Did Parker put you two up to this? He is quite the practical joker."

The two men's faces clearly showed that this was no joke.

"Professor, I work for a corporation called MESA." Kingston watched to see if there was any recognition on the professor's face. "What if I told you that if we worked together, we could shave a century or two off your timetable instead of merely a few decades?"

CHAPTER 12
BLACK MAGIC

Time: Current day, dusk

Scene: Desert village on the edge of the Jade Empire

A man dressed in beggar's rags slumps against a sandstone building in the fading moments of desert twilight. His alms plate holds a meager collection of coins and bits of food. He chants in a low voice as others shuffle past him on the dusty street adjacent to the now-closed open-air market. Unnoticed by the passing citizenry, no one thinks anything of him. He appears just like any number of other beggars throughout the village.

His soft chanting prayer continues uninterrupted as a merchant slowly wheels his cart full of wares past his spot of rest. The merchant scoffs at the beggar's ragged appearance.

"When will they take care of trash like you?"

The beggar says nothing but continues his chant. His

head moves to the left and then to the right in a slow, deliberate fashion.

The merchant leaves his cart and reaches down to grab the man, but then their eyes meet. Deep beneath the rags that cover his head, the orbs of this beggar bore into the merchant. The merchant takes a step back, almost as if the man in the rags had shocked him.

The merchant regains his composure. "Bah, you're not worth the time," he says, trying not to betray the fear in his voice as he hurries off.

For the past two weeks, this beggar has sat in various places around the market, seemingly collecting food and money to support his scant existence. The people of this area, like the merchant who just ran from him, noticed him at first, but as time went on, the beggar has become just another part of the village.

The beggar continues to stare across the almost vacant alley. Despite moving the location of his solicitations over the past few days, he has always faced the guarded door across the alley. The beggar sweeps his eyes from one side of the market to the other, taking in each person still lingering in the area. He mentally reviews the information that he has gleaned during his observations. He recalls the early part of his recon, as he had shuffled around the village listening to the merchants and townsfolk. The information he desired was easy to find. The target's location was within the confines of the very building he is now watching. He has sat observing the guarded door over the days that followed.

The beggar continues his chanting, bowing slightly as a passing woman leaves two coins on his plate. He counts down the seconds in his mind. He knows that soon the guard will call to his companion to cover for him as he goes to visit the harlots on the outskirts of the village. The beggar has witnessed this each night the guard has been on duty, tracking the time down to the very second.

His count reaches zero. Without fail, the fat guard picks up his timepiece and looks at it. He calls to his younger companion to cover for him. The stout man sheepishly looks around before proceeding to the end of the street. He turns a corner and is swallowed by the darkness. The beggar counts the seconds.

One, two, three... then very slowly and with wobbly legs, he rises to his feet with his alms plate. Just as he has done the previous three nights, he staggers across the alleyway towards the remaining guard. The beggar hunches over more and puts a deeper tremor in his gait, almost falling into a wall at one point.

He moves his head side to side in a drunken fashion as he clandestinely confirms that no other person is on the street. As the beggar approaches the guard, he sees the expression of recognition dawn on the young man's face. The beggar bows his head low as he comes closer. The guard holds out his hand shamefaced and speaks in a foreign language, insisting that he has nothing for the beggar that night. The beggar holds out his plate anyway, mumbling something in the same foreign language. The guard again repeats his protest and walks to the beggar to stop him from coming closer.

Just as the guard nears, the beggar stumbles hard, spilling his plate of coins onto the dirt. The beggar begins to wail and stoops down to retrieve his fallen donations. The guard, exasperated, squats down to help. As he picks up the coins, he stops, hand outstretched. He notices that the beggar's wails have ceased and that his posture is no longer unsure or unsteady. Slowly, the guard glances upward to look at the beggar. Only then does he see the dark, cold eyes that do not belong to a downtrodden vagabond, but rather to a trained killer.

The beggar's hand glints in the faint light of the crescent moon as it flashes forward. The young guard's eyes close, never to open again.

———

Dirk Garrett was screwed. Really screwed. He had been screwed before, sometimes even by choice and thoroughly to his liking. But this time, he was totally and utterly screwed. Dirk looked around the cramped cell he had called home for the last eight months. He honestly couldn't remember the last time he had been even remotely this screwed. Well, there was that one night with that cute Jadian woman from the brothel in the first of the Seven Cities, but that really didn't count. He had paid for that.

During Dirk's various incarcerations, he would always try to occupy his mind. When he would run out of rocks to scratch vulgar messages on the dingy cell walls, he would turn to pacing his cell. When that had lost his interest, he would start to sing. After realizing that he didn't know that many songs, he would turn to writing. Upon realizing almost instantly that he had nothing to write with nor to write upon, Dirk would settle into reviewing his life to see where he had gone wrong. And this ritual had only occupied the first two days of this particular incarceration.

Just like other incarcerations Dirk had survived, in his mind this one was just as bogus. He honestly could not believe that someone could get so upset about a bunch of stupid relics. Sure, they just happened to be located on so-called sacred ground. And he guessed he maybe, possibly could see their point about removing old artifacts from said sacred ground. But honestly, there wasn't a sign anywhere that said "Sacred Temple of the Goddess of Fertility." He was just attracted to the naked statues and all the gold. How was he supposed to know that they didn't want men entering the temple? If a restroom could be clearly marked, then so should that shrine.

It was similar to the situation a few years ago when those natives in the Burning Plains had chased after him because he borrowed that ancient scimitar. The thing had just been sitting there in the brass and gold mounts. Again, no signage. He had brought that issue up at his trial, but alas, the judge had failed to see how the posting of a "Do Not Pilfer the Holy Sword" sign would have saved Dirk so much trouble.

The remaining months of his current captivity had been spent solving the world's signage issues. He had completed most of the ancient sites that he had visited in the Jade Empire and had been working on the southern half of the UWC. Ever since he had overheard the guard mention that the transport escorting him to the Seven Cities would be there in the morning, Dirk had tried desperately to occupy his thoughts with things other than the impending doom that awaited him.

It seemed ironic that for months Dirk had been able to remain anonymous in the prison. It was one of his survival techniques, especially when he was locked up in the outer region where the technology wasn't that up to date. Then they had figured out who he was. He was sure that he had at least a few Empire warrants in his name. And sure enough, days after they linked his name, he was going to be on a transport heading to a very bad place.

Dirk tried to return his thoughts to his signage project. He thought about the cave he had visited in the southern region of the Collective, the one with all the platinum in it. Just as he was coming up with an appropriate sign for the massive store of metal, his skin started to prickle.

Dirk's skin was an amazing organ. Some people spoke of

the ability of ancient sages from the Jade Empire to see things before they happened. While Dirk was not from the Jade Empire, his skin apparently didn't know that. Every time Dirk was about to strike proverbial gold, or if trouble was on its way, his skin would ignite, his hairs standing on end. Dirk had learned to pay attention to this phenomenon, and it had saved him more than a few times.

Dirk sat watching as the hairs on his arm stood at attention. He noticed a sound that he hadn't heard before in his long months of solitude. A small metallic scratching seemed to be coming from his cell door. He stared at the iron door, focusing on the faint scratching sound. He slowly stood and crept towards the rusty old door. Just two paces from it, he heard a faint click. Dirk's skin almost leapt from his body.

With a sound that he had grown accustomed to all these months, his cell door squeaked open to reveal... darkness. No one was there. Dirk started to get antsy. He tried to peer into the darkness down the hall, but it was almost as if the hall was gone, replaced by... nothingness. He took a small step forward. Just as he picked up his foot to move closer to the door, a figure separated itself from the darkness. It looked to Dirk as if this person was at one moment part of the blackness just outside of his cell and then he wasn't. Standing before him was a man wrapped head to toe in what looked like black synthetic material. Parts of this man seemed to almost fade in and out of existence as Dirk continued to process what he was seeing.

The man raised one gloved finger to his covered face, right about where his lips should have been. It took Dirk just a moment to recognize the gesture, but Dirk found it absurd. If this man thought Dirk was going to yell out for help while standing so close to someone with that much of a creep factor, this guy would be sadly disappointed.

Dirk cautiously, and a bit nervously, nodded his understanding. The shrouded man made another gesture indicating for Dirk to follow him. Even more cautiously, Dirk reached out, grabbed the doorframe, and peered out into the darkness.

As soon as he looked into the black hallway, the other man disappeared completely. Dirk started to lean back into the poorly lit cell, but then felt a fierce grip wrap around his arm and propel him forward into the hallway. Dirk could not see a thing. He knew the prison had lights, but none of them were on now.

The iron grip on his arm relaxed to a firm squeeze that led him down the hallway. Calling on his skills as a relic hunter, Dirk imagined in his mind the path they were taking. He had kept good mental notes on the numerous times that he had been hauled back and forth from his cell through the maze of the prison. Foolishly, early on in his stay, he had entertained thoughts of escaping and had wanted to memorize the routes to aid his attempt.

The man led Dirk down various hallways, turning at some, pausing at others. If Dirk's mental map was correct, they were approaching a very special room. Dirk had only seen it once through the crack of a slightly open door. It was where they were keeping the artifacts that Dirk had so ineffectively hidden away. Who knew these guys would have searched everywhere? Dirk involuntarily shuddered at the memory. Two more right turns and they would arrive at the room. One right down, one to g—

They turned left. Dirk stopped moving his feet. His rescuer's grip tightened. If he was going to make his move, it would have to be now. Dirk stumbled and fell down to the ground. The invisible man tried to keep him up but released him as he twisted away. Dirk hit the ground for a mere instant, then popped up and sprinted back down the hall. He turned up the previous hallway and made the last right. He could see the faint shimmer along the bottom of the doorframe. He was not going to leave without his stuff. Three meters. Two meters. One met—

Thump!

Dirk hit the ground hard. Something had wrapped around his legs, rendering them immobile, but his upper body was still free. The arrested momentum propelled him hard into the dirt floor. He started to moan when a hand clamped down over his mouth. Dirk tried to yell; the hand just clamped down harder. This wasn't working. Dirk tried something else. He played dead. He let his whole body go limp and played dead better than any Fido he'd ever seen. The hand still did not loosen its hold. In the passing seconds, Dirk started to hear muffled sounds. He realized that since he was playing possum, he was not making them. He doubted his masked man was making any of them either. That only left...

He could hear it clearly now. The sound that he had heard so many nights in his cell. The thumping of dirty, ratty old boots coming down the dirt hallway. Dirk was paralyzed with indecision. They had to get out of there. Panic started to course through his veins. Harder than the metallic grip covering his mouth, adrenaline pounded through his system at a blistering pace. Dirk's skin crawled with goosebumps.

———

He had heard something. He knew he had heard it. One minute he was taking a piss, the next a loud thud. And this damned blackout wasn't making anything any easier. Why hadn't the generators kicked in? Without thinking about it, he unstrapped his weapon from its holster and rested his hand on it, just as a precaution.

He saw a faint light down at the end of the hallway. That had to be coming from the holding room. That generator was always on. He'd use that as a starting point since it seemed to be the only thing that was lit around here. He trundled down the hallway towards the light. Oh, Rajav would not be pleased if his satellite entertainment was out. He had told Rajav to put the unit in the holding room so it wouldn't be affected by the blackouts, but no one listened to him. The light at the end of the hallway grew a little brighter as he approached.

———

Yep, once again Dirk was screwed. Cosmic fate had dealt him a sucky hand for what seemed like the umpteenth time. He could plainly hear the boots pound the ground as that lard-o night guard came lumbering towards them. Enough possum. Dirk started to quickly sit up. He got about five centimeters from the floor when the hand covering his mouth prevented him from going any further. Whoever this dude is, Dirk thought, he must have steel rods for bones and carbon fiber for muscles. He had never encountered such strength, not even from those goons guarding that Ganga shrine.

Dirk looked upwards. With the light seeping from the door, he could almost properly see his rescuer, or substitute captor; Dirk hadn't made up his mind on that one yet. The man's head was turned towards the sound of the guard coming down the hallway. Dirk seriously hoped this guy could fight. If not, at least he would get a potential cellmate out of the ordeal. Dirk wondered if the man liked chess.

In one fast, efficient motion, the man in black silently scooped Dirk up off the floor and pinned him against the wall, all the while never removing his other hand from Dirk's mouth. Dirk saw the faceless head turn towards him. Again, the black man's finger rose in front of where his mouth should have been and silently told Dirk to be quiet. Dirk nodded vigorously. The man regarded Dirk for a few more seconds, removed his hand from Dirk's mouth, and spun right next to him, pressing himself flat against the wall.

————

Almost there. He hoped that Rajav hadn't been watching the World Finals. Rajav would be pissed for weeks if the power had gone out during the games. He would check the holding room and then go out back to see what was wrong with the generators. Kishiv had probably forgotten to put fuel in them again. Well, if Rajav was angry, he could be angry at Kishiv, not him.

He rounded the last corner and saw the light coming from beneath the holding room door. Something at the corner of his eye caught his attention, and he turned his head. For a brief second, his conscious mind struggled to put the pieces of what lay before him together. It never did catch up to his involuntary nervous system, whose alarm bells had started to clang the moment he had turned the corner.

————

Dirk closed his eyes. Six more steps, four steps, two... His heart was now exploding through his chest. He opened his eyes and turned just in time to see the rotund, hairy man round the corner. Dirk saw the man almost go right past them. Then it happened. In slow motion, Dirk saw the confused look dawn on the man's face. In what was probably a millisecond but felt like minutes, the black man's fist flew towards the guard. Dirk thought he saw sand fly at the guard, but as the man tumbled towards the holding room door, Dirk could plainly see glints of light reflecting off hundreds of tiny glass shards that were now buried in the guard's face and throat. When the tubby man stumbled and crashed through the holding room door, Dirk saw the bits of broken glass plainly. He continued to stare at the now dead man even through the first blares of the alarm. It wasn't until he felt the hard tug on his arm that time sped up to normal.

They were dashing through the maze of passageways. Dirk, despite his mental map, had no idea where they were, but the man seemed to know every nook and cranny even with the lack of light. He saw flickering lights coming down the hallway. More guards with torches. Just when he had thought that karma was smiling down on him, more guards with torches. The man stopped in front of Dirk. Through the flashes of the beams of light, Dirk saw the man hunch over like he was squishing an inflated ball. He felt the air around him change, then grow colder. His ears popped painfully as the pressure around him grew. He felt some force starting to bear down on him. Then a giant blast of air whooshed away from him. One by one, each of the guard's torches flew wildly into the air and smacked against the wall. Dirk's ears were ringing as the two of them moved up the hallway where the guards had been. In the light of the now motionless torches, Dirk could see that all of them were unconscious and bleeding after being thrown against the passage walls by the sudden gust of wind.

Faint lights started to appear. They looked like emergency lighting and only barely lit the ground. As they rounded a corner, the door of the only modernized room in the whole facility came into view. Just as they approached the kitchen, it started to open. The black man jumped at the door, slamming it shut and throwing the guard on the other side back into the room. The masked man quickly squatted down and placed his hands along the threshold. Almost at once, Dirk felt the air pressure around him drop. Again his ears started to hurt from the rapid change in environment. The screams from inside the kitchen told him that the guards in there were suffering from it too. Then they stopped, and all he heard was moaning. The man whipped open the door and dragged Dirk behind him as they moved through it. All around the kitchen, guards were lying on the floor, some clutching their heads. Each had blood oozing from their ears and nose. Those closest to the door weren't moving at all. Dirk's skin, while all this time looking like a human-colored pickle, did the impossible – it prickled even more.

They raced through the back door of the kitchen. Two more guards came hurtling up the hallway just outside the kitchen exit. Dirk watched as the man pulled thin metal rods from a sleeve on his arm. Making a move like he was fanning a deck of cards, the small rods became saw-like discs. The man chucked the discs, impaling the two oncoming guards squarely in the throat. Down a second hallway, Dirk witnessed the same type of rods become thirty-centimeter blades that the man used to skewer two more approaching guards.

Three hallways later, they reached an outside door. Dirk was yanked down into a squatting position as the man knelt on one knee at the door. He produced two black bags, dipping each of his hands into a separate one. Black and silver dust glittered as the man proceeded to crush the two handfuls of material together. He repeated this process two more times. When he was done, the man held five balls; two light gray, two a darker charcoal gray, and the remaining ball was as black as the man's clothes and slightly larger than its friends.

Dirk heard more running from the hallway that they had just come from. The man seemed not to notice, or not to care. He carefully palmed the four balls in one hand and pressed the fifth into the locking mechanism of the larger outer door. The noise was growing louder. The man adjusted the fifth ball and then leaned back to look at his work.

Dirk could now make out individual voices as the mob came closer to their position. The man looked at Dirk, nodded, then simultaneously pounded the fifth ball with his fist while tossing the four others in the direction of the oncoming noise. Dirk once again felt the man's strength as he covered Dirk's eyes and pulled him down into a fetal position just as the guards rounded the corner. Even through the gloved hand covering his eyes, Dirk saw through the glove what must have been a blinding flash from the hallway and felt a wave of compressed heated air rush out from the door. Seconds later, amid the screams and wails, Dirk was forcefully brought to his feet and shoved out of the now-open doorway. As he looked back, his eyes adjusted to the retreating scene of a hallway filled with thick gray smoke, a partially blasted doorframe, and for the first time in months, the clear night sky.

———

They had been walking for what seemed like hours. Dirk had asked the man where they were going at least thirty times. Each request was met with the same answer: silence and no change in the black man's rapid pace up the hillside. Dirk had started to wonder about his current situation. Something inside him was telling his brain that he just might have been better off inside the prison than outside with this one-man killing machine. Dirk replayed the events that had happened earlier that night and found they were all very fresh in his mind. After the initial shock of actually being outside of the prison, the fact that he was not out of the famed woods hit very close to home. Where was this psycho taking him? Why was the psycho taking him there? Was the psycho working alone, or did someone send the psycho to get Dirk? If so, who had sent the psycho and what had Dirk stolen from them? Why couldn't the psycho have just let him grab a few pieces of his find before they left? All these were very pressing questions in Dirk's mind.

Finally, after walking up a particularly steep set of hills and rocks, the man in black slowed his pace. They entered a mass of trees. The man grabbed Dirk's shirt to lead him through the dense thicket. Soon they exited the trees, and Dirk saw a wide clearing before him. The man stopped just short of entering the cleared ground.

"Why did we stop? What are we doing here? Is this where you're going to kill me?"

Again, silence. Dirk heard it before he saw it. A faint humming noise coming from above the clearing. Once again, his skin prickled.

———

The chopper pilot hovered over the clearing and scanned the edges with his advanced Extra Sensory Goggles, or ESGs. The cloaked NightHawk was definitely military issue, but this pilot did not wear the uniform of the UWC or the Jade Empire. His sensors alerted him to one heat signature approaching from the southeast, and he notified the extraction team in the belly of the copter. The pilot saw the image approach as his goggles gave him a composite of its thermal, electromagnetic, and low-light resolution signatures. Walking next to the composite image was a moving void. The pilot brought the throttle of the copter down and triggered the de-cloaking protocols.

As the supports of the craft touched lightly upon the ground, the rear hatch opened to allow four armed men, all equipped with the same ESGs, to pour out and take up flanking positions across from the two now-visible figures. A fifth man exited the belly of the aircraft and ducked low as he met the two men. He took the bewildered-looking one, shoved his head down, and led him back to the open hatch. Once there, the fifth man radioed to the four sentinels, then to the pilot, and then placed a headset on the man's head. Instantly, Dirk could hear the chatter from the six-man team.

"Dirk Garrett, you are one expensive acquisition. Not that I don't know the answer to this question already, but do you have any injuries that I need to be aware of?"

Dirk stared at the man. "No, I don't think so. Who are you guys and how do you know my name? You UWC Ultra Forces or something?"

The engine of the copter started to whine higher as the hover engines gained more power. The four flanking men slowly retreated into the craft.

"Nope, not Ultra Force. Well, at least not anymore. Private sector pays better. As for us knowing your name, well let's just say your benefactor has tasked us with getting you out of this place. He needs you for some reason, and all the persuading in the world that you weren't worth the effort wouldn't sway him, so here you are."

The whine of the engines reached their pinnacle of sound, and the pilot started to engage the throttle again. Dirk looked out and could faintly see the shadow of the black man just where he had left him.

"Wait, what about him? Isn't he coming too?"

"Remember when I said you were an expensive acquisition? Well, that's cuz we had to hire him to get you out. His contract ended when you stepped onto the floor of this bird. Besides, as I'm sure you've already figured out, he doesn't exactly need any help."

Dirk watched as the hatch started to close. He felt the electric field grow around him as the cloaking engine engaged. The last glimpse he saw of the black man faded as the lights blinked out inside the chopper, the hatch sealed, and the copter rose into the night.

CHAPTER 13
HAVE CREDITS, WILL SHOP

Time: Current day, late afternoon
Scene: Mega Lots Shopping Center

"Sam, you're really starting to piss me off." Cammie set down six or seven outfits in a range of colors and styles. "This is for graduation, probably the last time that we will all be together. You aren't taking this seriously enough."

Richard looked up from his tablet. "This is the last time we'll all be together? Oh hallelujah, there is a god. Consider the debate settled; all hail the mighty creator."

Cammie ignored him. "Sam, seriously, time is running out. If you don't talk to Adam soon, there might not be another chance. You need to pull out all the stops for graduation and the after-party."

Sam modeled another dress made from liquid silk. It was silver and looked terrible on her, not to mention that it was way too expensive. Sam stepped back into the dressing room and ripped off the dress. She picked another one, a brand she didn't recognize. She put on the dress and glanced at herself in the mirror.

Now this didn't look so bad. Sam pulled at the pay strip, touching the holographic tag to get the price. Her face went white.

"Cammie, this was a terrible idea."

"Why, does it look bad?" Cammie slid back the curtain, causing Sam to reactively cover herself despite being fully dressed. Sam walloped Cammie on the arm. "How many times do I need to tell you not to do that? I could have totally been naked."

"And who are you afraid of seeing you?" Cammie said as she inspected the dress. "The only person here is Dick, and he's too smart to have delusions of that sort about you. Right, Dick?"

"The only delusion I have, Camille, is that someday you'll put together a semi-rational thought. But alas, we can all dream, right?"

Cammie stuck her tongue out at Richard as she pulled back the curtain so Sam could change again. "I liked it better when you were in the hospital. You're not going to get your appendix out again any time soon, are you? The time you were gone was so delightful."

"For me as well, Camille. For me as well."

Sam frowned slightly, sticking her head out from behind the curtain. "You don't really mean that, Richard. You missed me, right?"

Richard glared as he looked at Sam's pout. She sighed. He was still mad at her. She stomped the floor in frustration. She had let it slip to one person during the break that Richard was going into the hospital. One single stinking person. Unfortunately, that person just happened to be Cammie, and telling Cammie a secret was the equivalent of painting that secret on the side of a building, shooting a pic, and sending it to every person on the Interweb.

"Come on, Richard," pleaded Sam. "I told you I was sorry!" Sam put on her cutest puppy-dog face.

A half-smile broke on Richard's lips that traveled briefly up to his eyes. She had caught him! He forgave her. She smiled back at him. This was one of those rare moments that Richard showed any sort of emotion. Well, excluding his usual haughty discontentment. "Yes, of course, Samantha. I missed you while I was gone."

Sam giggled and pulled back the curtain. She had accomplished her mission, but as the feeling of elation came, so did the guilt. She really shouldn't do that to him, try to charm him like that. She didn't want to give him false hope, and acting all girlish and cute was not the way to avoid that. Sam's conscience nagged at her.

Three months ago, Cammie made the observation that

Richard might be in love with her. There was no explicit evidence, and he never said anything to make Sam think that, but now she was so conscious of everything he did that it often stressed her out. She really didn't know what to do. She didn't want Richard to go after graduation, but how could he stay?

She grumbled inwardly. Ever since they had become friends in their second year of Secondary School, Richard had been a rock for Sam. He had been there no matter what. Now that she thought about it, it would make sense that he had special feelings for her. What guy did the things Richard did – does, is doing, will do – for her and isn't in love? She didn't think that kind of guy existed.

Of course, she didn't think of him like that. She just wasn't attracted to him physically, as painful as that was to admit. But she also wasn't ready for Richard to disappear from her life either. She did not want him to go, though she knew that keeping him around was going to be impossible. Richard was on the fast track. He was going to enter the United Western Collective's most prestigious school, Western Advanced Research, in two months. There, Richard would be treated like royalty because he was a genius amongst geniuses. He could do anything, be anyone. All he had to do was try.

And then there was her. She was average in every sense of the word. Sure, her body had finally caught up to her age, and now she actually looked like an 18-year-old girl, but there were a lot of semi-talented pretty girls in the world. There was only one chubby, sarcastic genius boy out there, and he had proven to be a good and trustworthy friend, one that she was going to sorely miss when he was gone.

"Okay, I found the one. I think. Richard, don't you dare laugh."

Sam stepped out from behind the curtain. Cammie's voice sounded astonished. "Oh my George W. Bush! Sam, this is perfect. You have to get it!"

Another warm smile lit up Sam's face as she spun in a circle, admiring herself in the full-length mirror. The dress really was a thing of beauty. Demure and elegant, this dress was everything Sam felt that she wasn't. A spiking desire surged in her gut. She really wanted this dress.

Nervously, Sam touched the holo-tag. Her heart dropped out of her chest right onto the floor. Cammie caught a look at the holo-tag and whistled.

"This thing better be made of spun platinum. That is expensive!"

Sam stepped back into the dressing room. "I can't get this thing. It's way out of my league."

"It's on me, Samantha." Richard stepped forward, looking at her with open admiration and wonderment. "You and this dress were made for each other. You have to have it."

Sam studied Richard, confused. Not at his act of kindness – he did stuff like this all the time for her. She had grown accustomed to his habit of buying her things for no reason at all. No, what bothered her was that Richard knew what the dress was for, and yet he still offered to buy it for her. Some people were too kind for their own good.

"It's not like I'm really paying for it anyway," Richard continued. "Besides, it's nice to do things like this every once in a while."

Cammie raised an eyebrow. "Richard, that doesn't make any sense; if you're not paying for it, then who is?"

Richard ignored her question.

Sam watched Richard log onto the store's net and pay for the dress. He always said stuff like that too, brushing it off like it was normal to spend ungodly amounts of money on things like dresses. Just when she thought she was starting to understand him, he would do something like this. He always hid behind a cold, sarcastic exterior, but she knew better.

"I told you he was in love with you," Cammie said very quietly. "You'd better stop that real quick before he goes all crazy like those genius types do."

"Cammie?"

"Yeah, Sam?"

"Shut up."

"Chz. Well, I never!"

Ten minutes later, Cammie, Sam, and Richard strolled out of The Fox and into the shopping center. On the outskirts of Academy City 676, Mega Lots Shopping Center was the center of fun in town. They had the latest games, clothing, and accessories, not to mention a testing outlet for the electronics conglomerate Apples, Oranges, and Pears. The abso-lute highlight, however, was probably the military-grade survival combat tag played in the indoor weapons arena. Sam absolutely loved Combat Tag with the full-body suits and energy weaponry. It was like she was in a virtual game room, but much more intense. It was the same rush of war without all the downside of blood and death.

They wouldn't be playing today, however. Richard hated it, and Cammie wasn't much of a fan either. Plus, it had been so long since they had hung out that Sam was reluctant to do something she knew Richard wouldn't participate in. So instead of tag, their little group headed to Foodopolis to find some eats and meet up with Coda and his recently acquired girlfriend, who was the current topic of discussion.

"How could he have a girlfriend?" Cammie asked in exas-peration. "He's supposed to be in part seven of Cammie's patented 'How to Capture a Boy's Heart' plan. Stupid boy, he's messing up my timeline. Rival girls aren't supposed to show up until later, somewhere in the last third of the 57-part plan. I can already tell she's a homewrecker."

"I guess he must have missed the memo." Sam dodged a group of boys about her age, not noticing their gawking looks as she passed. "Just goes to show you, can't fight fate. If it's meant to work out, it will."

"Well, fate is about to have an encounter with a cleavage-maker bra and a high slit dress. Let's see him fight that one."

"You're impossible."

They both looked at Richard.

"Don't look at me. I can feel my intelligence diminishing just by suffering through this conversation."

The group found the main pathway that led from the shopping portion of Mega Lots into Foodopolis and stopped to get their bearings. Sam hated places like this. They were so large it was hard to know where to start. An artificial river cut across an eating area the width of a game field and probably twice as long. Restaurant after restaurant lined the walls in neat little stalls and served every style of food from the baked beef of the Deep South to the Gangan Super Spice of the Burning Plains. At the far end of the common eating area, an artificial waterfall gave the ambiance a particularly refined effect. Sam thought it was overdone, but she was about the only one who did.

She grabbed her screen and searched for Coda's avatar. It would have been a total nightmare trying to find Coda and his girl in this zoo of a dining area by sight alone. Sam quickly located him, and they headed over to his table, a more private eating area that sat right in the middle of the river, connected to either side by attendant-lined walkways stretching to the raised platform. Sitting at a table in the center of the platform was Coda and a girl with striking blonde hair. Coda smiled once he saw Richard and the others approach.

"Guys! You made it!"

He stood, nodded to Richard, and then gave Sam and Cammie a hug, one that Cammie held almost uncomfortably long. Coda didn't appear to notice though, as he sounded perfectly normal when he spoke.

"Take a seat, boys and girls. Have you guys ordered?"

Richard nodded and held up his interface as Cammie and Sam found chairs. "I took care of it."

"Perfect. Now then, let me introduce you to someone pretty special."

The blonde girl blushed, rosy patches of color blossoming on her cheeks. She smiled and twisted shyly.

"I'm Lacey. Tis a pleasure to make your acquaintance. My Coda Bear over here has told me so much about you all. Camille, Samantha, and of course Richard, thank you so much for watching over him. You have my gratitude."

Sam stared at her in awe. Was she serious? Coda Bear? Who comes up with pet names after a week of dating? And they had her gratitude for what exactly? This was weird; totally and completely weird.

As lunch progressed, Cammie was less than impressed. She looked downright incensed, which made for an awkward time. Sam could feel the murderous intent leaking out around Cammie. She severely hoped that Lacey didn't make any sudden movements or things could get real ugly, real quick. Lacey, on the other hand, hadn't noticed a thing, at least that Sam could tell. Either that or she controlled her emotions as well as a covert operative. Conspiracy theory aside, Sam was thankful when Lacey got up to take a vid call from her father.

"So what do you guys think?" asked Coda as soon as Lacey was out of earshot. "Isn't she wonderful?"

Richard was the first to cut in. "Absolutely delightful, Coda. I think you should propose right away."

Richard shot Cammie a half-smile, one that Cammie returned with a glare. "I guess she seems nice enough. You know, if you like that type."

"And what type is that?" asked Richard in mock interest. "I think we're all dying to know."

Again Cammie glared. "I was merely stating that she's nice. I just don't think she's for you, Coda. You need someone with a bit more culture. Maybe someone...ethnic."

Coda chewed on the inside of his cheek. "You think I need to be with someone more ethnic? She's totally ethnic, Cammie. Hello, she has blonde hair and blue eyes! Who has blonde hair and blue eyes?"

"Half of the Jade Empire."

"And let's not forget her totally cute accent!" Coda continued.

Sam tried to hold in her laughter but was having a hard time. Richard also seemed amused, which was out of the ordinary for him, though admittedly he also appeared slightly preoccupied. Cammie and Coda's back and forth continued for a long while, and Sam quickly lost interest in their increasingly crazy point and counterpoint. About twenty-five minutes passed like this, with Sam and Richard finding refuge in Richard's screen and a riveting game of World of

Warmongers. A buzz on Sam's own tablet and a flying envelope indicated a message from Cammie. Sam tapped the envelope and rolled her eyes. If you wanted to talk to me, why didn't you just say so? she thought.

Sam casually read the message.

I see you smirking over there; you'd better wipe that little grin off your face and look to the other side of the bridge.

Amazed at Cammie's ability to keep up two conversations, Sam shot Cammie a quizzical look and then turned in her chair, only to whip back around instantly. She slouched down.

Adam was only six meters from them, sitting with a group of his friends. A giggle and another envelope with the words OMGWB, you should have seen your face indicated Cammie's witness to Sam's humiliation. He was here. Right here. Right now. What should she do?

I could talk to him, she thought as she again glanced over her shoulder. Sam felt her breathing growing heavier. She had never been this close to him outside of school. Well, except that time at Camelot, but she was too embarrassed to remember anything about that.

Up close, he was much more handsome. His features were regal, his build perfect. He could have passed for a Vii-theater star if he wanted to; shoot, even if he didn't want to, he could pass as one. She wanted to talk to him. She had never wanted to do something so bad in her whole life.

"Well, I'm sure you're going to be very happy together."

Cammie's voice was more than angry; it was downright venomous. "If you'll excuse me, I just saw someone I know." Cammie stood, hooked Sam's arm, and pulled her away. Sam was too startled to resist.

"What are you doing, Cammie?" Sam protested.

"You want to go and talk to Adam."

Sam's face went white. "Like right now? Just walk right up to him?"

"Of course not, silly. See those guys at the other private table there? Up the center bridge and on the left?"

Sam attempted an inconspicuous peek to her side. She found the group of guys. There were five or six of them lounging at another private sitting area probably ten meters away. They were definitely not Academy City 676 students. "Yeah, what about them?"

"We are going to go talk to them," replied Cammie.

"Cammie, those guys aren't even close to our age. They're at least post-secondary, if not older." Sam looked again, this time a little more closely. "Definitely older."

"Come on, Sam, don't you want to go in for the kill?"

"Cammie, I don't know what that means!"

"Adam has his eyes on you. He's watching you this very instant."

Sam froze and started to turn around.

"No, don't look, idiot, he'll see you!"

"So what do I do?"

.   .   .

"Just follow my lead," Cammie instructed.

"Fine."

Before Sam knew what she was doing, she and Cammie were at another private sitting area talking to a group of absolutely gorgeous men they didn't know. And yes, they were men; there was no way they were students at Academy City 676, or post-secondary. They gave Sam a bad feeling.

"The small one over there is Samuel, the tall guy is Mark, and that's Tony, Jack, and Mitch. And I'm Rob," said the apparent leader of the bunch. He was probably the least handsome, but rugged and scarred, like he had been in a fight or two. He was a big guy too, much bigger than Sam was used to seeing. "And no, we aren't from around here. We're just passing through on our way to a match. We're with Southern University's Combat Tag team."

"That is amazing," simpered Cammie, trying to sound interested. "My friend Samantha here loves combat tag. We play it all the time!"

Ugh. Totally and completely, ugh. If this was flirting, then Sam would pass. To make a guy interested in you, you have to pretend to be interested in what they like? Cammie could not stand Combat Tag. As a matter of fact, Sam couldn't think of something she liked less, except for Richard, of course. Sam stopped paying attention to the conversation after a while and simply took it all in; the way the guys moved, talked, and smiled. The way Rob rubbed his chin and wrung his hands as if he was growing impatient. A prickle on the back of Sam's neck jolted her. Something wasn't right.

The prickle turned into a breath that caught in her throat. This man, Rob, was growing impatient; all of them were. But why? What were they waiting for? Sam instinctively grabbed Cammie's hand. "Cammie, you know that I've got to get home. Say goodbye to your friends."

"Sam, what the heck are you doing?"

"Never mind, just follow me."

Rob and the other guys watched as they walked away. Samuel was the first to break the silence. "What about those two? They seem like pristine property. Especially the brown-haired one. She was totally yummy."

Rob smiled. "Yeah, I don't think we're going to find much better candidates than that for today."

He glanced around at his crew. "Saddle up, boys. It's time to go to work."

CHAPTER 14
ADAM AND EVENING

Time: Current Day, early evening
Scene: Mega Lots Shopping Center

Sam tried to speak, but words simply wouldn't come. She was also having problems breathing, as if inhaling and exhaling had ceased to be an autonomic process.

"Sam! What the oven brick are you doing? Answer him!"

Sam smiled vapidly. "Hi, umm... it's nice to see you."

"You too. I'm—"

"I know who you are."

Sam cringed and raged inwardly. Did I really just say that? 'I know who you are'? Oh, he's going to think I'm a stalker now. Stupid, stupid, stupid!

"What I mean is I know of you... wait, no. I mean, I've seen you around."

He smiled at her. It took all of her strength not to go weak in the knees. "I've seen you around as well, and I've heard a lot about you too."

"Oh, have you?" said Sam with a giddy voice. "All good things, I hope."

"Mostly, but I'm more interested in the bad."

Cammie shot Sam a glance and mouthed, *He's interested in the "bad." Sexy!*

Sam forced another laugh, but it sounded more like a cow hacking up a hairball. Adam looked at Sam with concern as she tried to hide her embarrassment.

This was not going the way she had envisioned. Cammie came to the rescue. "So I was thinking we should totally get together tomorrow and do some Combat Tag."

Adam looked over at Cammie as she eagerly engaged Adam's friend, Howard. Adam pushed his dirty blond hair out of his face with a small gesture. Sam couldn't help but stare. Oh, his profile was so beautiful. He was almost too cute.

Sam felt her stomach churn. The fact was, he was too cute! How could they get married when he looked so much better than she did? No, no, that was not the case. She was hot. Okay, so she had about as much fashion sense as a blind, deaf Ganga, but she was working on that. Oh, if only he had seen her wearing that dress she just bought... that Richard just bought.

Reality re-engaged. They had been with Richard and Coda, and then she and Cammie had left because Coda was stupid. They had gone and talked with those guys, the really cute but really creepy ones, but what happened to Richard? Did he leave?

"So what do you like to do for fun, Sam?"

Adam's smile hit her like an old Louisville Slugger. She was having a hard time thinking. She knew that she should be worried. She knew that she should be sorry, but she just couldn't be, not at the moment.

I'm so sorry, Richard, she thought. *I promise I will make it up to you. I swear it.*

"Actually, I'm a big fan of Combat Tag. Do you play?"

Adam's soft baby blues lit up. "Combat Tag? That's amazing! I love Combat Tag! I've played since I was little."

Sam sat comfortably as hours with Adam melted together. They had come to the mall for a reason, and she had been really worried earlier, but now she couldn't remember why she had come at all. None of it seemed to matter. Adam was simply more amazing than she could have ever hoped for. They had so much in common, from the foods they liked to the programs they watched. It was just perfect. He was just perfect. She was so happy she couldn't see straight.

Dinnertime came and went with Cammie, Howard, Adam, and Sam dining in the upper echelons of Foodopolis, where several breezy outdoor gazebos provided music, food, and a breathtaking view. Sam spent the time learning more about Adam, eagerly listening to any detail he would voluntarily divulge.

"I transferred from Academy City 781, in Sigler Providence, for a change of scenery more than anything else." Adam sipped at a glass of wine. Sam found that his older age just added to his hotness. "My father is a consultant for a large multi-providence conglomerate, so we move around a lot. My mother is from the Jade Empire—"

"Your mom was from the Jade Empire?" Cammie blurted out, looking amazed. "NO WAY! I've always wanted to go to the Jade Empire. How did your mom and dad meet?"

Adam chuckled, warm and low. Sam wanted to put her head on his chest and listen to him laugh or breathe, or just listen to the thump of his heartbeat. Adam took another sip of wine. "The Post War constrictions aren't as tight as you might think. While the Chancellor and Emperor have a lot of bad blood, they also understand that if they don't deal with each other, there isn't exactly a third market option. I mean, there is some business with rogue states, but the smugglers garner most of the profit from that."

"So where in the Empire is your mom from?" Cammie's enthusiasm surprised Sam. She didn't know that Cammie was so into geography.

Adam hesitated briefly, then whispered, "The Seven Cities."

The table went silent. Howard looked just as shocked as the two girls. Cammie, having no filter, almost combusted from excitement and was halfway out of her chair when Sam placed a hand on her arm.

"Thanks, Sam," Cammie sat back down. "So your mom is

from the Seven Cities. Unbelievable. Why would she ever leave?"

"Why indeed, Camille, why indeed?" They all waited, each holding their breath in anticipation. Adam paused again, the hesitation becoming that much more obvious. "She had her reasons, trust me." He looked directly at Sam. "Important ones. That's partly the reason I'm at Academy City 676. For my mom."

The rest of the evening melded into an endorphin-induced blur. They talked. They laughed. They touched. They flirted—a lot. They flirted a whole lot. Sam couldn't remember the last time she had piled on so much charm. She laid it down thick and was rewarded with Adam's full and undivided attention. It was truly a night to remember, a night that Sam would share with her and Adam's children on family vacations to the mountains.

Oh girl, Sam chided. *Don't get too ahead of yourself.*

Sam, Cammie, Howard, and Adam separated at the underground parking structure on the North end of the Mega Lots Shopping Center. They said their goodbyes, Cammie and Howard locking lips in a fervent attempt to devour each other's faces while Sam and Adam stood across from each other awkwardly. He smiled and put out his hand.

"It was nice to formally meet you, Sam."

"Umm, yeah, it was great talking with you as well." Sam took his hand. "We should do it again sometime."

They released their handshake.

"I'd like that. You have my ID, right?"

Sam nodded. "Yeah, I'll ping you."

Adam looked around. "You know it's pretty late; are you sure you don't want me to take you home?"

Sam tried to control her grin. She was about to say yes but then saw Cammie shake her head. She answered before she could get her tongue around the words.

"No, that's okay; we've got it. The tubes aren't far."

"As you wish, My Lady."

Adam grabbed her hand and kissed it. Sam could have died right there. She was never going to wash that hand again. Ever!

With a last look and smile, Adam moved off in the direction of his transit bike. Howard and Cammie only broke off their PDA when Adam called out, "You'd better hurry, Howard, or I'm going to leave you behind."

Howard wiped his mouth. "Um, well, it was nice to meet you, Miranda."

"Samantha, Howard. My name is Samantha."

"Yeah, Samantha," answered Howard, preoccupied. He looked to Cammie. "And you, my little lotus blossom, I will hit you up later."

Cammie looked off into the distance thoughtfully. "Yeah, we'll see."

Howard's eyebrows rose in confusion. "What do you mean—?"

"Howard, I'm leaving you," Adam called out from a considerable distance.

Howard gave Cammie a torn look then marched off after Adam. Sam and Cammie watched him descend into the darkness of the lot. As soon as Howard was out of sight, she pulled out her screen and started hammering at it.

"What are you doing, Cammie?"

"I'm updating my status, duh."

"Your VIIS? Why are you doing that?"

"Because I was just totally smackin' with Billy Bob there."

"Don't you mean Howard?" Sam asked.

"Yeah, that's his name," Cammie replied distractedly.

"You forgot his name?"

"I'm not sure I ever knew it."

"I'm so confused," Sam sighed.

"Sam, hello! I was just smacking with him to make Coda jealous."

Sam couldn't hold back her sarcasm. "Oh, now it all makes sense. Why do you think it will make Coda jealous?"

"Because he totally wants me; he just doesn't know it."

"Keep telling yourself that. And just so you know, what you said just now didn't sound crazy at all. So topic change, why didn't we go home with Adam?"

Cammie touched her nose. A stupid gesture if there ever

was one. "Too fast; you need to build it and then take him for everything he's worth."

Sam didn't get it but felt too happy to argue. The girls started to move off to the tubes. It was well into the evening now and noticeably less crowded.

"So what about you and Adam? You two seemed to be getting along swimmingly."

"'Swimmingly'?" asked Sam mockingly.

Cammie sighed. "I've been hanging out with that walking dictionary you call a friend too much. Swimmingly. Who says stuff like that? Anyway, you've made some progress; I'm impressed."

Sam giggled idiotically. The girls rounded a corner on the far edge of the lot leading away from Mega Lots. They followed a long, dimly lit pathway that would take them to the underground transit.

Sam hated walking at night. She hated the dark, hated not knowing what could be watching her this very second. Her body shivered involuntarily. The sensation was creepy until she realized that the shaking was originating from her bag. She pulled out her tablet, shifting it to get around the weird silver box that she was almost surprised to see. She had forgotten to take it out again. While she didn't understand it, somehow it felt wrong to leave it behind. A small envelope sat on the screen.

Hey, did you get home okay?

Sam flinched as if the message had stung her. She

couldn't tell Richard that they had stayed and were just now leaving. Public transit could be dangerous at night, and Richard would definitely be paranoid. She couldn't tell him the truth. She started to type back.

Yeah, I'm fine; I'm home already. It's a long story. I will catch you up tomorrow.

Sam waited for the reply. She really hoped he wasn't paying attention to her VIIS locator ID. If he saw that she really wasn't home... Richard's message came quickly.

Bravo then. We'll converse tomorrow.

Sam put her tablet away as the guilt set in. She hated lying to Richard, but she didn't want to admit that she had completely disregarded Richard's long-standing advice, "Get Home Before Dark." He was awfully paranoid about potentially dangerous situations. But even beyond that, she really didn't want to have to discuss Adam with him. She didn't know how Richard would react if she got a boyfriend, and for right now, she just wanted to enjoy the small victory.

A sudden noise startled her from her thoughts.

Tap, Tap, Tap.

The odd percussion displaced the sounds of the normal concrete jungle. The sound stirred her insides, creating a certain amount of anxiety in her otherwise relaxed state.

Tap, Tap, Tap.

Sam stopped, throwing out a hand to halt Cammie as well. The noise... it was closer, more distinct. Cammie pulled her head out of the social clouds.

"Sa-man-tha, what is your deal? I'm trying to give Ashley a play-by-play of our date with Adam and Leonard."

"You mean Howard."

"How about I call him Sheldon?"

"Cammie!"

"I was just kidding."

"So you don't hear that?" asked Sam, instinct telling her to lower her voice.

"Hear what?"

A strange intrusion swept over every synapse of Sam's senses. She could feel it bristle on her skin, hear the rumble of it in her ears, and could taste the musk of it on her tongue. Her heart started beating faster, the pounding of her blood flowing with her anxiety. She turned around and stared off into the darkness. She tried to hear the noise and separate it from the background.

Then Sam's throat closed up in fear.

In the bushes, just beyond the light of the walkway. She could hear... she could hear... breathing.

Sam casually turned back around, making eye contact with an unnerved Cammie.

"Something is here," she mouthed. "Get ready to run."

For once, Cammie didn't argue.

Sam took a step towards the tube station. One. Two. Three steps. The rustling in the bushes was accompanied by the snap and crack of small twigs. Sam had taken a fourth step when a dark mass emerged from the shadow just beyond the walkway light. Sam had had enough. "Run!" she yelled.

Sam and Cammie took off, running full out. More crashing came, followed by the smacking of boots on metal. Sam didn't look back but could again feel the presence of whoever was behind them. She knew that their pursuer was not alone.

The end of the pathway was in sight. Another ten meters maybe. If they could get around the corner, they might be able to get to a guard post and—

Sam's flight came to an abrupt stop as an iron grip clamped onto her hair and jerked her back. Pain erupted in her scalp and neck as she whiplashed back. Unable to stop her momentum, Sam felt her body slip out from under her. She hit the ground with a thud.

She looked up into the face of a person she hadn't expected to see again for the rest of her life, let alone that evening. Rob, the supposed captain of Southern University's Combat Tag team, stood over her, still holding a handful of her hair.

"Hey there, pretty girl." Rob touched her face, stroking her cheek gently. "Oh yeah, we are going to get a sweet credit for you."

Slavers. These men were slavers. Modern-day human traffickers! She and Cammie were in big trouble. These were the kind of guys that didn't mess around. If they didn't get away, they were going to disappear forever.

"Arrgh!"

One of Rob's goons backhanded Cammie across the face. His hand was bleeding.

"What the hell, Samuel! You're going to mess up the merchandise."

Samuel scowled. "The little beast bit me. Took a chunk of my hand."

Rob and the others started laughing as they lifted a dazed Cammie to her feet. She didn't fight back. Briefly, they took their eyes off Sam, not noticing her slow movements towards her bag. Sam knew they had one chance to get out of this, just one. If she didn't take it, there wouldn't be another opportunity. Sam found what she was looking for and slowly slipped it into her hand, palming it out of sight. She steadied her own breath.

Rob looked down at her again. She curled up in a defensive but defeated position that Rob took as acceptance of a hopeless situation.

"Good girl. I know some plantation owners who are going to pay top dollar for a looker like you. It won't be so bad, you know. Once they break you in." He pulled her up from her hunched position. Sam stood, waiting for the chance.

Once he turned his head to talk to the other guys, Sam struck Rob with the gas blaster square in the jaw as hard as she could, knocking him back. As soon as he stumbled away, she discharged the can right into his face. Rob started choking and spewing everywhere. In the confusion, the others looked towards their choking boss, attempting to get a handle on what had happened.

Cammie, without any prompting, sprang back to life. She kicked one of the guys standing directly in front of her, putting the tip of her very pointy shoe squarely between his legs. The strategy seemed to work, and she repeated it, driving her fist into the crotch of the guy behind her. Cammie broke free.

Sam fired another dose of the gas blaster at the remaining two goons, emptying the contents. The effect was far less potent. They reacted better than Rob, who was still choking. Sam knew that it wouldn't be enough, so she turned and ran, Cammie not far behind her.

"Get them," spewed Rob, choking on his vomit.

Behind them, in the distance, Sam could hear the shuffling of bodies and the pounding of boots. She was at a loss. If these men closed in again, they would be beaten and gagged. They couldn't get caught. It was all over if they did. They ran down long stretches of walkway, the men coming fast behind them. Two discharged energy rounds struck the wall next to them.

"Sam! What are we going to do? We can't outrun them!"

"I know, Cammie, I know! I'm working on it!"

Sam tried a door out of the building. Locked. She tried another, and this one opened. They both ran through and dodged around a corner. They came to a skidding halt at a dead end. If they didn't find another path, it was all over.

They searched to their left, then their right, only to see concrete walls and a zoned-off workspace. Sam ran to the only other door in the area, pulling on it desperately. The door didn't budge. They turned back to run the other way. Maybe they could try to get back to the corner.

Too late. The men were already in sight. There was nowhere left to go.

Sam looked around for something to defend themselves with. She grabbed a couple of steel pipes from the edge of the work area and moved back in front of Cammie, handing one to her.

"I'm going to try to create an opening. When you see it, run," Sam whispered.

"I'm not going to leave you."

"I'm not giving you a choice. Do it, and tell... well... tell... you know."

Cammie's eyes welled up with tears. "Yeah, I know."

The men slowed as they closed in, Rob in the middle, the others fanned out around him.

"You've been bad girls, you know," said Rob, his tone playful but his eyes deadly. "I'm going to have to punish you now."

"Bring it!" growled Sam, swinging her steel pipe in front of her.

Rob's face lost its playful quality. He pulled a small metal rod from his pocket. "Enough messing around, girl. Drop it or I kill your friend."

Sam's mouth ran away with her. "Wow, only thirteen centimeters? I thought alpha males were supposed to be better equipped."

Rob's grin broke out again, but this time it was slightly demonic. He moved a slider forward. A thin plastic-looking rod shot out of the handle.

"So it's a bit longer," said Sam. "Still not very impres—"

Her voice trailed off as a yellow glow formed around the energy lines that stretched out and connected on different points, forming the outline of a blade. Rob put his arm straight out and swept the blade across his body. Instantly, the smell of ionized air wafted towards Sam.

"Oh... oh no. Sam, that's a Light Shiv! He's ex-military," Cammie moaned.

Sam looked over at Cammie. "What are you talking about, Cammie? I thought the UWC didn't use Light Shivs!"

"I wasn't talking about our military, Sam."

"Excuse me, folks, what seems to be the problem here?"

A man walked out from the other hallway. He was wearing a disheveled shopping center security uniform, complete with goofy hat and sunglasses. The man looked like he had just crawled out of bed, uniform and all. He had a small firearm, and he was pointing it directly at Rob. All but one of the men turned to face him; one remained staring at Sam and Cammie. Rob stepped forward and addressed the officer, seemingly unperturbed by the small gun leveled at him.

"This isn't where you want to be, rent-a-sec. We've got a job to do, and you're in the way. So back off, or I'm going to introduce you to Sally here."

Rob swung the blade, charring some nearby construction.

Sam couldn't help but feel sorry for the officer. He didn't have the training for something like this. Maybe he had called the real security. If they could just get here in time.

The man's answer surprised her. "We've both got our jobs to do, and we both can't have any witnesses. So maybe I should remove them."

In a blur, the man swung his arm around. Two shots shattered the silence and scattered the goons. Everything moved so fast that Sam wasn't aware, didn't really know what was happening. Confused, she reached down and felt her chest. Pain burned through her. She was growing weak... so weak. She couldn't stand up anymore. At first, she thought she had seen the officer's gun smoking slightly, or maybe it was the light. She saw fuzzy images of men being tossed around the room. She felt herself fading as pain and darkness took over.

A guard... he came to help us... why do you look so familiar?

She couldn't hear the other men yelling any longer. A blurry security guard stepped into her view, directly under one of the hazy lights in the ceiling, casting his shadow over her. She thought she saw him remove items from his jacket and... Sam knew no more.

CHAPTER 15
PINK PJ'S

Time: Current day, middle of the night
Scene: Partial Palace

I lay motionless, the bright jagged pillars of light cutting through the darkness, making it hard to see anything but shadow and glare. The forceful vibration of a fossil-fuel engine rumbled as we traversed a bumpy path. I moved, testing my body, and found my extremities bound. I attempted to move my hands but found it painful.

I was sweating all over. I smelled the stench of days past. How long had I been here?

A cylindrical light streaked past a face, and I saw her. A girl I knew to be a friend lay right next to me. She, like me, was bound and gagged, but she wasn't moving. Her head was bleeding; some of the blood was dry. I tried to nudge her. She still didn't move. I whispered to her.

"Hey, wake—"

A hand cracked me across the face. It stung from the impact.

I wanted to retaliate. I wanted to see if my friend was all right, but I couldn't. I couldn't do anything. My body ached from my wrists to my feet to my head. The dull ache of restraints pulled at my wrists and ankles. The path of barely dry tears was wet again as new droplets flowed downward. I tried to speak to my captors.

"Please," I said, trying desperately to make myself heard. "Please, it hurts."

They didn't answer me.

"Please," I said a little bit louder. "You're hurting me."

Something prodded my head. It really hurt.

"Please!" I screamed through the gag, "It hurts my mind. Stop! Please stop..."

The face of one of my captors leaned forward. He was wearing a mask covering half his face and magnification specs. He spoke in soft tones, but I couldn't hear him.

I looked around and tried to focus.

My head continued to pound and ring.

I wasn't in a vehicle anymore. I was somewhere else. More light, brighter and hanging directly overhead, blinded me completely. I shifted my head once more just as it turned off. The shadow of a multitude of people and whispered conversation hung in the air as I glanced down at my hands. I checked the left hand and then the right. They were shackled, tethered to the bed with thick bands. My hands wouldn't budge, but that wasn't what scared me. What really scared me was that when I watched my fingers twitch and my wrists pivot, I noticed they were too small and too delicate to be mine. I realized then that the hand I was moving wasn't my hand.

———

Sam awoke with a start. She was sweating, and tears were running down her face. It was dark. She couldn't see a thing. She didn't know where she was. Was she alive? Was she dead? Was she—

"Samantha?"

A sweet voice that held a hint of concern pierced Samantha's thoughts. She couldn't have felt more relief in that moment.

"Mom, is that you?"

The light flipped on, and Sam was momentarily blinded. Her sight adjusted quickly, but not before a familiar sensation touched her. A hand caressed her forehead.

"Hey, honey," Sam's mother said, "You look like you were having a nightmare."

Sam sat up. "I was. The dream couldn't have been more—"

A shooting pain racked Sam's body. She drifted backward toward her pillow a ways before she caught and righted herself. Dizziness made her feel sick and disfigured her mother's face into something that wasn't so motherly. It was then that she looked down and noticed she was wearing pajamas.

"Sam, is something wrong?" asked her mother.

Sam looked up at her. "Mom, did you put my pj's on?"

Sam's mother gave her daughter a quizzical look. "Samantha, are you feeling okay? You know I couldn't have put on your pj's. I was at work all night."

That should have been obvious. Sam's mother was still in a semi-crisp uniform that sagged from the weight of a whole day's work. Sam hung her head shamefully, upset at her own insensitivity. Her mom worked long hours, and asking silly questions made it look like she didn't notice her mother's hard work, which wasn't the case at all.

The head of household for two different High Tracks families, Sam's mother was a manager extraordinaire. She had a commanding presence and executed her duties with military precision, which was to be expected of the overseer of hundreds of employees at four different manor houses. Sam knew that her mother could be severe if the circumstance called for it. Actually, she could be downright mean, but there wasn't a trace of that severity now. Sam's mother looked tired and more than a little worried. Sam forced a smile.

"I'm sorry, Mom. I'm just a little out of it tonight. I'm glad you're home."

Her mom smiled. "Me too, honey. You were shopping,

right? How was your meet-up with your friend, oh, what was his name?"

"Coda?"

"Yes, that's the one."

Sam's stomach churned as she hesitated. "So it wasn't a dream."

"What was that, Hon?"

Sam snapped out of it. "Nothing, Mom. I'm just tired. Shopping was good. We met Coda's new girlfriend, Lacey. She was a looker."

Her mother's face soured slightly. "Oh, I'm sure that Camille was happy about that."

Sam shrugged as she started to get up out of bed. "Thanks for checking in on me, Mom. Have you eaten?"

Sam's mother placed her hands on Sam's shoulders, pulled her in to hug her, and then gently pushed her back. "You are more than exhausted. You look sick, and I'm perfectly capable of making myself some food, Sam. You go back to bed. It's quite apparent you've had a long day."

Sam did as she was told. "Good night, Mom. I love you."

"Goodnight, honey. I love you too."

The minute the door shut, Sam popped out of bed and started to pace around the room. She attempted to remain calm while she replayed the events, which until moments ago she had thought were a dream, in her mind. Images of the mall, Richard, Cammie, Adam, older guys. Crappy and unsure feelings, impatience, Adam, wonder, warmth, and smiles. Walking, running, fear, pain, and then... Blackness raced around her mental vision. Now she was here. She was in her pj's, sleeping. It couldn't have all been real... could it?

She continued to pace. The men were slavers, human traffickers that took and sold girls to the plantation owners of the Burning Plans. The only way that she and Cammie had survived—

"Oh my George W. Bush! Cammie!" Sam rushed to her wall vid and called up Cammie. She waited impatiently as the connection finalized. Cammie's butler, Alfred, answered.

"Ahh, Ms. Montgomery," said the sharply dressed butler, "It is quite late. Do you mind me asking the reason for your call?"

Sam hesitated. He was speaking completely normally to her; no hint of drama or emergency. It gave her hope that Cammie was all right.

"I'm sorry, Alfred, I was just hoping—wondering if—is Cammie okay?"

Alfred's eyebrow rose artfully. "An odd inquiry, Ms. Montgomery. You know very well that my Lady is recovering quietly from your adventures."

"So she got home okay?"

If Alfred was confused by the question, he didn't show it. "Were you not the one who brought her home this evening after your outing? It was your code that accessed My Lady's wing of the complex."

Sam again hesitated. Now that didn't make any sense.

Nobody had her access code. Nobody. Was she the one that brought Cammie home?

Sam fought the urge to shake her head. She smiled sweetly instead. "Alfred, what is Cammie doing right now?"

"She is sleeping, Ms. Montgomery. Will there be anything else?"

Sam shook her head.

"Then good evening. I will inform my Lady of your call."

The vid blinked out.

Sam resumed her pacing. Her worry lessened slightly as the knowledge that Cammie was home and safe sunk in. They had both gotten home with no apparent injury. This sent Sam's mind whirling.

She spoke aloud. "This doesn't make any sense! There is no way those slavers would have let us go and no reason to think that rent-a-sec could take them. They were military, right? How is that possible?"

She kicked over a bag in frustration. "What's even weirder is Cammie and I got home without incident. I'm even in my pj's. That means that the person who saved us knew where we both live, but how could they know where we live unless—"

Sam tripped over the bag, falling flat on her face. Pain shot through her hands and head as she fell to the floor. She swore aloud and looked at what had caused her fall. It took her a second to recognize it. The contents of the bag from her shopping trip were jumbled with her half-open school bag. It seemed so long ago that they had been in the store looking for the perfect dress. She reached over the bag and grabbed the dress that Richard had bought her. A gesture of affection and one of the few ways he reached out, but not one that she understood. No one understood him. Sam had a sudden desire to speak to Richard, to hear his voice. Richard usually went to bed early unless he was caught up in some sort of academic "I'm smarter than you" pursuit. She also knew that he would be super pissed at her if she called and woke him up. No, she couldn't just call him.

Sam went for her interface. She would check Richard's ViiS locator before she tried to call him.

Sam opened her school bag and felt around for the thin device. Involuntarily, her hand clamped down on something that was not her tablet. She tried to let go, but her fingers wouldn't listen. It was strange. She could move her muscles, just not in the way that she wanted. Sam pulled her hand from the bag. It was the tin box she had found in the lake. Sam stared at it.

What in the—why can't I let go? she thought. Sam worked her fingers, trying to get them open for a brief span. They wouldn't let go. She centered the desk's corner in the middle of the box and pushed. Again her fingers would not let go. She was just about to lie down on the ground and start pushing with her feet when the box released her. She could move her fingers again. She dropped the box.

The metal hit the ground with a heavy clunk. The sound resonated, but not the way a metal box should. Sam was no physics expert, but she knew enough to know that the size, weight, and density of the box shouldn't have been enough to make that sort of sound. She half expected the floor to be cracked.

She moved to pick up the box and then stopped. What would happen if she got close to it again? She didn't want to touch the box with her hands, so she did the only thing she could think of; she kicked it.

It slid unremarkably across the floor. At least it didn't stick to her foot.

Sam checked the place where the box had hit. The plywood floor looked as it always did, gleaming and polished. Sam stared at the spot in disbelief, then looked over at the box. This was very strange.

What the devil are you?

Her curiosity got the better of her, and despite her earlier apprehension, she reached down, using the corner of her pj's to buffer her touch. She moved in slowly, edging closer and closer until—she touched it.

Again, nothing strange happened.

Sam felt a bit of disappointment, though she really didn't know why. She should be happy that her hands weren't acting like a magnet, but still, she was disappointed. She hadn't imagined it, had she?

Sam pulled her hand out from under her pj's and tried again.

For a third time, nothing happened. Baffled, she gripped the box with both hands and walked slowly back to her bed and plopped down on it. She held the box aloft. Her mind wandered.

Was she just so tired that her mind was playing tricks on her, or had that really just happened? What about the date with Adam and getting attacked by the slavers? How much of that was real? If her ordeal at the shopping center had not been a dream and indeed happened, then she had definitely been through the ringer. Perhaps right now was a dream.

Sam shivered and shook her head, remembering the dream and the scary way it had unfolded.

The road, her dead friend, the rumble of the transport. Then there was the feeling of restraints and the bright light overhead. They had felt so real but were different from what had happened at the shopping center. That had been real. She was sure of it. Those men had attacked her, a security guard had showed up, and now she was home wearing her pink pj's. Things had grown weirder from there. She had been looking for her interface and had grabbed the box on accident.

No, that wasn't right.

She hadn't grabbed the box; it was the box that had grabbed her. Thinking back to the sensation, it was slight, but it was there. The box had attached to her, and for a brief moment, didn't want her to let go. The question was—

A throbbing white light exploded around her. She didn't know the source, but the sensation ate her up completely. All she could see was light. She heard a scream but couldn't tell where it was coming from. She felt the sting of a knife cutting skin but wasn't sure if it was her skin. She witnessed the heartfelt plea of someone begging another not to go, but she couldn't tell for the life of her who was leaving, who was staying, or why.

Still, other emotions flooded her. Anger, rage, depression, pain, jealousy, disgust, respect, happiness, joy, and love all mixed together into a stream of unending color. She didn't just feel the emotion; she saw it in a lightwave structure of hues.

Pain erupted. The colors and feelings retreated from their assault. All of it drained from her faster and faster until nothing was left.

Sam opened her eyes barely and noticed that her face was wet. She touched her own skin and pulled her hand away so she could see it. She realized that her tears were mixed with blood.

CHAPTER 16

MESA LABS

Time: One week after the start of the college semester
Scene: MESA Labs main entrance

The beefy-looking man behind the desk continued to scrutinize the identification summary on his screen. He looked up at the small gray-haired man in front of him and then back down to the screen. The small man looked around nervously, hoping to find a familiar face. He was just about to tell the guard to forget it, that he must have come to the wrong building, when Kingston strode out of the security doors behind the desk and up to the Professor.

"Good morning, Professor. I'm glad to see you made it to our cozy home."

"Oh, Mr. Kingston. I'm glad... well, I was beginning to wonder if I had the right place at all," replied the Professor.

"Yes, you are definitely in the right place, Professor. As soon as we finish logging your credentials into our security matrix, I'll give you a tour of the facilities." Kingston glanced towards the beefy guard, who nodded and handed him an ID card.

"Good, good. Here is your temporary badge, Professor. You'll need to use it until we can get you wired up." Kingston handed the Professor the badge as he escorted him to the security doors.

"Wired up?" inquired the Professor.

"Just a phrase we toss around here. You see, our security uses state-of-the-art biometric locks, including rapid DNA scanning and encrypted RFID proximity authentication. We took your DNA at the desk from the epithelials you left on the desktop and coded them into our system. Later we'll get you fitted with one of these."

Kingston held up his right wrist and pointed to the faintest of scars. The Professor had to lean in close to see the very faded dot right above the area that Kingston was pointing to.

"And what is that?" asked the Professor.

"It's our RFID chip, designed and produced all in-house here at MESA. The head of our interface lab has a lot of neat little gadgets that the company takes advantage of."

The Professor's face grew a little apprehensive.

"Oh, don't worry, it's painless and so small you'll never

notice it. It samples the DNA surrounding it and then transmits the coded data to the receivers. The radio used is pretty limited, so it only transmits your credentials when in close proximity to a security station here on the grounds. For now, you can just use your badge. It takes a few hours for your profile to load through the matrix, so we'll get you wired after the tour."

The Professor's apprehension ebbed slightly as they continued down the hallway.

The two came to a large sealed door with another guard station off to the side. The Professor was so busy staring down the various offshoots and hallways that when he saw the tall, slender strawberry-blonde goddess standing at the desk, he let out an audible gasp. She was dressed in a version of the security uniform that the front desk guard had on, but noticeably different. It was almost as if this one had been tailor-made to accentuate the woman's ample curves. She looked up from her screen at the noise, appraised the Professor, and then glanced at Kingston.

"Ah, what a happy coincidence. Professor, I'd like to introduce our head of security, Ms. Green. Ms. Green works very hard to make sure all of us are safe here at MESA."

"How do you do, Ms. Green? Is it normal for employees to be unsafe working here?" asked the Professor.

The woman smiled a knowing and somewhat flirtatious smile. The Professor only grasped the knowing half of it.

"I run a very tight ship here, Professor. The safety of our employees and the company's assets is paramount. Aside from the secured areas of the grounds, you will hardly know that we are even here." Again, the smile crossed her lips.

"Yes, well, Professor, you will be seeing more of Ms. Green later when you get wired, but for now let me show you your new home, so to speak." Kingston glanced at the clock on the wall, nodded to the woman, and then led the Professor off. He did not, however, notice her following him with her eyes as he passed through the security doors. Kingston led the Professor down another hallway with the same offshoots and conjoining corridors as the first.

"My goodness, a person could get very lost in this place," remarked the Professor.

"We've thought of that as well," replied Kingston as he moved over to a screen on the wall. As soon as he approached, the screen flashed a holo-message, "Welcome Kingston. You are in corridor 1 Alpha, section 8. How may I assist you today?"

Kingston motioned to the screen. "Again, the head of the interface lab's idea. Each section of the grounds has these terminals lining the hallways. From here you can access unsecured mail or make a non-private vid call, among many other things. You can also send a message to an employee, and the terminal matrix will find that employee anywhere in the grounds and flash the screen nearest them to give them your message. Everything is read from your RFID, so the system automatically knows who you are."

The Professor eyed the screen. "So if I do get lost, I just need to remember someone's name to call and come find me," he said with a laugh.

"Even better, Professor," Kingston stood in front of the screen. "Directions to the Professor's lab, please."

The screen projected a hologram of the MESA logo that then morphed into an arrow flowing through a series of hallways and turns until it terminated at a point on the map. The map continuously changed from 2D to 3D and back again, showing the path.

"Now watch as we walk down the hall. The screens that we pass will light up with our next direction as my RFID transmits my identification," explained Kingston as he and the Professor continued walking down the hall.

To his surprise, the Professor saw each of the screens they approached flash with an arrow pointing the way they should go. Projected animation accompanied the screens where a turn was required, showing the two when to head left or right.

The Professor was very excited to see the next screens and eventually got a little ahead of Kingston. As he was making a right-hand turn, Kingston called out to him.

"Professor, one moment. I wanted to make a quick stop to show you something I think you will find interesting."

The Professor popped back around the corner as Kingston walked up to a large secured doorway.

"Each section of the grounds is coded to that employee's security level. I wanted you to be able to see this place with me, as your clearance isn't set yet."

The door opened, and a slight breeze from the negatively pressurized area behind it swept outwards with an accompanying "whoosh."

The two men walked through the entryway into a brightly lit lab filled with a host of terminals and personnel working away. The Professor saw glass enclosures with people inside them performing the strangest of tasks and making a myriad of humorous-looking faces in the process. There was a man hooked up to what looked like an EEG with wires streaming from his head. He looked as if he was attempting to win a staring contest with a robotic arm that was gripping the lid of a jar. Another person had a very large backpack of metal, antennas, and wires and was paying attention to a small remote control car that was zooming about the room. Yet another had a headband on and was staring at a projected chessboard as unseen masters played out a game.

The Professor continued to look around, completely forgetting about his tour guide. He moved from enclosure to enclosure, watching and wondering what these subjects were doing. It wasn't until he bumped into a lab tech that he remembered where he was and who he was with.

"Oh pardon me, I am so sorry, dear," said the startled Professor. "I didn't see you there. I was so fascinated by what was happening to that man that I completely forgot to watch where I was going. In fact, I seemed to have wandered off a bit. Do you happen to see Mr. Kingston around?"

"Over here, Professor," called Kingston from across the room. "I'd like you to meet someone."

The Professor again apologized to the lab tech and walked toward Kingston and a taller man, who by his demeanor was very experienced and wise but didn't look a day over forty.

"Professor, I would like you to meet the head of our Interface Lab, Charles Jameson."

"Please, Professor, call me CJ. All my friends do." The taller man greeted the Professor with a firm handshake.

"Well, CJ, I'm pleased to meet you. Do you often make friends of strangers so quickly?" asked the Professor congenially.

"Forgive me, Professor," said the taller man smiling. "I am a closet fan of your work. Have been since you began it. I've read every paper you've published, and I watch every lecture you have on the feeds. I guess I feel that I know you already."

"Oh, well now I am the one at the disadvantage of not knowing you so well. But from what Mr. Kingston has shown me, just with your contributions to the security around here, I do say that I am intrigued already by your work. Tell me, what are all these people doing that had me so engrossed?"

The taller man smiled and motioned for the Professor to come with him to the glass enclosures. "Here at the interface lab, we work on perfecting the synergy created by connecting the human brain to an external processor. These trials you see here are all iterations of types of computer/human interfaces or CHIs that we have developed."

The three men started to cover the same route as the Professor's previous solo trek around the lab.

"This subject here is interfacing with the robotic arm to give it commands to unscrew the jar. Here, a modular interface is assisting this subject to send radio waves to control the car. It's been doing left-hand circles for 20 minutes now, so we're trying to get the darn thing to change its direction. We just can't seem to find the right frequency."

"What was that? Did you say frequency?" asked the Professor.

"Yes, we tuned the pack to emit different frequencies that match with different simple commands. Forward, backward, right, left. However, it seems that the subject is having difficulty adjusting his focus as the car is doing dizzying circles."

"And what about this man staring at the chessboard?" inquired the Professor.

"Not staring, Professor, playing. This is one of our most advanced iterations. And one of our most gifted subjects." The three men watched as virtual pieces were moved back and forth across the floating board.

"Extraordinary!" exclaimed the Professor. "Tell me, do you have any contracts for this work? I mean, who funds your research?"

Jameson was about to answer when Kingston cut him off.

"Mostly pharmaceutical companies. Although we do have large contracts with various defense departments from across the collective, a large part of our research is self-funded as well. MESA Labs has quite the portfolio, and we've done well over the years."

"Most interesting. The university is just now getting interested investors to look at my research. It was most exciting."

"Yes, well you are in for a rollercoaster ride here at MESA," Kingston replied. "You'll be a kid in a candy store with all the resources and personnel you'll need to bring to fruition your passion for Harmonicum research."

"Yes, well I am looking forward to furthering Harmonicum. So many possibilities." The Professor turned again to look at the virtual chessboard. "I dare say, Dr. Jameson—I mean CJ—that Harmonicum would be of great worth to your work here in your lab."

Kingston sharply met Jameson's eye.

"Yes, well I am sure that it would. Perhaps in the future we could harmonize the frequencies of our efforts," Jameson replied.

The Professor turned around slowly to look at Jameson.

"Well, Professor, we have a lot of ground to cover. We should get you to your new lab. Jameson." Kingston nodded curtly and whisked the Professor off.

"It was nice to meet you. Thank you for the tour," called the Professor as he and Kingston exited the lab.

A few hallways and corridors later, the terminal screens showed they were approaching the Professor's lab. Just before they arrived, they passed a woman entering the largest secured door that the Professor had seen thus far.

"My goodness, that lab looks enormous," said the Professor, craning his neck to see past the closing door. "Looks like a whole array of human and animal trials. Could we tour this lab just for a moment? It looks fascinating."

"Unfortunately no," Kingston quickly replied. "That lab has the highest security clearance of all the labs on this wing. Our contracts dictate that all personnel who work or even merely visit are vetted and cleared by the contract holders. Perhaps when you're settled in a few weeks or months, we can arrange a tour."

The Professor watched as the door slowly closed. "Yes, I would appreciate that very much, Mr. Kingston."

The two made a few more turns and finally arrived at another secured door. Kingston showed the Professor how to operate his security badge and temporary DNA scan. The door swung open, and they walked into the new lab. Lab techs were running around calibrating instruments, working with technicians who were setting up large racks of equipment, and generally looking busy.

The Professor noticed that the area was divided into three main sections. He could see an office section complete with open area workspaces and a few closed offices, a main lab area that took up the majority of the space, and a third area consisting of sealed experiment bays.

"Amazing. This is impressive indeed," marveled the Professor. His eyes swept the room, taking in the various areas, machines, equipment racks, terminals, monitoring interfaces, and all the people. "This is at least three times the size of my university research facility."

"Actually, about four times. There is an additional set of experiment bays off to the right there," indicated Kingston.

The Professor's eyes grew wide. "And the staff? Certainly, all these people are just getting things in order. How many will stay once the lab is set up?"

"All of them, Professor. Each one of these employees is at your disposal to further your work. We provided you with a team of lab techs, analysts, experiment coordinators, assistants, and technology managers. All of their previous assignments have been retired, so there will be nothing that will divert their time from you."

The Professor turned slowly towards Kingston, a look of astonishment and giddy anticipation on his face.

A small wiry man approached Kingston and the Professor. "Ah, Kingston. So good to see you. This must be the great Dr. Thurman." The man extended his bony hand to the Professor.

"Professor, this is your head research assistant, David Warrick," said Kingston.

"Very nice to meet you, David. Please, Professor is just

fine. I've grown accustomed to it over the years of teaching," said the Professor, shaking the young man's hand.

"Likewise. Everyone around here just calls me Warrick. Shall we introduce you to everyone else in the lab?" Warrick turned to address the room. "Excuse me, everyone." All of the employees in the lab immediately stopped what they were doing and turned to look at Warrick. "I would like you to meet Dr. Eli Thurman, the head of MESA's new Harmonics Lab."

CHAPTER 17

BIG SISTER

Time: Three weeks into the Professor's employment at
MESA Labs
Scene: Harmonics lab

"These results are most impressive, Warrick." The Professor
reviewed numbers as they scrolled down a screen. "Far better
than I had hoped for. And the work on the interval
frequencies?"

"Just as impressive, Professor. The interval team is
making great strides in documenting the passive oscillators
that show promise. We should have a list for your review by
the end of the week." Warrick stood in the Professor's office,
delivering his daily update. "And I'm happy to report that the
modifications on the spectral array seem to be giving us a
more accurate reading."

"Very good, all very good, Warrick. I had no idea that this

much could be accomplished in such a short amount of time," mused the Professor.

"Well, it seems that we have a good partnership between your mind and MESA's resources. Is there anything else you need an update on, Professor?"

The Professor looked up from the scrolling numbers. "No, no, that's fine for today. Besides, I need to drop off some notes I've been working on for CJ at the interface lab."

"Oh, I can do that for you, Professor," offered Warrick. "I'm heading past there on my way to Security. My RFID chip has been acting up. Just need to get it checked."

"Oh, well, I was hoping to go over some suggestions with CJ about one or two of his interface trials. We haven't been able to line up our schedules recently."

"It wouldn't be a problem at all, Professor. Like I said, it's on my way. I'll go and load these updates to the lab server and then head over there." Warrick reached out and took the mini-drive from the Professor's desk. He started to walk out of the office and then turned back.

"I know Jameson has been busy with a new interface iteration. I'm sure you two will find some time to chat soon." Warrick smiled and then left the office.

He went to the office next to the Professor's and sat down at his terminal. He loaded the mini-drive and called up the files. He scanned through them quickly, previewing some and skipping others. He bundled the files and called up his encrypted mail server. He attached the files with some simple instructions and sent the message. A few seconds later, a message was returned. Warrick read the message, deleted it, and then set the server to scrub his recent activity. He hid the server app and then locked his terminal. Warrick rose from his desk, picked up his tablet, and proceeded out of his office.

He walked through the work area to the secure exit door. Exiting the lab, he took the quickest route possible to a short hallway off to the side of the interface lab. Two secured doors, a security post, and an elevator ride later, Warrick walked into the boardroom.

"You're late!" barked the old man.

"My apologies, sir," started Warrick. He then cleared his throat and spoke in a much deeper tone. "I was smoke screening Jameson's lack of availability."

"Still trying to foster that relationship, is he? Well, continue your efforts. The work in the Interface Lab is too close to Thurman's. We need the Professor isolated from it for a while longer." The old man shifted in his leather chair. The floating heads on the monitors grumbled their agreement. "Just the same, we may need to review our social isolation efforts."

"Of course, sir. Shall I continue with my update?" asked Warrick.

"That is why you are here, Warrick," said Kingston from behind the old man's chair.

Warrick glared at Kingston and then addressed the other members of the board sitting in the darkened room.

"The progress in the lab over the last period has exceeded our projections in all categories. At this rate, we will be able to start feeding the Interface Lab data in four or five more cycles, which is two periods ahead of schedule. I will coordinate with Jameson to make sure his lab will be online and ready to receive the data earlier than planned."

"And what of the other related experiments in the wing? Is the isolation plan working?" asked a floating head.

"It is," replied Warrick, "aside from the close call on his first day." Warrick stared at Kingston. "The secured lab has been apprised of the Professor's movements throughout the wing using his RFID locator. They are adhering to the no-contact policy quite well."

"Speaking of no contact, Jameson is behaving himself, isn't he?" asked the old man.

"Yes, he is. The Professor had worked on some suggested updates for the Interface Lab and was going to walk them over, but I intercepted them before I came here. I sent them to the isolation team, and they are currently working on drafting a response from Jameson. They will brief him on the surrogate contact. Aside from these infrequent attempts to interact on the Professor's part, Jameson has adhered to the no-contact policy. Personally, I think the Professor was taken by the Interface Lab's research and nothing more. I believe he is trying to be friendly and social."

"Well, it's a good thing you aren't paid to think," retorted Kingston. "What you haven't noticed," continued Kingston as he read Warrick's confusion, "is that Ms. Green has recorded no less than twelve attempts by the Professor to visit Jameson in his lab. If that's the Professor trying to be friendly, then our reconnaissance team needs to be terminated. The Professor is normally consumed by his work and previously had very few professional associations, and almost no social ones that we were aware of. This effort to form a relationship with Jameson has me, for one, concerned. One false move and we have a serious liability on our hands."

"Well put, Kingston," commented the old man. "I want a full review of the isolation team's protocols to ensure we keep the good Professor where he needs to be: in his lab making MESA very wealthy."

"Of course, sir, I'll have that review scheduled immediately," said Warrick. He tapped out a few commands on his tablet and then returned his attention to the board.

"As for the progress on the equation, the Professor has made some very intriguing insights. The interval iterations are progressing faster than projected, and he believes he is close to starting work on the element trials as soon as the week after next."

"And has he made any indication that he recognizes any of the work from his early experiments?" asked another floating head.

"No, sir, I don't believe so," answered Warrick. "While his early work was the foundation for our work here, we have not only surpassed his expectations but, by ultimately using the

Interface Lab as the end game, we've taken his work in a direction that he could not have even dreamed of. I understand the need to keep the Professor in the dark about what he is working towards, but I am still pleased at the progress we are making despite the inconvenience of indirect application."

"That's all wonderful news," remarked the old man. "If we can get that equation built, Jameson's progress in the Interface Lab will skyrocket. Gentlemen, I believe we are closer than ever to being able to terminate the original prototype and proceed with our efforts on the second generation. Jameson's last report on Proto 2 showed promising acceptance of the latest round of coding trials." He turned to Warrick. "Anything else to report?"

Warrick looked uneasy. "There is one concern that may be approaching faster than anticipated. We are coming up on the physical trials. Since the Professor is the expert on Harmonicum, I wish to raise my concerns that the cover story explaining MESA's considerable quantity of Harmonicum may be insufficient to curtail his curiosity in the matter."

"Warrick, your clearance, let alone the Professor's, isn't high enough to even begin to discuss that," replied Kingston. "The original response is the best response. Simply tell him it's classified. Even you don't know where the resource comes from. And since you don't, you won't even have to lie."

Warrick again stared coldly at Kingston. "Very well. That

is my update, ladies and gentlemen. I will file my report and return to the lab."

Warrick returned to the elevator and proceeded down.

The old man touched a spot on the table, and the floating heads all returned to MESA logos. "Kingston, I told you not to aggravate the situation with your petty pissing match with Warrick. I need him at his best, not being reminded of his inferiority to you."

"Yes, sir. I'll watch that," replied Kingston.

The old man stood and walked to the window, his hands folded behind his back.

"Where are we on the facility break-in investigation? Heaven knows I've already spent a barge of credits to smoke screen the media. Please tell me you have good news."

Kingston called up a report on his screen. "Well, the scrub team has completed their trace, and they have only been able to come up with partial results. The data servers were infected with a rage worm that tunneled through the security wall. That prevented a complete backup from being made before the alarms were triggered."

"Enough with the tech talk, Kingston." The old man turned from the window to stare at Kingston. "Do we have a lead on the lost project or not?"

Kingston slowly looked up from his tablet. "Yes, sir. We do."

———

Warrick continued down the hallway towards the lab. He was fuming over Kingston's snide remarks about his security clearance. Just as he was concocting things he would say and do to Kingston if he ever had the chance, a screen flashed his name, and a message icon bounded outward. Warrick looked behind him and down the hallway and then came to the screen. He tapped a spot on the screen to silence the voice commands and responses. A keyboard floated towards him, and he signed in. He first checked the proximity matrix. The nearest RFID beacon was three corridors over and moving away from him.

Next, he signed into his encrypted email server and read the message. He fished out the mini-drive and held it against the small square on the terminal. A progress band rapidly filled as the contents of the drive were swapped with the information from the encrypted server. Once complete, Warrick pocketed the drive. He called up the swapped files and quickly searched through them. Most were replies and notes that appeared to come from Jameson. The isolation team had done quite well in masking their origin, and most even sounded like Jameson's style of writing. Warrick double-checked that Jameson had been informed of the counterfeit response.

He then logged in to the server's impersonation app and called up Jameson's mail. He drafted a quick note thanking the Professor for the suggestions and mentioning Jameson would get to them as soon as he could. He apologized for not being able to accept them in person as this new iteration was consuming all his time. He also mentioned that he had jotted down a few ideas for the Professor and had given them to Warrick. Warrick added a few more details, read through the message once more, and then sent it.

The proximity icon flashed as a tech exited a lab five doors down. Warrick cleared the activity, signed out of the server, and continued down the hallway towards the lab.

———

Ms. Green watched as the activity from the encrypted server flashed across her screen at the security command post. She sipped her rare and illegal jasmine tea, smuggled in as a result of the trade embargo, and observed as Warrick stared back at her on an adjacent screen. She didn't care for the little man at all. Small, scrawny looking, and not very well endowed with manly features, Ms. Green was actually slightly repulsed that she was forced to constantly watch the man. Her good taste prevailing, she darkened the camera behind the screen that Warrick was using. She could monitor his activity without having to stare at the ugly man's face.

She watched as he swapped out the files, drafted the fake message from Jameson, and then cleared his activity just as another tech was starting to come down the hallway. She glanced at the giant 3D map of MESA's entire grounds and saw a dot walking away from the terminal Warrick had just used and another dot approaching it in the same hallway.

Small dots, all in various colors, buzzed around the hologram. Some were in labs, others in offices, yet others in hallways. Some dots were even outside of the buildings. The entrance guard station had a few, and so did the parking lot beyond MESA's perimeter fence, as did the restaurants and shops near the grounds.

From this map, Ms. Green could identify, track, and record the movements of any employee, security officer, or visitor. She noticed the group of blue squares congregated in the main lobby. She checked her watch and then called up the lobby cams. She had almost completely forgotten about those wretched children on their field trip. She looked back at the map. The deep red dots of the security guards and the green dot of the public relations director were clearly visible amid the sea of forty or fifty blue squares. She had assigned one of the S&D commanders to escort the group. She quickly located him at the security station and flashed him a message to report to the main lobby.

She felt a sense of relief that she wouldn't have to deal with the snot-nosed kids. Secondary school or not, all kids were nothing but little brats. She was the head of security, so she had the power to delegate. It had come in handy so many times throughout her career at MESA. She supposed that this was the very reason she was so bitter about the Warrick assignment. Watching and tracking that unattractive man day in and day out, reviewing his messages and monitoring his communications, she hated all of it. Kingston would seriously owe her one.

She knew that the orders came from the old man, but this was Kingston's project. He was the one who suggested she take this on personally, as opposed to delegating it to one of her team members. Sometimes that man made her blood boil. He could be so infuriating... and that's what made him so appealing at the same time. Oh, he definitely owed her for this. Her eyes closed as she pictured Kingston. She could think of a number of ways that the man could repay her. After a brief moment of daydreaming, she opened her eyes.

The commander had reached the lobby and was doing his song and dance about security at MESA Labs. The man was good at it, too. He looked like ex-military, and in fact was, which usually impressed the little kiddies. Something about a beefy man with facial scars seemed to add a little something to the tour. Ms. Green started to stare at the beefy man on the lobby cams and then noticed that she was biting her lower lip. No, she thought. "One man per day. You'll have to wait until tomorrow," she said as she tapped his image on the screen.

She looked back at the hallway where Warrick was and saw that he had reentered the Harmonics lab. He was sitting in his office as other colored dots moved around the lab. Next to him was a bright orange dot that marked the Professor. It was the only orange dot on the whole map.

———

The Professor read the note from CJ. Warrick had dropped off the mini-drive and had been in his office next door ever since. The Professor scanned through the files looking for anything of interest. Some of the comments and notes were very insightful to the work the Professor was doing. He had implemented many of the previous suggestions CJ had sent him, and the results had been very good. Other notes were very benign, helping the Professor understand the inner workings of MESA's systems and procedures. These too were helpful, but in a different way. The only downside of reading CJ's notes was that it only increased the Professor's desire to sit and chat with him about their work. He felt that they could accomplish so much more if they weren't reduced to this back-and-forth messaging.

That's why CJ's last line about being consumed by his latest iteration was so frustrating. Warrick had said the same thing earlier. Still, the Professor had his doubts. Something about the messages from CJ lately had been off. He couldn't quite tell why or how. The reality of it was that he had only met the man a short time ago, and their subsequent interactions had been limited and brief. Still, the Professor felt a connection between them, a budding synergy almost. He hoped that Jameson felt the same way.

CHAPTER 18

BOXED IN

Time: About one month after the attack at the shopping center

Scene: Chem lab, Academy City 676

"There's just something about you, isn't there?"

Sam sat alone in the chem lab, lounging at her table. It was lunchtime, and she was starving, but she didn't want the company of her friends in the lunchroom. The small tin box sat on the table before her. She touched the cool surface. "I wish I could at least make sense of one thing in my life."

Involuntarily, Sam touched the place on her chest where, less than a month ago, she could have sworn she had been shot with some sort of projectile. The experience had not only left her with nightmares of Rob and his band of slavers but also with visions of locked rooms and hospital beds, chains and wrist restraints, all accompanied by an overwhelming pain. She didn't know if the sensation was in her head or if it was real, but the ache festered within her, joining the myriad of questions that weighed heavily upon her mind. No answers were given or received. No relief could be found. She was left with the pain in her body and mind, blood in her tears. Now that scared her.

On the night of the attack, she had awoken to find herself in her own bed. Impossible. Comical, even. There was absolutely no explanation for her waking up in bed, but she did, pajamas and all.

The questions were starting to eat at her. The one thing anchoring her sanity was the fact that she didn't experience it alone. Cammie had been there, had witnessed the events of the night, but even that connection was starting to feel hollow, like they were both hallucinating. Cammie's story was similar to hers, but with slight variations. Cammie awoke not in her bed but in her bathtub, as weird as that sounded. Cammie didn't like to talk about the events or the weird aftermath, but Sam couldn't get it all out of her head, partly because of Cammie's unwillingness to discuss what had happened and partly because of her own real or perceived isolation. She sat and wondered contemplatively, alone in a room, asking herself the same question.

How had she and Cammie survived?

Those men, human traffickers that catered to the plantation owners of the Burning Plains, were trained professionals. Ex-military, if Cammie's information was to be believed.

There was no reason that she and Cammie should be here today, and yet they were. They were here, alive and in one piece, like nothing had ever happened. And what about that security guard? Did he really save them? If so, why not say something, get some sort of reward? It just didn't make any sense.

Sam pulled a water bottle from her bag, took a long drink from it, and eyed the silver box sitting complacently upon the table. If it wasn't one question, it was another. The box was just as frustrating as her nightmares, maybe more so because of its tangible presence. Basically, the box pissed her off.

Sam placed her bottle on the table next to the box. She picked it up gently and held it closely in her hands. She closed her eyes, enjoying the quiet.

Soon the weight of it became more noticeable, but not burdensome. It was comforting to a degree. Ahh... yes, it was the peaceful feeling right now. She had missed this one.

The situation confused her. She couldn't leave the box alone and couldn't explain what it did to her. Sometimes she felt at peace when she held it, like she had connected to a deeper part of herself. At other times, she couldn't help but feel fearful, angry, or irritated. The emotional continuum changed frequently but also stayed consistent. Different feelings came at different times, but always the same range of emotion, if that made any sense.

Sam didn't know why these feelings always came when she held the box, but they did every single time. Then there was that incident in her room, the night of the attack. It was like the box had been a magnet and her hands metal, which was absolutely mystifying. Now she was wondering if her hands sticking to the box had even happened. It had not happened since. Perhaps it was all in her head.

Sam opened her eyes to stare at the box. What was so special about it? Why did it make her feel this way? Why couldn't she bring herself to tell her friends about it? All these questions continually plagued her, but if there were answers to be found, she didn't know where to look.

A distraction came as a message flashed across her screen. It was from Cammie. Sam reluctantly tucked the box back into her bag and scooped up the tablet.

Have you made up with Dick yet?

Sam typed back. *No, not yet.*

OMGWB, it's been almost a month! He can't still be pissed because you lied to him.

You obviously don't know Richard very well, and I don't think he's really pissed about the lying anyway.

.   .   .

Is it about Adam?

No, I don't think so. Haven't seen much of him either.

I noticed. What's up with that? Why hasn't he been around?

Who knows—I haven't talked to him.

Coda's been MIA as well. He's been skipping to spend time with that skank, what's-her-brick again?

Lacey, and stop pretending you don't know.

Whatever. The point is, what is going on with our boys?

"Samantha, what are you doing?"

Sam looked up from the conversation as Richard walked into the room. He looked haggard; a far cry from his usual haughty self. Sam didn't care, though. He had just spoken to her! She was going to take advantage and not ruin the moment.

"Would you believe that I was doing homework?" she said, covertly slipping her bag under the table.

A half-smile formed on Richard's lips. "You were talking to Cammie, weren't you?"

Sam giggled slightly. "Yeah. She was just wondering about you."

"Well, if that isn't the logical quandary. Cammie expressing an emotion beyond the insatiable need to shop. Amazing."

Awkward silence settled upon the two. Richard's trademark wit felt comfortably familiar, and yet the punchline didn't have the same impact. His delivery was off slightly.

"What's wrong, Rich?"

"Don't 'what's wrong' me. I'm still not real happy with you, that's what's wrong."

Sam nodded her head. So that's what it was. He still hadn't forgiven her.

"Richard, I told you I was sorry. I promise I will never lie to you again. Can you just stop? Please? Just stop."

Richard studied her. "You promise you will never lie to me again. You promise?"

"Yes, I promise," answered Sam quickly, feeling that she was finally getting somewhere with him.

"I'm serious, Samantha, no more lies."

Sam paused ever so slightly. This was really important to

him; she knew that much. She wasn't sure why, but if her promising and meaning it was the only way to get Richard back, then she would do it.

"I promise you, Richard, that I will never lie to you again."

"Okay," stated Richard matter-of-factly. "Then you are forgiven."

"Really?!" Sam's face broke out in a huge grin. "You're going to stop acting all weird now?"

Richard nodded.

Sam wanted to do a backflip right then and there but was reluctant to believe him. "Really? No lecture? No telling me how I don't think, and how you're right and I'm wrong, and that I was stupid for not going home when I should have, or for listening to Cammie? Nothing?"

Richard scoffed. "I've prepared remarks. If you like, I'd be more than happy to lecture you for the next couple of hours."

"No! That's okay. I'm just surprised you let me off the hook so easily." She smiled. "You must have missed me."

Richard shrugged. "It was about that time, and there is no way that I missed you."

Sam bounced out of her chair and threw her arms around him. "Well, I missed you, Rich!!"

"Yes, yes, throw our arms up in the air. Huzzah for the long-awaited reunion." Richard gave another half-smile. "Shall we, my dear? The lunchroom awaits."

Sam beamed, ran over, and grabbed her stuff. "Oh, I thought you'd never ask!"

.   .   .

As they walked side by side to the lunchroom, Sam felt alive again. Richard was talking to her! He had forgiven her for lying to him about being home that night. She was elated. Her doubts still gnawed at her, but she felt only passing concerns, conversation points instead of true problems. Still, she needed to focus. She now had the chance to ask the question she had been waiting to ask Richard. She took a deep breath; for some reason, she was nervous.

"So, now that we're talking again, I need to ask. Did you check up on me that night?"

Richard leaned into her, moving over so he could get out of the way of some oncoming students. "Now, of all the questions you could have asked after our long-anticipated reunion, you choose that one? I wonder why. In answer to your query, no, I did not. When I say I'm going to be somewhere, I'm generally there."

Sam rolled her eyes. "I told you I was sorry, Richard, and you already forgave me. You have to let it go now; that's how it works."

Richard contemplated this. "Really? That's how it works?"

Sam nodded.

"Well, that certainly seems unjust, but to each his own, I suppose. I appreciate the lesson on social mores. Please continue."

Sam started up again. "So I told you how Cammie and I were attacked by those human trafficker guys, right?"

"Yes, I think you may have mentioned it, Samantha," answered Richard sarcastically.

Sam stuck her tongue out at him but continued. "So I told you I got shot and right after passed out?"

"Is this also a social convention? That people have to rehash events in a highlight-reel pattern of storytelling? Because if that is the case, I might have to teach a seminar on the proper way to analyze a sequence of events."

"Here's my point, jerkface, so you'd better listen. After I passed out, I mean, when I woke up, I didn't come to on a slab of cold cement outside Mega Lots Shopping Center. I woke up in my bed. In my bed, Rich. I was even wearing my pajamas."

"So someone undressed you? They saw you almost completely nude?"

Sam's face went scarlet. "That's what you got from that story? That someone saw me naked? Focus, Rich. I'm telling you that someone knocked me out and then took me home, dressed me, and put me in bed."

"And in the process saw you naked."

"Why aren't you focused more?"

"Why aren't you more concerned? I would be if someone had the misfortune of seeing me naked. Then again..." he looked Sam up and down, "I suppose that seeing you naked would be a far more desirable experience than seeing yours truly."

Sam punched Richard's arm.

"Ouch! What was that for? Totally uncalled for."

"It was for talking about me naked and not even blushing. I'm pretty rockin' in the buff; the thought should at least make you pause."

"I see. If the occasion of discussing your personage au naturel ever again presents itself, I will try to act more appropriately."

Sam smiled and said mockingly, "And people say you have no social skills. Now come on, I'm starving. Let's go get some food."

———

Ten minutes later, Sam and Richard had trays heaped with food. They sat down at an out-of-the-way table, like they usually did.

Sam sighed, completely forlorn. Richard rolled his eyes. "Samantha, is there something else troubling you, or are you still preoccupied with the thought of someone seeing you naked?"

"You're hilarious."

"Yes, I know; it's my burden and curse. So, are you planning to share, or can I go back to eating my vegetables and dietary supplements in peace?"

"Richard, I can't shake the feeling that I knew him."

Richard popped a supplement and a couple of cherry tomatoes into his mouth. "And who do you supposedly know?"

"The sec-guard. Well, I guess I don't really know he's a guard, but the person who helped us."

Richard chewed his food slowly as if he were preparing himself for something unpleasant. "So you feel as if you recognize this knight in shining armor who saved you from the bad men?"

"Yes. I swear. It was a little thing; small, tiny, every other similar adjective I can think of. There was something about him that I recognized."

"So who is he then?" asked Richard with little to no interest. "Who is your mysterious savior?"

Sam gave Richard a scathing look. "You'd better not laugh, Richard. I think... I think he reminded me of Adam."

Richard burst into laughter. "Samantha! Don't be ridiculous. What reason, what possible reason, could Adam have to hide his identity from you?"

"What do you mean? Weren't you the one that said he was untrustworthy?"

"Of course, but only within the context of the everyday adolescent construct. What you are saying is just crazy."

Sam scowled. She knew she shouldn't have told him, but she wasn't backing down. She had only seen the man for a few seconds, but the way that he talked, walked, acted, the way that he moved; it all had the air of familiarity to it. Sam had had plenty of time to run the scenario over and over again in her head. She knew that man, and the only one that made sense from the build to the height to the hair was Adam.

"I don't know. He's from the Jade Empire, did you know that? Maybe he's a spy and he's trying to protect me."

"Protect you? Protect you from what, Sam? If he's a spy from the Jade Empire, what could he possibly want from you?"

Good question. Sam mulled it over. Maybe it wasn't her at all... but something else...

Sam's mind reverted back to the box. Why hadn't she thought of that before?

"You do realize that if it's true and the person that undressed you without your knowledge was in fact Adam, then he saw your nude figure in all its glory."

"Yeah, so?"

"Well, after he saw you in your birthday suit, he disappeared for weeks. That doesn't say much for your naked body. Also, riddle me this: Did you know that in 18th century

England there was a tradition that unmarried women could not marry if they were seen in the nude before their vows were taken? It's too bad that the Victorians destroyed their own traditions."

Sam scowled again. He was having way too much fun. She spoke without thinking. "If it was Adam and you know that I like him, then he saw me naked and you haven't. Shouldn't that upset you?"

Richard's face contorted in surprise. "In reality, Samantha, I would hope that you would be the one upset about Adam seeing you in the buff, as you put it."

"Attention students, attention. An assembly will be taking place immediately. Again, please assemble in the complex. Please gather with your instructors and proceed to the Central Chamber. Attendance is mandatory for all students."

The students in the lunchroom started to move, dumping trays, returning plates, and gobbling up what was left of their food. Richard looked down with melancholy at his barely touched lunch.

"They'd better have a damn good reason for interrupting."

Sam gathered her stuff, and then she and Richard started down the hall. Richard pulled out his tablet and started tapping away vigorously, the sound drowned out by the chatter of the crowd. Sam gave them all no notice but continued to ponder the events of the past few months, especially the day that she and Cammie got attacked. Her conversation with Richard had left her wanting and had simply restarted the cognitive process that so many times before had left her irritated and disappointed. She just couldn't leave it alone.

What bothered her most was the distinct impression anchored within her subconscious that the man who had saved them was Adam. His actions, his body language, everything about their rescuer during that brief interaction was just too familiar. It had to be him. But if it was, then why not show himself? Why not take credit for helping them? It didn't make any sense.

Worse still was the fact that no one, including Cammie and Richard, gave credence to her theories. It ate at her in the most grating of fashions. The whole mess jumbled in her mind whenever she tried to make sense of it.

Still, she tried to shake the feeling that she was missing something obvious. She couldn't help but believe, somewhere in the pit of her stomach, that these strange feelings were somehow connected to the box she had in her bag. She felt all of this was connected; finding the box, her sudden rise to fame at school, Adam taking notice of her, she and Cammie being attacked; so many random events in such a short time. They all had to be related somehow. But how? And why would she be at the center of it? Sam closed her eyes briefly, centering her thoughts as she clutched the bag to her chest. Richard's increasingly vigorous tapping on his tablet irritated her.

"Rich, can't you do that a little quieter —"

Sam stopped mid-thought. Richard was staring at his screen, his expression one part confusion and one part anger. Richard continued to read with lightning speed. The further he moved down the page, the more his anger and confusion morphed into deep thought. Sam was almost too startled to ask.

"Rich, what's wrong? Why do you look so upset?"

"This assembly. It wasn't on the schedule, and they don't have any information on the server indicating its purpose."

Sam let out a breath of relief. "Is that all? And here I thought you were really mad about something. Not everything goes according to plan, Rich. Someday you're going to have to learn that."

Richard didn't answer.

The students pushed through the many sets of double doors leading to the huge centralized auditorium located at the center of Academy City 676. Sam saw that they weren't the only ones being called in for this assembly. All the younger kids were being rounded up as well. More disturbing still was the presence of many unknown men and women. Some of them were in black suits and some in lab coats, but all were mulling around and directing students. Medical and lab equipment were out in abundance, not to mention, though they tried to hide it, many men with guns. And not just any guns. Highly advanced-looking guns. Something was not right here.

The older students were pushed to the outer ring near the

walls while the younger ones were herded towards the center. Right smack in the middle of the building, a circular stage was erected with nothing on it but a podium and two people. The first Sam recognized: Peter Thomson, the principal of the school and Mayor of Academy City 676. The second was a woman who wore a unique black bodysuit that fit as if it was tailored to her every curve. It was almost like a black-skinned suit of armor. The woman wasted no time coming to the podium.

"Shut your traps, you brats."

The room instantly went silent. Every eye was on the woman. "Now that's better. I have a special assignment here today, and if all goes well, we can exit quickly and quietly. The government has commissioned my company to find something very special, and I need your help and cooperation. Can you help me with that?"

There was a murmur of assent.

"Good. My name is Ms. Green, and I'm from MESA Labs." She continued in a more mocking tone. "It's a pleasure to meet you all."

CHAPTER 19
AN INDECENT PROPOSAL

Time: Current day, right after lunch

Scene: Main assembly hall, Academy City 676

"MESA Labs? As in the weapons manufacturer?" Sam looked at Richard, who was still deep in thought. "What could they be looking for here?"

Richard shook his head and kept tapping away. Sam caught a fleeting glimpse of what looked like blueprints flash across his screen.

"Rich, come on, can't you get off of that thing? I'm a bit on the freaked-out side."

"I apologize. I was attempting to ascertain what a company like MESA would be doing here. I can't seem to find anything about it on the school's server. They appear to be just as surprised as the students are."

Sam squeezed her bag instinctively, her thoughts jumping back to the box. She shook her head, trying to clear it. She was just being paranoid; there was no way they were looking for the box... right?

Sam shook her head again. Of course, they weren't looking for the box. That didn't make any sense. Why did her mind keep going back to that stupid thing?

"Now, my little experiments, if you will all sit down for the moment until you receive further instructions, this will go a great deal smoother." Ms. Green pointed to the young students in front. "Please, no talking. I don't want to have to cut out your tongues."

The woman smiled sweetly. Sam's jaw dropped.

I don't want to have to cut out your tongues? Sam thought. *Can she say stuff like that?*

The room was quiet for the most part, the stress of the situation keeping the crowd under control. Yet as time passed, the younger students gave in to their nature. A nine-year-old boy started messing around in the front.

"Excuse me, little boy," Ms. Green pointed and again smiled sweetly at the kid, who simply went on playing.

"Excuse ME, LITTLE BOY!" she said with heavy emphasis.

Again, he ignored her.

"LITTLE BOY!"

Ms. Green's hand flashed to her side. The next thing Sam

saw was Ms. Green posed with her foot forward and right hand out.

A scream mixed with additional yelps and cries sounded from the front of the crowd. Sam didn't know what had happened until the younger children scrambled away, literally stepping over each other in panic. Apparently, Ms. Green found their fear rather humorous as she began to laugh openly. Sam's face twisted in anger as she realized what she was laughing at.

Now that his classmates were gone, the nine-year-old boy sat wide-eyed in a perfect combination of terror and embarrassment. The source of the terror was a 30-centimeter throwing knife glowing with a faint blue light, lodged deep into the floor right between the boy's legs, nestled next to his crotch. The sight of it made Sam's anger towards the black body-suited woman turn to rage. The boy was terrified. He looked like he wanted to crawl into a hole and die. Tears and snot were running freely from his face, and he was sniffling incessantly. It was then that Sam noticed the puddle of liquid the boy was sitting in and the wet splotch on his pants.

"He soiled himself," said Richard in a flat voice.

Sam wasn't listening. She started to her feet, already thinking about moving towards Ms. Green, intending to give the leather-wearing devil woman a piece of her mind. Who throws glowing knives at little kids? This woman was going to pay for that. Sam was going to make sure of it.

———

A ragtag bunch of men and women with seriously antiquated equipment checked their weapons as they drove cautiously in a series of street vehicles. No nationality or even gender could be determined, as each person wore masks of presidents of the former United States.

In the front seat of the first vehicle, a particularly burly individual spoke into a shortwave radio. "We just got word from our guy inside. MESA has come in strong. We might encounter S&D. We've got to get in, gather what intel we can, and get out. No dicking around or a lot of people are going to get hurt."

"Washington, sir," came a voice from the back of the black transport, "how are we supposed to find whatever it is we are looking for? We have no idea what MESA is after."

"We've been over this, Nixon. We don't know exactly what MESA is after, but the underground chatter is way up. MESA's in some kind of corner. They are desperate. Something is going down today at Academy City 676. Something big. This could be our chance, so don't screw it up. Palin, be careful with that tech flow cell. They might be old, but those high-energy fusion rounds can be nasty."

"Yes, sir."

Washington put his radio back up to his mouth. "ETA five minutes. Beck, Johnson, Wilson – ready the blast core and muffle drum. Palin, you're on point. Let's go find Teddy."

———————

"Put the motherly instinct in check, Samantha." Richard threw a beefy arm around her, picking her up off the ground. She tried to get away from him, but he was strong. Surprisingly strong—it appeared that all the supplements were starting to work for him. But Sam wasn't the only one who was pissed. Many others, including teachers, were muttering under their breath, though Sam was the only one attempting to do anything about it.

"No way, Richard. That psycho doesn't get to throw knives at little kids and get away with it. There is no way."

"Samantha, listen to what you just said. She threw a knife at a little kid. Think of what she'll do to you. The boy is embarrassed, but he is fine. No use in bringing attention to yourself."

Sam's fighting spirit lessened. Richard was right, of course. He always was. Now that she thought about it, she hadn't even considered what she was going to do when she made it over to the woman. Richard felt her reluctance.

"Let it go, Samantha."

Sam's body completely relaxed, going limp in Richard's arms. Richard didn't set her down, though, but slung her over his shoulder and carried her back to where they had been sitting. She felt like a sack of potatoes.

"Richard, you can put me down now. I won't do anything."

Richard shook his head. "Absolutely not. I'm not fast enough to stop you if you go all mother-hen again."

From Richard's back, Sam saw Cammie standing ten meters away next to the most unlikely of students. Coda was grinning outlandishly, watching with an evident amount of interest. He came across as way too excited in light of what was going on. Cammie was attempting to engage him with little success. Another three meters to his left, Adam lingered against a wall, totally relaxed, watching the knife-throwing psycho lady with little to no interest. He seemed preoccupied.

Sam couldn't help but stare. Oh, was he a sight for sore eyes. Richard moved back towards their original spot, causing Sam to strain in an effort to maintain her view of Adam. Her mental function skipped a beat.

Adam was talking intimately with a girl that Sam didn't recognize. The girl was really pretty and standing way too close to Adam.

"Richard, put me down. I need to... I need to... to go."

"Now, my darlings, I would like to start with the young ladies sixteen and older. If all of you would be so kind as to make a line over here." Ms. Green pointed to her left, indicating the group of lab techs. "Once in line, you will disrobe, allow our techs to run their tests, and then redress. Once you are done, you will be escorted back to your central pod." Ms. Green's voice had regained its sweet quality, though to Sam it was like nails on a chalkboard.

A confused mumbling swelled through the room. Everyone stopped what they were doing. Their faces reflected their confusion. All were asking the same question, wondering if they had heard right? Did she really say that all the girls in the room were to go and disrobe? Right here? Right now?

"Chop, chop, ladies. Get to the side of the gym and take off your clothes. I don't have all day."

Well, that answered that question.

An instant outcry sounded, replacing confusion with a horde of other emotions: anger, outrage, incredulity, rejection, and eventually an embarrassed sort of acceptance. Over the pandemonium, Sam could hear the Principal of 676 yelling.

"Now, now, Ms. Green. We can't have the young women undressing in front of the young men. That is just improper. The school board and city council will not stand for it."

Ms. Green ignored the Principal. "Children!"

The noise increased, and chaos snowballed as the students fed upon each other's emotions. Sam wondered what Ms. Green was going to do to subdue the mounting anarchy when the woman pulled something from her belt. Slowly she raised the black device and—

Boom!

An explosion shredded the din as a ball of super-heated light hit the wall and literally melted a chunk away.

The room went silent as a graveyard. The only residual sounds were of those who were unfortunate enough to be splashed with some of the gooey debris from the now porous wall. Every eye stared wide at Ms. Green, who waved her weapon around nonchalantly.

"Now that's better. Ladies, if you please."

Sam took deep, steadying breaths. She didn't see how this could get any worse.

———

One hundred and fifty meters in the air, a stealth hover transport descended rapidly into Air Space Zamar, the air traffic designation located right above Academy City 676. The aircraft was completely invisible to the naked eye and untraceable to most forms of electronic detection. Really, the only thing that this craft had to worry about was the Gamma Star Detection Platform, but the UWC almost never patrolled this far inland. They had the advantage for now. The Assault Captain of the elite Móguǐ unit spoke to his men in Mandarin.

"Intel says that the package has been identified. We infiltrate, pick it up, and exfil. You are to keep casualties low, but kill anyone—man, woman, or child—who sees you. There is no room for error. If you see weaponry beyond C class, do not engage if you can avoid it. The suit's energy field won't last against A or B class weaponry. Have Light Shivs ready for close quarters. Do not discharge without prior approval. Is that understood?"

"Yes, sir!" came the reply.

The Assault Captain gave his men a reassuring smile. "We take it back today, brothers. Our long period of dishonor is almost at an end. The advance squad is already on the ground, and the landing area is secure. Any questions?"

"No, sir."

"Good. Code phrase only until we know what we are dealing with. Our man on the ground says that the area is crawling with MESA. If they call in their S&D force, it could become complicated."

Explosions, one right after another, caused the transport to shake slightly.

"Did you hear that, sir?" said one of the soldiers from the back.

The Assault Captain put his hand out to steady himself. "Isolate the location."

The soldier turned back to a free-floating monitor. "Sir, both explosions came from the school. Energy weaponry detected."

"I see." The Captain pulled out a medium-sized bottle and passed it around to each of his men. Each poured a small amount of the contents into different containers.

Once the bottle made it back to him, the Assault Captain held it up. "To victory, gentlemen."

They all drank.

———

The hole in the wall from Ms. Green's gun struck fear in students too young to remember the news reports of past conflicts. They gawked at the power of the weapon and the lack of hesitation in using it. The second explosion didn't seem as scary as the first. It was distant and muffled. Yet in a way, it was scarier. The student body had seen Ms. Green discharge the energy pistol into the wall and completely vaporize a section of it. They had no idea where the second explosion had come from.

Ms. Green seemed just as surprised as the students. She barked out orders, and some of the armed MESA patrols responded by filing out of the assembly hall. For the first time since they saw her, Ms. Green looked a little unsure.

The Principal of 676 was not impressed. He got right up in Ms. Green's face. "You cannot do this! This is a school! I will have you act appropriately!" He pointed to the wall. "This is why I hate the private sector. Always acting any way you want. Well, I've had enough. I am contacting the Governor. Security, detain Ms. Green and kindly escort her people off school property."

The school's security forces appeared and started to move into position.

"This is why I hated school." Ms. Green glanced from side to side, totally unconcerned. "I guess I will have to make myself clear to you, Mr. Principal man whose name I have forgotten."

Ms. Green turned and pointed her high-energy hand

cannon at the principal, who froze and stared in wide-eyed disbelief.

"What do you think you're doing? I am the Mayor of this City. You can't just point weapons at—"

Ms. Green fired her gun, and the principal melted into a puddle of goo. Screams and panic erupted. Students started trampling over one another, all heading towards the door. They ran headlong into a wall of armed MESA guards. Without a word, the men opened fire.

———

Washington's voice came angrily over the squad's radios. "Status report! Who the hell started firing?"

Palin checked the hallway, looking for any hostiles that might have been around when they had blasted into the building. "No one fired, sir. There isn't anyone here. The place is completely deserted."

"Damn. If that wasn't you firing then... squad one! Move! We have hostiles here in the building. Engage at will. Be careful of the students; do not engage any of them. Squad two is breaching now. Move!"

Palin started moving up the hallway, Beck, Nixon, and Wilson in tow. They silently stepped down the hall, checked their corners, and started moving again. They needed to find who was shooting.

Palin threw up her fist and gave the other three directions

to move out. A flicker caught her eye. The slightest of disturbances in the hall directly ahead of them floated in the air. Not so much a movement, but a shimmer of light across her vision.

"Palin, we have to move."

"Shut your can, Wilson. Something is wrong—"

An unnatural glow materialized. A blade made of pure light came out of nowhere. Nixon was sliced clean in half.

"Waste it!" yelled Palin. She and her men opened fire.

———

The sounds of gunfire bellowed like a million angry bulls. Bodies, one after another, dropped where they stood, the students no more important than clay targets. Ms. Green discharged her weapon again, this time firing at the ceiling. A chunk of ceiling melted away, the ooze again splashing down on unsuspecting students. Ms. Green's flashy display, coupled with the additional use of stun batons after the first wave of students was cut down, enabled MESA to regain order. Beaten down, many of the students were sobbing uncontrollably, Sam included. The tears ran down in an irrepressible river.

The scene was horrific. Bodies strewn everywhere, the echoing wails of lamentation, and the harsh bark of heartless ordering. Sam was at a loss as to how things had gone so quickly downhill. Why were so many of her schoolmates lying dead on the ground? Why would MESA do such a thing? How could they think they would get away with it?

Maybe they plan on killing all of us, Sam thought. *That would be the easiest way to cover up something like this. Simple.*

Sam felt a renewed round of tears well up. She needed to keep it together. She needed to think and try to figure a way out of this.

Sam glanced at Richard, her go-to reaction when something didn't make sense or she had a problem in need of answering. Richard didn't seem to be fairing any better than her. His head was bowed, cradled in his arms. He was muttering senselessly to himself, and she could only hear bits of words like "lethal" and "target."

Sam put her arms around him, touching his skin on his neck. It felt clammy. Richard was not doing well.

"You don't have to worry, Rich. I'm here. They aren't after you, remember? They're after the girls. I'll protect you."

Richard looked up, and their eyes met. His expression was strange. It was familiar, but somehow not. It was an expression that Sam had seen before, but not on his face. Richard forced a smile, picked up his tablet, moved to the back wall, leaning heavily against it, and started tapping away. She took this as a sign that he wasn't going to give up, so she knew that she couldn't either. She grabbed her bag.

Sam made her decision as her mind went right back to the silver box. MESA was looking for something here, and she didn't know what. But there was something different, something special about this box. She didn't know what that damn thing had to do with this, but she was certain it was somehow connected. This might get her killed if she was wrong, which she probably was, but she was going to Ms. Green, was going to give the accursed silver box to her, and hope that the action would stem something.

Inadvertently, or maybe not so inadvertently, she found Adam in the crowd. She wanted to see his face, wanted to look at him before she moved towards her goal. Their eyes connected. One single, crystallizing moment. She knew what he was thinking. He wanted her, but she didn't know what that meant. He started to run, tearing up the ground in front of him as he dashed towards her. He was coming to her, to save her. Sam's heart leapt.

More explosions, this time one right after another, rippled all around them as hot steam shot out from the walls and surged into the assembly hall. Chaos resumed with the steam's arrival, accompanied by the clangor of machinery. Barely seen through the swell of vapor, the room's floor started to move. Sam didn't know what to make of it.

An incredibly strong hand grabbed onto her bag. With one sharp heave of an arm, she was thrown onto a shoulder. She couldn't fight back. She couldn't move, and she didn't know why. Her rescuer navigated effortlessly through the maze of steam, students, and lab techs. Before she knew what was going on, Sam and her savior were at the locked door. They went right through it with no problem. The clouds of steam billowed out with them, but after a few steps, it no longer impeded her vision. Sam looked down at the sprinting legs that were carrying her. She reeled with shock.

CHAPTER 20
DOUGHBOY

Time: Current day, mid-afternoon
Scene: Hallway in Academy City 676

Sam gawked at her savior in complete and utter disbelief as he moved effortlessly down the hall with her in tow.

It was Richard. He was holding her with such incredible strength that she couldn't move. No. That wasn't right. It wasn't strength; it was something different than just strength. It felt as though he was restricting her joints, somehow holding her in a way that locked up every major joint in her body. Was that even possible?

Richard didn't say anything as he navigated the halls. Sam tried to speak to him but found that her words disintegrated against the precipitous change in circumstances. With his weakened heart, Richard shouldn't have had the strength to carry her for more than a few feet, let alone down hallway after hallway. Yet right before her very eyes, he was doing just that. Not only that, but his whole demeanor had changed, the way he carried not just her, but himself as well. She couldn't articulate what she felt coming from him, but it was different. Maybe it was fear. The adrenaline could explain his strength. She knew that people did strange things when they were afraid. Sam herself had just tried to do something out of the ordinary. That Green woman had opened fire on an assembly hall full of students, and Sam had been ready to confront her! What was she thinking?

The sound of rapid gunfire echoed off the walls, creating in Sam's mind the momentary image of a trench-dug, enemy-infested battleground. She could hear the gunfire and the lingering screams from the assembly hall but couldn't see anything. Richard continued to move with Sam on his shoulder until they were a good distance away from the assembly's main door. He put Sam down, and she found she was able to move again.

"What the hell, Richard?!" Sam bellowed. "You don't just go picking people up and throwing them over your shoulder—"

Richard shuffled to Sam's side and placed his hand over her mouth.

"If I'd thought you were going to start screaming like a wounded hippo, I wouldn't have given you this."

Richard showed her the most miniature of accelerator pins. Sam stared at it wide-eyed. What was Richard doing with an accelerator pin? They were old military equipment, very old in fact. They were used during the Third Great War to counter bio and chemical weapons, but nobody used that stuff anymore. It was easily counteracted. Why did Richard have old military-grade weaponry?

"I bought this on EarthBay. You'd be amazed at what you can get on the interweb. Anyway, I gave you a dose of a rapid paralyzing agent while I was carrying you. I had to get us out of there before we got caught in the crossfire. This is the anti-dote. I assume from your outburst it worked."

Sam was angry now. Richard had just scooped her up without asking, drugged her twice, and was now trying to convince her to run.

"Richard, we can't just run away. Our friends are in there; Cammie, Coda, and—"

She stopped herself. Adam. Oh, to all the gods, real or make-believe, she hoped he was all right.

"You're wondering if Adam is okay."

Sam didn't answer.

Someone began yelling from just ahead of them, effectively ending the conversation. Richard grabbed her wrist and ran. The previous strength wasn't there, and neither was Richard's apparent change in demeanor. He was back to how she remembered him, back to the Richard she knew. She was beginning to think that the drug, whatever it was, must have done a real number on her, making her see and feel things she knew had to be incorrect. She tried not to think about it.

Richard was Richard, and if she knew him at all, he had a plan to help everyone survive this. That is, if they could stay alive in the process.

Richard was scanning their surroundings. Sam could hear the voices getting closer. They ducked into one of the secondary connection hallways that the administrators used in case of an emergency. They sprinted down it and were just about to round a corner when chaos reared its ugly head.

A four-way fight had laid waste to the western main hall. Two of the groups Sam recognized—MESA's men and the school's security forces—were readily identifiable. But who the other two were, Sam had absolutely no idea. The first group was wearing the most peculiar collection of equipment, like they had found their tools of destruction in a junkyard. The second was just as unrecognizable but dressed much more like a military unit. Their weaponry was slick, like nothing she had ever seen in the Vii-R shows or games. Each of these men was wrapped in a strange blue hue, like they were being protected by an invisible field that wasn't quite invisible. The one weapon that Sam did recognize was the unmistakable glare of Light Shivs. The sight made Sam's throat go completely dry. An image of Rob, the human trafficker, popped into her head, making her recoil slightly. Who were these men?

Scraggly Unit, that's what Sam decided to call them, was boxed in between MESA and the Fancy Uniform Unit. With seven or so men, Scraggly Unit fought off thirty-plus soldiers from the combined force of the Fancy Uniform Unit, MESA, and the school's security force. Sam and Richard remained hidden in the secondary hall, undetected.

"Should we go back?" Sam was relieved to find that her voice was quite stable. "We can't just walk out there; we'll both end up dead."

The word came out of Sam's mouth. Dead. They would both end up dead. Actually, compared to the way she was feeling now, the prospect of being dead wasn't as scary. At least she wouldn't have to worry about being sold to a plantation owner in the Plains.

But Sam rebelled against the thought. She had people that cared about her and that she cared about. She couldn't give up now. Did she really want to end up like the Principal or one of her classmates?

Another mental image wormed its way into her mind, this one seeming to move at the speed of a snail. She watched as her classmates, friends, and teachers were mowed down like cattle. She could see Ms. Green's face through all of it. That evil woman would pay.

Richard's voice brought Sam back. "No. This is the quickest route to the mainframe room, and that's where we need to go."

"Why do we need to get to the—?"

"Not now, Samantha, I'm thinking."

Sam's jaw dropped in surprise. Did Richard just hush her?

Richard was back on his tablet and muttering under his breath. "Oh, this would be so much easier if I could work unfettered. Why isn't he answering?"

Richard shut his mouth as he rolled his neck. Sam heard the muffled crack of bone and joints pop. Another one of those unfamiliar expressions crept onto Richard's face. Sam really had trouble placing this one. Stress, from what it looked like. Richard paused as he studied some sort of gauge on his tablet. He spoke but more to himself than to Sam.

"We've got to get out of here. These fools are going to kill each other. It looks like we've got just enough power to get there."

Sam was about to ask what he was talking about, but before she could, Richard touched the upper left-hand corner of the tablet and then took a step back.

The sounds of battle were overpowering, but still not enough to cover the sudden onslaught of clacking that accompanied the pitch and grind of shifting gears. One compulsive step later, Sam retreated back and was now standing next to Richard. She watched as the floor in front of her started to shift.

The moving floor startled every soldier in the western hall. The walls started to retract, rotate, and move while the floor folded over itself. Carbonized steel lowered from the upper reaches of the ceiling, covering the windows. Sheets of the same steel stretched out in front of the combatants, blocking their line of sight and boxing in groups of soldiers.

Richard touched two more buttons on his tablet and then touched the wall to their left.

"Get ready to run," he said simply.

"Why do we have to—?"

Steam burst through one of the few walls that was not covered in the carbonized steel. Richard caught Sam's hand and stepped into the gushing vapor. They navigated almost completely blind, Richard guiding Sam, stepping lightly and shifting through the soldiers, security officers, and MESA paramilitary. Sam closed her eyes as they went. The steam was hot and stung her. Even worse was the fear she couldn't shake, the fear that the warring factions within their school would just start randomly shooting, taking her and Richard with them.

Stepping out of the steam was like stepping out of a sauna microwave. Relief rushed over her. They were past the soldiers and moving into another hallway. They were going to make it. They were going to get through this. She and Richard rounded another corner.

"Duck!" Richard pounced on Sam, driving her hard to the ground. A conglomerated ball of super-heated plasma passed less than a half-meter above them. Backdraft and a concussive wave came next, followed by the rush of rapidly retreating air. Screams of terror pierced her eardrums. Sam and Richard, still on the ground, were pushed back by a backlash of wind. She didn't know what was going on.

A few more seconds ticked by, then additional plasma

balls sped down the hallway, aimed straight for them. The balls missed their mark and instead hit the walls to either side. Panicked, Sam tried to scurry away from the burning walls. She was unsuccessful. A pinch of charred material landed on her arm.

Pain erupted across her skin, and without realizing it, she started screaming. She couldn't see. She couldn't think. She felt someone tug on her person, but it was disembodied, not real, a dream in which she was merely a spectator. She felt her consciousness slip farther and farther down a hole filled with nothingness. She didn't know if she would return from it...at least the pain was going away slowly... slowly... slow—

Beeping... where are those sounds coming from? Oh, the pain!! Is that my body that hurts so bad? Where—where am I?

Sam opened her eyes, but nothing was in focus. Everything was out of whack, like her brain could not process what her body was telling her. She let her concern fade as she took inventory of her senses. Taste. Ugh, she had blood in her mouth. Smell? Sweat and fear. Touch? Even worse than the nasty taste of blood, every inch of her body hurt. Sight? She already knew that one. She couldn't see, but that particular sense was making a comeback. All that was left was her hearing. She couldn't really hear anything at the moment, except for the stupid beeping. She decided to sit up.

Nausea swept over her, and she had to lie back down twice before she could sit up properly without feeling sick. She looked around. She was sitting on a table in a room full of servers and six-by-six holo terminals. This was the type of room that came right out of the Vii-theaters, a place so high-tech it was alien. She knew this room; well, of this room at least. This was where the central mainframe was located. This place acted as the brain of the entire city complex. Why was she here? Sam moved her attention back to the holo terminals and saw one of them alive and kicking.

Richard was standing in a glowing space, moving screen projection after screen projection around as he scanned each of them. The glow of the conductor's hands, a special glove used to interface with the holo terminals, was making him look like some sort of raver at a party. Programming codes, vid feeds, gauges, and charts of all kinds swirled around him as he called out commands in a knowing and authoritative voice. He moved about, inputting and taking information at light speed through hand and voice.

Sam got to her feet and instantly felt woozy. She stumbled and was saved from a full crash only by catching the corner of a nearby desk. Once she felt right again, she moved forward. "Richard?"

Richard didn't turn around. He simply answered, "Sam."

Sam paused. He had just called her Sam. He never called her Sam. What was going on with him?

"Richard, what are you doing?"

Again he didn't turn around. "I am clearing out some very sloppy security jamming protocols and hiccup routines within the school's anti-terrorist shield program. No one is going to know what's going on unless I can cut off their communications expert; otherwise, our chances of calling in the cavalry are close to zero. If I can un-jam the system, the security protocols will trigger, and the army will be alerted. I need to enable at least one more interface so I can hack the system remotely again. At the moment, it's keeping me and at least two other hackers out of the system. I'm fighting with them and the system. Now, Sam?"

"Uh—yes?"

"Shut up. I need to concentrate."

Sam's jaw dropped. Again. He just told her to shut up!

"You just told me to shut up."

"Yes, I did. Was I unclear as to my meaning?"

"No, but— but you never talk to me that way."

"And look where it's gotten me."

"What's that supposed to mean?"

He didn't answer her, and once again she was left in bafflement, at a loss as to what to say next.

Richard. What happened to you? she thought.

Something in Sam's peripheral vision caught her attention, and she turned. Vid feeds from various parts of the building played on the few screens that were still active. One particularly large screen showed the Western Hall. Sam crept closer. The hall was unrecognizable. Sam inspected the image on the screen, running a keen eye over it. The hall was destroyed, mangled beyond belief and repair. How did that happen?

"That part of the Western Hall was pressurized."

Richard's voice didn't sound like it was talking to her, but to the empty space in front of him. She answered regardless. "And how do you know that?"

"Because I pressurized it." Richard finally looked at her, moving one of the screen projection boxes out of his way. "The school has a locking and pressurizing system in case of biological attacks. Using that system was the contingency in case we were spotted and attacked. It's quite difficult to maintain battle formations when you're being sucked through holes in walls."

His gaze bored into her like it never had previously. The look scared her slightly. "So what now?"

Richard moved the screen projection back, impeding her view of his face. "Now we get out and run like hell."

"Why?"

"MESA."

Boom.

The room started to shake, tossing Sam and Richard, causing them to stagger.

"What was that?" Sam braced herself. "Do they have an earthquake machine or something?"

Richard steadied himself on the rails of the holo terminal. He almost laughed an ironic sort of laugh. One more thing Sam wasn't sure how to take.

"Richard, you're scaring me. They really don't have an earthquake machine, do they?" Sam asked again.

He went back to his work. "It doesn't matter. We're getting out of— Yes!"

A surge lit up the room, actually making the dome light above their heads brighter. Sam didn't know what it was, but whatever Richard just did collected around them. She could feel it on her skin. The gauges on Richard's screen projections skyrocketed upward from black to yellow, orange, and finally red. A bunch of equipment around the room sprang to life and went to work doing unknown tasks. The area buzzed with artificial life.

"Come on." Richard stepped from the terminal and picked up her bag. "Take this."

He handed it to her. She took it and then looked from him to the bag and back to him. He studied her.

She felt the corners of the box. It was still there. The cursed thing was still snuggled neatly at the bottom of her bag. Perhaps now was the time to show Richard. Maybe he could make sense of the thing and tell her... and tell her if this box was what they were looking for.

Richard picked up his tablet. He was still wearing the

conductor gloves. He took four or five swipes at the holo terminal, pulling the information to his tablet. Satisfied, he addressed Sam.

"It's time to go. We have the intel, power connections, and escape route set. We've got a chance now."

"We've got a chance of what?" she asked, confused.

"A chance to get out of here alive." Richard pulled up different feeds from the various cameras, all of which were suddenly working. "You see these men?"

Sam nodded.

"These men are part of a special unit from the Jade Empire. They are called Móguǐ. It means Devil. They come in as ghosts and don't leave anyone alive. Any person—man, woman, or child—who sees these men is dead, no exception."

Sam glanced half-heartedly at the tablet, then jerked it out of Richard's hand and felt her heart jump into her throat. Adam was running full speed down the hallway, the Móguǐ right on his tail, light shivs at the ready.

"Richard, look!" Sam showed him the feed. "They're after him! We've got to help him!"

Richard pulled the tablet back from her. "What are you talking about, Sam?"

"The Móguǐ, they're after Adam. They're going to kill him!"

"Sam, it's too dangerous for you to— argh!"

Sam, without thinking, kicked Richard in the crotch. He buckled forward in pain.

"I'm so sorry, Richard. I'm so, so, so sorry. But you aren't going to let me go, and I can't let Adam die. It's been so great having you as a best friend. I couldn't have asked for a better one. I wish... I just wish that... well, you know."

Sam bent down and kissed Richard on the cheek. It was extremely cool to the touch. She ran out of the room, taking the tablet with her.

————

Sam tried to run and keep an eye on the tablet but was having difficulty. She wasn't the greatest multitasker, and her nerves were wound so tight it hurt. She was cursing her idiotic action. Why hadn't she thought out some sort of plan? She wasn't sure where she was or how she was going to help Adam. If the Móguǐ unit was as bad as Richard said, then she was in for the fight of her life. Further complicating her emotions, she felt sorry for kicking Richard in the man-berries. There was no justification for that. He would certainly hate her after this... if there was an after.

She stopped at a four-way intersection. She was starting to recognize where she was. The hallways were painted in warm earth tones of brown, green, and sand. Some genius from the Committee of Education had ordered the colors for their postulated effects on student hormones. Who could get romantic in a place that was so aesthetically dreary?

She checked the camera feed on Richard's tablet, attempted to locate her position, and decided to turn left. She moved fifteen meters up the hall, then threw herself against the wall in an attempt to hide. Just ahead of her, a man was yelling in Mandarin and pointing weapons at a group of her classmates. She couldn't see if Adam was among them. As she listened, she thought they seemed to be arguing about something.

Sam crept forward, trying to sneak up on the soldiers, then stopped, quickly ducking into one of the rooms right off the hall. She cursed in a whisper. I don't have any weapons. How do I help them?

That's when she saw it. A gun sitting near the body of a dead masked man. She crept out softly and picked it up, gingerly holding it at arm's length. She didn't know how to check if it was loaded. She knew how the Combat Tag weapons worked, but this was the real thing. Sam glanced from the weapon to the men holding her classmates at blade and cannon point. The soldiers continued to argue, gesturing at different students and back at tablets. The soldiers' actions didn't resonate with Richard's description of them. Why were they hesitating? Don't they kill everything on the spot?

She pushed it out of her mind and stepped out from her hiding place. She tucked the butt of the gun into her shoulder and pointed the weapon at the back of the nearest soldier.

A beefy hand moved over her mouth, and something hard jabbed her in the ribs.

"Don't move."

Damn, she thought. Game over.

Everyone is dead. They were all going to die, and there was nothing she could do about it.

The person behind her moved, directing her back into the classroom. Had he been there the whole time? She had not looked when she entered the room. She probably should have.

The hard object, she assumed it was a gun, was removed from her back, and she felt the person behind her shift, drifting something slightly through her hair. He or she, or whoever they were, was going to execute her. She hoped it would be quick.

Crack.

A hand whacked her upside the head. It was hard, but it didn't kill her. What was going on?

"Next time you kick me and then go marching right into the midst of a Jadian death squad, I am so not coming to help you."

"Richard?" Sam whipped around. "I thought, well I thought that I... well, you know."

"You thought you nailed my boys to my pelvic bone? You tried, but..."

Richard knocked his crotch. "I come prepared."

Sam smiled. She was relieved that he was here. "Richard, we've got to do something. We've got to help."

"Sam, we can't. What can we do? We'll die. You know we'll die."

Sam sighed. "Then I will die, but I am going to help." Sam snatched up her gun and made for the door. In the corner of her eye, she saw Richard's hand move to his forehead in a gesture she recognized. He was frustrated. He muttered to himself, and while she shouldn't have been able to hear him, she could.

"Gently. No breaking. Do as you're told. Gently. Son of a —." Richard pulled his hand from his head. "Sam, wait."

She stopped. He did it again. He called her Sam. "Yes?"

"There's a way. I can help, but do you promise we can leave after? You won't put up a fight?"

Sam nodded, "yes, but we save the group outside and Adam. Deal?"

Richard rolled his eyes. "Okay. But you don't fight me, understand?"

She nodded again.

Richard picked up his tablet. "Fine. Let's go."

They both moved to the door and stepped over the threshold. They crouched behind some of the debris created from the fighting. As Richard was tapping madly on the tablet, Sam pointed her gun down the hall, not knowing what else to do.

"What do we do now?" asked Sam in a nervous whisper. "How are we going to fight off those goons?"

Richard looked up from his tablet. "It's simple really. Will you do me a favor and fire that weapon at the soldier on the far right?"

Sam hesitated. Richard saw her hesitation and placed a hand on her shoulder. "Just think of it as Combat Tag Pro."

Sam nodded and whispered, "Richard, you hate Combat Tag."

She leaned up, aimed down the barrel of the gun, and squeezed the trigger.

Kaboom!

In a reenactment of what had happened to her and Richard right before she had passed out, superheated plasma streaked from the gun, striking the wall right next to where she was aiming. The soldiers realized they were under attack and moved into cover, maneuvering from point to point like gears in a well-made clock. Slowly, they converged on Sam and Richard while the students cowered in the background.

Sam fired off a couple of shots. "Rich, I hope you weren't bluffing about the brilliant plan, because we're in trouble!"

Richard smiled. "I never bluff, Sam."

Richard tapped a large red button in the middle of his tablet that said, "Execute." Then he ducked his head and tugged Sam down beside him.

Sirens screamed, bright lights flashed, and a corny computer voice sounded down the hallway.

"Terror threat level currently at red. System will engage in three seconds. All unauthorized personnel leave the premise immediately."

The soldiers were momentarily caught off guard but then laughed off the threat of the computerized voice. They called at each other in Mandarin, continuing their advance on Sam and Richard. The lead man was grinning a yellow-toothed smile from cheek to disgusting cheek. He stared triumphantly at the two, raising his light shiv.

Pat, pat, pat, pat!

A scream, and the man's light shiv fell right between Sam's legs. She didn't understand. She looked up to see why he had dropped his blade and screamed in horror as the headless corpse of the soldier fell to the ground.

Giant rapid-fire laser weaponry had appeared from panels in the walls and lit up the area with their blasts. The "pat" noise resounded again and again. The soldiers fell where they stood, huge gaping holes in their chests and heads. Blood and the smell of burning hair and flesh threatened to overcome Sam. She didn't want to be sick. She didn't want to vomit. She tried to stop it, but she was unsuccessful.

The lasers eventually stopped firing, and the sentry guns retreated back into the walls. The sounds of pain-filled death slowly faded, leaving only the smell. Richard was the first to stand. He appeared unfazed by the violence. He moved towards their classmates, who were beginning to stand up slowly. The only one Sam recognized was Dice Dyson.

Dice looked like he was going to cry. "We didn't die. We didn't die. How—how are we still alive?"

Richard answered. "The school has a terrorist alert system just like the jet way and marine ports all over the UWC. If you turn the terror threat high enough, anyone not programmed into the system is seen as an enemy, and the school fights back, which is probably why MESA gathered everyone in the gym in the first place."

Nobody answered; nobody had an answer to that statement. Sam did, however, punch Richard on the arm.

"Why didn't you do that earlier? You could have saved a lot of people in the assembly hall."

Richard scowled at her. He obviously didn't like being hit. "I did. How do you think we got out? I initiated the grid lockdown system. You remember those lines that stretched across the assembly hall?"

Sam nodded.

"Those lines mark the system. They rise out of the floor, creating a protective shell around anyone who is within their confines. Once they're activated, only the governor of the province can open them."

Sam shook her head. "What about the people that MESA gunned down? Why didn't you save them?"

"Because none of them are dead, Sam." Richard gestured in the direction of the assembly hall. "The group that MESA shot was only hit with pulse rounds. They hurt like hell, but they are made to incapacitate, not kill. Any more stupid questions?"

Sam glared at him. Richard turned back to Dyson.

"Here, take this." Richard handed him his tablet. "It's useless to me now, and you'll probably need it to get out."

Dyson took it from him. "Why is it useless? Can't you use the security system to fight?"

Richard shook his head. "No, this network is a learning interface and has at least two other hackers in the system. I won't be able to hack it again from a remote location. I was saving it for our escape, but Sam wanted to save you."

Richard pointed at an icon. "This route will take you to a passage that will allow you to meet up with the rest of the school. I'd suggest you take the weapons from those dead soldiers. I doubt you'll meet up with more of the Móguǐ on the lower floors, but if you do, fire first. These men won't hesitate to kill you."

Dyson nodded his head.

"Then go."

Dyson and the rest of the students started down the hallway and disappeared into a classroom. Sam glanced nervously at Richard. He spoke without looking at her as he led her up the hall.

"That room contains a passage to the underground tunnel

system. It's used for an emergency just like this. The tablet will tell them where to go. We should leave too, before something happens."

Sam turned to Richard. "Now we find Adam?"

Richard sighed. "Now we find Adam."

Just as Richard finished his sentence, a smaller ball of bright blue energy struck right where they had just been standing. Farther down the hall, a group of soldiers ran towards them, light shivs and arm cannons at the ready.

"So much for that." Richard grabbed Sam and started to run. They avoided the fast-moving balls of light, bobbing and weaving around the school and jumping over bodies, debris, and smoking infrastructure. Sam didn't know how they were going to dodge this bullet. She sighed. She wished she could have said goodbye to Adam.

As they rounded another corner, Richard spoke, but not to her, and it was obvious he was trying to speak quietly. Nevertheless, Sam heard him over the din of her heavy breathing and the constant discharge of gunfire. "Doughboy to Big Daddy. SIT REP as follows: Package in hand. Environment is tango heavy. All exfil options exhausted. Permission to engage?"

"Richard, what are you talking about?"

"Nothing, Sam. It's a password to get us out of here. The school should react."

Sam called over the noise. "Where are we going then?"

"There's a passage that leads out of the school. It's just ahead. If we can get there, we can lose these losers."

A half-smile crossed Sam's lips. Richard always did have a way with words.

The two friends took a final turn and ran headlong into a dead end. Where a door to another part of the school should have been, a mess of mask-wearing bodies now sat. Just beyond the bodies was a large pile of rubble made from the destroyed building materials and classroom debris. The halt of their flight took time to sink in. They were cut off. There was nowhere to go.

The soldiers turned the corner after them and saw that they had Richard and Sam trapped. The leader grinned and walked slowly towards the two. He laughed and said something Sam didn't understand to his comrades. She knew Richard might have understood them. She watched as the leader flicked his light shiv from side to side.

"What do we do?" asked Sam.

"Nothing. They're a death squad, remember? We're dead."

More arguing broke out among the soldiers. They were gesturing towards Richard and Sam and hovering over a tablet.

Sam leaned in toward Richard. "Now what are they doing? Why don't they just kill us?"

Richard shook his head. "I'm not sure. They seem to be looking for something."

Sam glared. "And it's just now coming up? They were just shooting at us!"

"Pulse rounds, Sam. They weren't trying to kill us. If they were, we'd be dead already."

Richard moved in front of Sam. A romantic gesture, albeit a silly one.

The man Sam assumed was the leader of the small squad spoke again to the group, and they powered down their shivs and moved in around Richard and Sam slowly.

In a sudden and violent action, the leader gave Richard a quick punch to the face and then a swift kick to the side. Sam saw the man grimace in surprise for some reason, but Sam wasn't sure at what. Richard hit the ground and started to spit blood.

She felt tears form at her eyes. So much for them not trying to kill them. Richard was finally wrong about something, and she wouldn't even be able to gloat.

The group of them laughed as the leader kicked Richard again. Sam wondered if what they had in store for her was much of the same. It was not. It was much worse. The lead soldier pulled out a long wicked knife with a rippled blade. He calmly strolled up to Sam. He took the hem of her shirt and made a small incision.

Ahhh... she thought. So that's it. 'Tis a fate worse than death for me; well, isn't that nice.

The leader apparently cracked a joke to his comrades as they laughed at his words. He started to split her shirt right up the middle; once her shirt was split, he grabbed her and spun her around.

Suddenly the man released her. He fell back. Sam oriented herself and realized Richard was in front of her, holding out his arms to either side of his body like a cross of protection. He growled at the men. "Back off."

The others pointed weapons at him, and light shivs were turned back on. The leader barked at them from the ground. Sam didn't understand the words, but she understood his meaning.

No. He's mine.

Weapons still pointed at Richard, the soldiers backed away. The leader approached slowly. He was very angry.

Richard wasn't done yet, though. "Answer. Damn it, I know you're there. Answer me!"

"Richard," Sam said softly. "It's okay. Get out of the way. Maybe they will keep us both alive if I..."

Richard ignored her.

"Please, Richard, get out of the way!" She touched the nape of his neck and was once more amazed at how cool his skin was.

No time to think. The leader was in front of Richard and glaring heavily. He struck without warning. The leader jabbed the knife into Richard, but it wasn't a blow that was designed to kill quickly. The leader yanked the blade straight down into the top part of Richard's protruding gut. He laughed wickedly, slicing farther down until he stopped abruptly. He looked confused.

Sam's screams shattered the air. She started to cry uncontrollably. "No, Richard! No, no, no!!"

She repeated this over and over; it was all she could say. Blood oozed out as the soldier pulled out the blade, and Richard fell to his knees. Was he already dead?

Everything went quiet. The men were staring at Richard, completely silent, frozen with strange expressions on their faces. The leader looked livid. He flipped the blade around and brought it down sharply, aiming for Richard's spine. Sam closed her eyes in terror as the knife plummeted towards him.

Suddenly Sam heard a crackling disembodied voice, like the righteous word of God himself, coming from Richard's ear. Richard immediately threw up his arm and caught the soldier's wrist in an iron grip, halting the plunging knife centimeters before it sank into his neck.

The voice rattled off commands one by one.

"Big Daddy to Doughboy. Permission granted. Protect package at all costs. Bravo weapons use only. Engage tangos at will. I repeat. Engage tangos at will."

CHAPTER 21
AN UNEXPECTED HERO

Time: Late afternoon
Scene: Academy 676

All thoughts of screaming or crying melted away as the voice came. The words echoed in her mind.

"Big Daddy to Doughboy. Permission granted. Protect package at all costs. Bravo weapons use only. Engage tangos at will. I repeat, engage tangos at will."

Slow motion, the everlasting cliché from so many a story and Vii theater experiences, commandeered her cognitive function. She could hear and see everything as the bloody mess unfolded.

Richard's lips moved in a slight whisper. "Bravo weapons, huh? About brickin' time."

Richard's head tilted skyward to meet the gaze of the Móguǐ soldier trying to skewer him with the wicked-looking knife. Richard smiled a half-smile as the soldier's eyes went wide in surprise. Sharp movements so fast Sam could barely make them out and the unmistakable cracking of bone replaced the echo of the crackling voice in her head. The soldier's scream of pain was abruptly cut off by an odd gurgle.

Next thing Sam knew, Richard was standing tall and undaunted, while the soldier was on the ground, his arm horribly disfigured and obviously broken in several places. Blood flowed across the scarred tile, coating the space with red. The soldier's lifeless eyes distracted from the gaping hole in his throat. Sam took an involuntary step back. Icy indifference rolled out from Richard in cascading waves of cold.

Richard was saturated with blood. Sam could see it soaked into his clothes and running from his gut. She knew he was hurt. How could he not be hurt after a blade to the stomach?

Light shivs stretched to their full length as the reality of the Mógui's downed leader set in. Murderous eyes fixed themselves on Richard as the Jadian unit fanned out.

"Sam."

He said her name, but she didn't recognize the voice. Sam couldn't answer him.

"Sam!"

Sam gulped, "Yeah, Richard."

He looked over his shoulder at her as he flicked the switch of a light shiv. Now where did he get that?

"Get behind me."

It was a command. No room for dissent or argument. Sam didn't think to argue.

Just as she retreated behind him, the first soldier attacked. A fast cross-body blow aimed directly at Richard's neck swiped out but struck nothing. Richard didn't block; he didn't even try. He simply leaned back, avoiding the tip of the light shiv by centimeters or less. Richard's counter was a quick spin and slash from hip to shoulder that ended with Richard facing Sam. It was like Richard was trying to give the man a piggyback ride. Sam instinctively found the man's face. It was lifeless.

Richard ripped the dead soldier's light shiv from his hand and dumped the body just as the other soldiers leveled strikes from the left and right. With a reverse and fore grip on the shivs, Richard blocked both blows, put an elbow to the nose of one soldier, and a quick snap kick to the gut of the other. He finished the two men with thrusts to the heart. Four men lay dead at Richard's feet. Blood was everywhere; Richard's, the soldier's, and probably Sam's, though she couldn't remember getting hurt. She didn't know anymore. Conscious thought had all but deserted her.

The rest of the soldiers met similarly gruesome fates. They fought and died in a heaping gory mess. Richard dealt with them with speed and violence like Sam did not think possible. She was dreaming. She had to be dreaming. Richard had been stabbed. He was bleeding. He should be dead. *She* should be dead. Had they had their way with her? Used her and thrown her aside? Had they killed her?

Sam fell to her knees and retched violently, spewing up bile and the lunch she had barely eaten. Lunch... she had just been sitting in the lunchroom with Richard worrying about a mysterious savior and the object of her budding affection, and now... now she sat crumpled to the floor, barely able to stand. It all just felt wrong, so very wrong. Richard was at her side. She couldn't remember him moving there. He held her hair out of her face and her sick on the floor. Instinctively she buried her face in the side of his neck. His skin was *still* cold to the touch. She felt him stiffen.

"Sam, we can't stay here. We've got to move."

Tears formed at the corners of her eyes and rolled down the side of her face. "What are you, Richard?"

Richard pulled away from Sam, moving a healthy distance from her. He stared at her with heavy, piercing eyes. Her blood slowed to molasses.

Who was this person?

Richard stood and pulled her to her feet. "We need to move. There are still Mógul, school security, Republicans, and MESA."

He looked at his timepiece. "I think it's safe to say that MESA has called both Containment and S&D. If we don't move, we're dead. Bravo weapons aren't going to take down those monsters. Same for the Mógul Heavy Ops. We could have a real fight on our hands."

Sam wanted to argue. She wanted to run. Her fear was consuming her loyalty and sense of friendship. Richard. Fat, genius, sarcastic Richard, had just slaughtered those men, butchered them without hesitation or remorse. Could she really go with him?

A terrible thought struck Sam.

It wasn't *could she go with him*, but *would he allow her to leave?* Would he let her go?

Sam shuffled her way along the hall, away from Richard. Richard's eyes narrowed as she did. Quick and graceful, far more graceful than his pudgy frame should have allowed, Richard moved in front of her, blocking her escape. Sam sucked in a deep breath. He wasn't going to let her go.

"Who are you, Richard? Why are you here?"

Screaming voices and the sound of gunfire echoed in the distance, close enough to be heard but not close enough to cause immediate concern. Nevertheless, others were coming. Friend, foe, classmate; at this point, it didn't matter. They had only a few moments, and they both knew it.

Richard's eyes didn't leave Sam. "I've always thought you were more intelligent than this, Sam. I would have thought the reason I'm here is obvious."

His eyes remained passive. Too passive, as if... as if he wasn't trying to look somewhere. The gears in her head dislodged themselves, a single thought forced its way in.

The box. He has to be after the box.

Suddenly Richard's eyes fixed on something above her

head. He flicked on the light shivs and dashed towards her with unnatural speed. Sam felt her eyes clamp down and her arms reflexively shield her face and body. Why was he charging her? Was he going to kill her? Did he know where the box was after all? Perhaps he didn't need her anymore.

Sam felt a *whoosh* as ionized plasma scorched the air overhead. A thumping noise to either side of her body forced her eyes back open. Sam looked into his eyes and felt... felt... fear. Their faces were centimeters apart as he held light shivs to either side of her body.

She had difficulty looking away from his eyes. They were cold and dead. No eyes should look like that. She glanced to the side and saw clumps of tiled ceiling. She understood. Richard had rushed her to keep the falling ceiling debris from crushing her head. She suddenly felt stupid for thinking he was going to kill her. After all, if he wanted her dead, he could have done that ages ago.

Richard grabbed her hand. "Come on. We need to leave now."

"But—but what about your wounds? Aren't you going to—?"

Richard pulled on Sam, and they set off back down the hall, Richard's pace not slowing in spite of his injury. They continued to backtrack, making a couple of turns before exiting the school hallways into the Academy City 676 central courtyard, a massive central yard that divided the different education levels. They made their way to the elementary level buildings where the youngest of the Academy City 676 citizens did their learning.

Sam and Richard ran, but hadn't moved more than a few meters when the sounds of fighting erupted once more. MESA, some of the rag-tag bunch of fighters, and the Móguǐ were on each other. To make matters worse, the school's defenses were finally kicking in, blasting just about anything that moved.

A concentrated blast of heat fried a patch of grass right in front of Richard and Sam, cooking it completely. Richard pulled Sam behind a row of unique trees, a cross between pine and oak. They rounded the edge of the treeline just as another group of Móguǐ soldiers came dashing from the other side of the treeline. Light shivs flickered to full length, and hands went for their waistbands. Each of the soldiers touched a large blue button, and a slight blue haze enveloped them. Sam knew instantly they were in trouble.

Richard hesitated, but Sam didn't know for what. Was he scared? That seemed unlikely, but he wasn't doing anything. He wasn't firing up his shivs or taking a fighting stance. Nothing.

Then Richard attacked himself.

Sam watched in horror as Richard extended his two stolen light shivs to quarter length and proceeded to shear off his own skin. Richard's actions were so jolting the soldiers stopped just short of their attack. They stared at Richard in disbelief. Sam just screamed.

"Richard, what in the hell are you doing?!"

Richard's skin fell off in long strips, the light shivs slicing through it like butter. Sam's head went fuzzy, her upchuck reflex reacting once again. For a second time, she fell to the ground, throwing up. She simply couldn't stand the sight of any more blood.

Her vision was blurry, but she picked up on Richard also hitting the ground. This made more sense than any of the events transpiring around her today. He had lost so much blood, yet he still sheared large chunks of his skin right off his body. It was like he was peeling an apple, a fleshy human apple. Perhaps he had lost it and was committing suicide. In the wake of all that had happened, *that* at least she could get.

The soldiers advanced, apparently recovering from their dismay at watching a man filet himself. The one closest took two steps forward and—

Crack, Crack, Crack.

Cracking sounds filled the air one after the other. The noise was beyond forceful and made Sam's ears hurt. Sam struggled to find the source but could only focus on the lead soldier. His blue hazy field flickered. He took two steps back, then dropped to the ground. The soldier's neck flopped to the side, allowing Sam a clear view of his face.

A 2-centimeter hole sat directly in the middle of the soldier's head. Life fluid trickled from the wound. Again Sam felt queasy. The cracking again commenced, the sound repeating over and over again as the remaining soldiers fell in

the same pattern as their leader, each accompanied by a fluc-
tuating blue haze and a hole in their head.

Sam searched their immediate area and found that she
and Richard were alone. Once more, all the soldiers near
them were dead.

Richard was suddenly in front of her, attempting to help
her up. He was too slippery, and she didn't know why.
Nothing about the situation was making sense.

Richard swore. "I can't get a grip on you. I need to get this
thing off first." Immediately Richard began removing parts of
his body, shedding his girth like clothing.

Like a lightning strike to the brain, abruptly it clicked.
Everything clicked. Sam finally got it. His cold skin, his
healthy diet with no change in physique, his reluctance to get
in the water, his disproportionate strength and speed. With
Richard, there truly was more than met the eye.

"Okay, get up. We need to leave."

Richard was, once again, back at her side picking her up.
This wasn't her Richard, though. He stood tall, muscled, and
ruggedly handsome. The fat from his face was gone, his hair
color different, and he handled Sam with forceful strength
and surety. Sam looked him up and down but quickly
whipped her head skyward. Her face went beet red. Richard
was bare-butt naked save a black bag in his hand.

For all that was holy, he was naked! She tried not to look,
but she couldn't help but watch him. He had scars on his
body. Healed wounds from the looks of it. His skin was

tanner than it should have been and warm. His body was incredibly warm.

A short distance away, the fat Richard, or parts of him, were stacked in a heap on the ground, burning like pig fat. Far from just a costume, Sam could see intricate biomechanical infrastructure, wires, leads, and other devices all meeting the same fiery fate as the fake skin. Sam was at a complete loss. She didn't know what to do anymore. Sam looked back and forth from the burning pile of artificial flesh to his body as they retreated back into the hallway.

Richard surveyed the area, looking for any hostiles. Sam allowed herself to be led. Satisfied she wouldn't run, Richard let go of her and proceeded to put on clothes, which he pulled out of the black bag.

Richard quickly dressed in a plain black shirt, pants, and boots. He then placed several pieces of equipment on his person. They were weapons she had never seen before, at least in real life. She had seen these guns on the classic 2D movie channel, but she didn't know any of them still existed.

The sounds of fighting could still be heard off in the distance.

"Richard, you're so skinny."

Richard didn't look at her as he checked his weapons. "Yes, sixty kilos of biomechanical weight tends to make you look chubby. How observant of you."

Without warning, Richard pulled two pistols up to eye level and pointed the guns in her direction. Sam reacted, trying to move out of the way, but Richard was too fast; more gunfire ripped the air.

"Sam, stop moving." Richard pushed forward and shot his arms out to each side of her head. The guns were loud and echoed off the enclosed space, deafening her.

The figurative dust settled, and Sam turned to see what Richard had fired at. She saw three downed individuals at the end of the corridor. Once again, Sam's breath caught in her throat. She tried to look back at Richard but was having difficulty.

Smoke trailed up from Richard's guns. His thumbs touched the side of each weapon, causing metal columns to fall out. Richard popped two more back into the bottom and pulled the tops of the guns backward. He placed the weapons in holsters on his thighs.

Richard turned his attention back to Sam. "Listen closely, because I am only going to ask you this once. Do you want to live through this little experience?"

Despite Richard's voice sounding like it was trying to escape from a thick blanket, Sam nodded.

"Good. If you want to live, then you need to do exactly as I say and stop flinching every time I get near you."

Sam's felt her skin go hot. "If you don't want me to flinch, then stop pointing guns at me. Anyone would flinch in that situation. And who says I need you to stay alive?"

Richard laughed. It was cold. It made her skin prickle.

"You think you can survive this? Fine, go on; I'll leave on my own."

Sam froze. He couldn't be serious, could he?

He was. Richard walked away, again displaying a grace and smoothness she would have never thought possible from him.

"Wait," she called out, attempting to be heard but not overdo it. They were still in danger after all.

He stopped but didn't turn to face her. He merely looked over his shoulder.

"Yes?"

"Please."

"Please, what?"

"Please don't leave me alone."

Richard returned to her side. "Remember you said that. Now follow and stay behind me. If I move, you move. That's it. Do you understand?"

Sam nodded.

"Then move."

They wasted no time returning to the courtyard. The smoldering wreckage of Richard's artificial body was little more than ash. Richard stalked past, not sparing it a glance. Sam used all her willpower not to throw up; she couldn't help looking. They approached the treeline more cautiously this time. Richard led, a pistol in each hand, the guns sweeping the area. Once clear, they moved from cover to cover as they crossed the courtyard.

Sam snuck a glance at Richard. No hint of expression, no acknowledgment of her existence. He came off calm, cold, and calculating. Scary. She was scared to be with him. Then again, right now, she was scared to be without him. Maybe she could ditch him once they made it to safety. *If* they made it to safety.

She and Richard entered one of the side doors on the far side of the courtyard. They were in the eastern wing now, hopefully far away from anyone else. Suddenly the report of gunfire rattled her. Flashes of bright light, the sudden starts and stops of screams, and then silence. She found the courage to open her eyes. Four more soldiers lay dead in front of her, all with gunshots to the head. Richard was reloading. He reholstered them and gestured to her.

"Come here, Sam," he said, walking over to one of the dead soldiers. "I want you to put this on."

He removed a belt from one of the dead men. It was of the same make and model as the dead soldiers' out in the courtyard. He wrapped it around Sam's waist and clicked it into place. His hands touched her exposed skin just above the line of her skirt. She became abruptly aware that her shirt was cut open, exposing her bra to Richard.

"What are you doing?" she said, sounding more embarrassed than she would have liked.

Richard glared at her but didn't answer.

Sam rolled her eyes, exasperated. "Okay, so I know you're the new super Richard, but if you ignore me, I'm going to continue to ask you questions until you kill me or answer me. Would it be that much harder to answer me than kill me?"

Richard cracked his neck. "Yes."

"Yes? Yes what?"

"Yes, it would be more difficult to answer your questions than to kill you."

He took a deep breath, apparently calming himself.

"This is a Jadian Oscillation Shield. The Jadians pride themselves on their martial talents, so most of their weapons and tactics highlight those particular values. The Plasma Scimitars I was using earlier are a prime example of this. What I'm putting on you now is standard-issue defensive equipment for Jadian Special Ops. The belt is like a force field that uses energy to absorb, displace, or flat-out block projectiles. It does have some—"

Sam interrupted him. "You mean like body armor? That doesn't make any sense. How can energy be used as armor?"

"Sam, energy and matter are all made of the same thing. If harnessed in the right way, energy can be just as effective as a plate of carbonized steel."

Richard engaged the belt. "This will keep you safe. The belt can withstand most low-velocity energy weaponry with near impunity. It will even take a strike or two from a plasma scimitar. Just be careful and watch the gauge."

He slapped a sort of wristwatch on her. "100%" appeared in the screen of the watch.

"Keep a close eye on this gauge. If the number goes down

to zero, then take cover immediately." He pointed to the watch. "Any center-mass hits after that, and you're dead."

She still didn't really understand, but she figured she really didn't have a choice. They proceeded on their way.

———————

Skinny Richard was like no one Sam had ever met. A personality and person so unique it was borderline exquisite. Ironically enough, this was exactly the same feeling he had cultivated the first time Sam met him so many years ago. Fat Richard had been so different in personality and action he couldn't help but stand out. Skinny Richard was more of the same, but in different ways. Incredibly different ways. Violence, aggression, and the single-minded certainty he displayed burned at her nerves and inflamed her fight-or-flight response. He intrigued her even while he instilled the fear of God in her. Yet she followed him without hesitation. She did not know why.

This whole escape experience was surreal. If she didn't know any better, she could have sworn they were in an especially intense game of Combat Tag. This feeling was only exacerbated when Sam actually saw weapons of similar make and model to the ones used at the combat range. The weapons didn't act the same though; there were no minuscule doses of incapacitating energy or subdued prickling feelings after the light blue balls of semisolid energy hit. No, these weapons used by these soldiers, these... invaders, were just as their title indicated. These were weapons: equipment designed to kill, and they fulfilled their purpose enthusiastically.

Soldiers continued to appear, only to be cut down by Richard with his archaic weapons. It was miraculous on every plane of reality, imaginary or otherwise, and it seemed every encounter would end the same. A gunshot wound to the head. Sometimes Richard fired once, sometimes as many as four times. Regardless of who stood before him, they fell like bricks.

It felt like hours had passed when they finally made it to the large underground building made to house personal transportation modules for those students privileged enough to have a personal vehicle. Richard hopped on a two-person open-hatch rocket with the name—

"Dyson?" said Sam, scandalized. "You're going to steal his bike?"

Richard nodded and put on a helmet. He threw a second helmet to Sam. "He owes me for not killing him."

"Kill him? Why would you—" Comprehension dropkicked Sam in the head, closely followed by anger, then rage. She punched at Richard, who dodged her hastily thrown fist.

"You jerk!" she shouted. "That's why Dyson never actually hurt you, isn't it? ISN'T IT? Do you know how worried I was? How I thought—"

Richard was upon her, his hand over her mouth. Again he

immobilized her. She thought that he had drugged her again, but she didn't feel any sort of poke or injection. How was he doing this?

"We don't have time for this," he whispered in a deathly voice. "This is your last chance, Sam. Do you want to stay with me and live or stay here and die? Your choice. Make it."

She tried to take a deep breath, but even that was hard. Richard seemed to feel and understand this. He released her.

"Sorry," she said. "I will be good from now on."

"Good," was all that Richard replied. "Now get on."

Richard and Sam climbed on the bike and sped away from the main building of Academy 676.

———

I could feel the rumble at the back of my knees and in my thighs as we roared down the road. The power of the turbo-charged hydrogen engine screamed as he throttled the bike, the whine of the gears pitching higher and higher as the speed increased... 50, 100, 150 kilometers per hour. I didn't know how fast he could go, but I could barely catch my breath as we pushed forward into the darkness. I held him tight, feeling muscle so taut it couldn't be real. My body and mind were like the aftermath of a warzone. I was hot. I was sweaty. I had bruises on my arms and shoulders from the grip of the soldiers. The soldiers who had tried... who had tried to... I could not say it. I would not say it. Saying it would make it all the more real. I buried my face in his back.

I did feel comforted. Those soldiers wouldn't be after me, not anymore. They wouldn't be after anyone anymore. I felt tears form at the corner of my eyes, tears that were instantly swept away into the night, lost to the wind and road. Lost like me.

My body shivered from the churn of rushing air pouring over my sweaty skin. My shirt was split, whipping up behind my back and exposing my skin to the torrent of the artificial tempest. The violence blocked my senses. I couldn't feel any more. I was numb; at least that's what I tried to tell myself. Actually, I was scared. I was scared of what might be following us up the road.

How many were dead? How many were gone? The faces of my friends one after another played over and over in my mind. Cammie. Oh, Cammie, you were so good to me even though I was from Partial Palace. Coda, dirty-minded Coda, how will things develop in the future with you and Lacey? Are you in love? Are you ever going to realize Cammie's feelings for you? Are you even alive? Mother, oh my poor lonely mother, for some reason I can't— remember your face.

The bike coasted, coming to the crest of the highest of the hills that circled the valley. We slowed unexpectedly to a stop at a place where I could see the valley we had just traversed. The lights of the city and the twinkling of the stars fought to hold my attention. Both of them, the stars in the sky and the lights of the city on the ground, sparkled in their respective element. Beautiful.

More tears formed on my face. I longed to speak. I longed to ask the question and finally found the courage to do so.

"We can't ever go back, can we?"

He didn't say anything. He just turned to look at me, the faint glare of the bike's headlights barely illuminating his face. We sat there staring until he opened his mouth and said a single word.

"No."

He spun the bike around and ripped down the backside of the hilltop to the inter-way. Once again, my breath was lost to the wind. We tore our way along the backcountry, whipping along the road faster and faster. My worry seemed lost to exhaustion, fear, relief, and then sadness. I didn't know anymore. I didn't care anymore. I let my hands go from his waist, feeling them catch the air as it rushed past. I felt the urge to let go completely. I just wanted to be free from all of this. Without warning, the bike skipped and skidded. I opened my eyes as I screamed and felt myself lifting from the seat as we tumbled over the steep cliffside.

CHAPTER 22
TWINKLE, TWINKLE
LITTLE STAR

Time: Current day, evening
Scene: Distant motorway outside Academy City 676 limits

I could feel the rumble behind my knees and in my thighs as we roared down the road. The power of the turbocharged hydrocell engine screamed as he throttled the bike, the whine of the gears pitching higher and higher as the speed increased. Fifty, one hundred, one hundred and fifty kilometers per hour. I didn't know how fast he could go, but I could barely catch my breath as we pushed forward into the darkness. I held him tight, feeling muscle so taut it couldn't be real. My body and mind were like the aftermath of a warzone. I was hot. I was sweaty. I had bruises on my arms and shoulders from the grip of the soldiers. The soldier who had tried... who had tried to... I could not say it. I would not say it. Saying it would make it all the more real. I buried my face in his back.

I did feel comforted. Those soldiers wouldn't be after me, not anymore. They wouldn't be after anyone anymore. I felt tears form at the corners of my eyes, tears that were instantly swept away into the night, lost to the wind and road. Lost like me.

My body shivered from the churn of rushing air pouring over my sweaty skin. My shirt was split, whipping up behind my back and exposing my skin to the torrent of the artificial tempest. The violence blocked my senses. I couldn't feel anymore. I was numb; at least that's what I tried to tell myself. Actually, I was scared. I was scared of what might be following us up the road.

How many were dead? How many were gone? The faces of my friends, one after another, played over and over in my mind. Cammie. Oh, Cammie. You were so good to me even though I was from Partial Palace. Coda, dirty-minded Coda, how will things develop in the future with you and Lacey? Are you in love? Are you ever going to realize Cammie's feelings for you? Are you even alive? Mother, oh my poor lonely mother. For some reason, I can't—I can't remember your face.

The bike coasted, coming to the crest of the highest hill that circled the valley. We slowed unexpectedly to a stop at a place where I could see the valley we had just traversed. The lights of the city and the twinkling of the stars fought to hold my attention. Both of them, the stars in the sky and the lights of the city on the ground, sparkled in their respective elements. Beautiful.

More tears formed on my face. I longed to speak. I longed to ask the question and finally found the courage to do so.

"We can't ever go back, can we?"

He didn't say anything. He just turned to look at me, the faint glare of the bike's headlights barely illuminating his face. We sat there staring until he opened his mouth and said a single word.

"No."

He turned the bike and ripped down the backside of the hilltop to the interway. Once again, my breath was lost to the wind.

I, Samantha Montgomery of Partial Palace in Academy City 676, had a crush on a foreign transfer student named Adam, was best friends with a high-tracks girl named Cammie, and had once or twice secretly fantasized about kissing Coda, the friend of a friend. I fought with my mom the morning it had all started and said some pretty mean things to her. I deeply regret that now. I wonder if I will ever get the chance to say I'm sorry.

Two months before graduation in the last year of my primary education, violence besieged my school, and I was whisked away from my home, my friends, my life, everything I cared about. Looking back, I think I knew, even as we sped down that motorway, that life—my life as I had known it— was never going to be the same again.